KARMEN LEE

Recycling programs
for this product may
not exist in your area.

ISBN-13: 978-1-335-04163-0

The 7-10 Split

Copyright © 2024 by Kristen Rhee

Harlequin Enterprises ULC
22 Adelaide St. West, 41st Floor
Toronto, Ontario M5H 4E3, Canada
www.Harlequin.com

Printed in U.S.A.

AUTHOR'S NOTE

This book discusses cancer, drunk driving and the loss of a parent.

One

"Whatever it is, the answer is no."

Ava knew that look. That look promised extra hours with no extra pay and a significant bump in her caffeine budget for the week. She already needed to cut back on that dark-roasted money suck and agreeing to whatever ridiculous school spirit activity Bradley Parrish was surely coming to convince her of was not the way to go.

"You haven't even heard what I have to say."

"And it's going to stay that way," Ava replied, ducking quickly into her classroom and attempting to close the door behind her. If she were the type to startle easily, the hand that slapped down on the other side of the door would have done it. As it was, she just sighed loudly before abandoning her moment alone before the staff meeting she didn't even want to go to.

It wasn't that she would get fired for missing it. Peach Blossom High School was understaffed, and they wouldn't risk losing an Advanced Placement teacher right now unless it was over something illegal. Maybe. No, she just didn't want to deal with the pettiness that was their principal, Robert, when he scented even a whiff of insubordination. Ava dealt with enough petty behavior at home being the middle child sandwiched between two sisters gung ho on always being the head bitch in charge. She didn't feel like dealing with it at work too.

"Leave me be, Brad," she huffed. "I have books to sort, lesson plans to finish, and wounds to lick."

It was the third year in a row that Robert had rejected Ava's plans for reviving the school's old bowling team. She had even downgraded it to an extracurricular club to reduce the costs, but still he had vetoed it. If Ava wasn't so used to it by now, she would have slammed the door on her way out of his office. Instead, she had calmly replied she understood before stuffing her feelings down and locking them behind a wall thicker than Robert's bullshit civility.

"Ouch. Let me guess," Brad said. "He rejected your plan for the new team and said the school had no money for it."

"Got it in one." Ava figured it was time for her to give up the idea in its entirety. "I'm not in the mood to do anything but finish this planning before this meeting so I can go the hell home and eat my weight in yeast rolls."

"So, you don't want to talk about who the new teacher might be?" he asked. Ava's curiosity was piqued but she refused to show it. No, if he was going to get her off-task, he had to work for it. She resolved herself to a couple more hours of sorting the books she had on hand and praying the ones still missing were enroute to arrive soon.

If anyone had told her five years ago she would be back at

her old high school teaching English, she would have laughed in their face. The Ava Williams of five years ago had big plans that included a PhD in Europe where she could walk the same streets as her favorite authors while churning out words that would one day earn her heaps of praise. Teaching AP English to high schoolers back in her small hometown of Peach Blossom, Georgia, had been nowhere in her plans. Yet, here she was about to start her fourth year and not completely hating life.

Usually.

Ava fell into her chair, her loose skirt wrapping around her legs. When she looked up, Brad's hulking frame leaned against her desk. His curly brown hair gleamed under the harsh classroom light with a few errant curls falling over his forehead and his lips were split wide in an eager smile. She was determined to out-stubborn him this time, but the angle was all wrong. If she stared up any longer, she would get a crick in her neck and then have to drive a couple hours to find a chiropractor. Sometimes small-town life was a pain in the ass.

"Don't you have your own lessons to finish planning?"

"Did them already," he replied. His wide smile and boyish charm were usually enough to pull Ava out of a funk, but not today. She had barely gotten any sleep last night thanks to her sisters having another argument over absolutely nothing and she was not in the mood. Despite having their own designated spaces in the large family home they shared with their father, it never failed that someone would get on someone else's last nerve and Ava would get roped into the middle against her will. She sometimes wondered if she should have just bitten the bullet and gotten her own place.

"I can't believe you really aren't the least bit tempted to talk about it," Brad continued. "Getting a new teacher is kind of a big deal."

She shrugged before reaching out to shuffle some papers. Small-town life meant any change, no matter how inconsequential, was a big deal. "We get new teachers sometimes. I don't see why I should waste my time talking about it."

He gave her a look that she refused to find amusing. She had too much to finish before school started next week to find his interruption entertaining. "When was the last time we got a new science teacher? Who was a woman *and* qualified enough to allow us to add an AP Chemistry course to the class schedule?"

Ava's mouth clicked shut. She had been about to interrupt him, until that last bit. He was right about that. The school hadn't attracted many women in the sciences or math subjects for quite a few years.

"And I heard they managed to get her to sign a two-year contract."

Ava widened her eyes. "That's a first."

Brad nodded, his grin growing wider. "I heard the school nurse talking to the assistant principal about it. Seems they are trying to figure out a way to entice the newbie to stay longer than that."

"Which means they have their golden goose for the next two years," Ava said, rolling her eyes. "Well, hopefully the person isn't a total dick, otherwise we will be the ones dealing with it until the newbie wises up and fucks off to their next assignment."

He crossed his arms before shaking his head, curls falling

over his arched brow. "You are way too colorful to be so pessimistic." He waved a hand at her outfit. "How is it you look like a walking ad for the Black Ms. Frizzle and yet can somehow manage to turn the whole world gray with one sentence?"

Ava snorted. It wasn't the first time she had heard that comparison given her penchant for colorful skirts and dresses and the curls that adorned her head. She happily embraced the description. Still, just because she favored bright colors didn't mean she always had to be a ray of fucking sunshine.

"I'm an English teacher. Words are my weapons and I wield them with glee."

Brad's laughter was loud enough to vibrate her desk and despite wanting to hold onto her frown, Ava found herself smiling. He was infuriatingly good at that. Rarely did she manage to stay in a mood when he came around whispering observations about things and generally being a pest that she hated to like. His brown eyes twinkled as he pushed off the desk.

"You're a menace," he replied. "I'm going to go grab some stuff from storage before the meeting. Save me a seat if I get there after you?"

"Always. Now shoo, we both have work to do, and I refuse to stay any later than I have to."

Ava watched him leave the classroom, the door clicking shut behind him, before she sighed and looked down at the mess of papers on her desk. She really did need to finalize her lesson plans, but now her concentration was completely shot. She replayed Brad's words in her mind. She wasn't lying when she said the school occasionally got people to stick around, but she was still curious about who the newcomer could be.

She hoped they would all get along well enough, considering their classroom would be right across the hallway from hers. Otherwise, the school year wouldn't pass quickly enough.

"Hopefully whoever it is isn't a total asshole," she said aloud. The last science teacher hadn't been completely terrible, but he had let it be known that he had no intention of sticking around for longer than the contracted year. It would have been fine if he'd let only the administration know, but the attitude had carried over into his classroom. The students had all known he didn't give two shits about staying long-term and they had acted accordingly. Most treated his class with mild indifference. A few known troublemakers had taken a more active approach, cementing the fact that the guy was in and out in one academic year.

He hadn't even left a forwarding email according to the office assistant. Well, according to Brad who had gotten his information from the school nurse who had gotten *her* information from the office assistant. It was like playing the world's worst game of telephone.

Ava managed to focus for another twenty minutes, but eventually her mind wandered back to the latest hot topic. Who could the new teacher possibly be? Patience wasn't a virtue she normally had, and this time was no different. Did she really want to wait until the staff meeting to figure out who the mystery person was? She glanced down at the still disorganized papers in her hands before giving in to temptation with a put-upon sigh.

The lesson plans could wait.

She turned toward her laptop, intent on doing some sleuthing. Surely, there was information somewhere about the new teacher. Ava could have called the front office and made up a story to get the information, but people around here liked to gossip. She didn't want to leave any trail that might come back to her in case shit went down with the newbie and people would definitely talk if they heard she had been asking questions about them.

She went to the school website, but when she toggled over to the staff and filtered for science, only a placeholder came up. Even that didn't have any identifying information. Not to be deterred, she opened a new tab, determined to find some information she could use. Thirty minutes later, she threw in the towel.

Nothing. She hadn't found a damn thing. All the school's social media accounts were focused on the start of school but nothing about new teachers. There was a vague post about adding AP Chemistry as a new course offering for seniors and juniors, but nothing about who was teaching them. If Ava were a parent, she would want to know that information. That seemed perfectly acceptable. Right?

Voices filtering in from the hallway caught her attention and she cursed herself for not having the door open. It would be weird now if she just happened to open it when they were standing in the hallway and Ava wasn't even sure if she wanted to engage in conversation. What if they were a talker and never shut up? She already had a couple of those in her life and her introverted ways would not allow for another one. Instead, she sat as still as possible and strained her ears to try to discern the voices.

She could recognize Robert's overly pleasant tone that belied the fact that he was often on some bullshit. Ava had been briefly taken in by his faux pleasant demeanor when she first started, but it only took her a couple months before she realized that the promises he made were hardly ever carried out unless they made him look good. His continuous rejections of her bowling-team idea was proof of that even when she showed him the interest in it and how little it would eat into the school budget. No, here football was king with basketball coming in a close second. Anything other than those was expendable or frivolous by comparison apparently.

The other voice was higher, and Ava frowned. There was something familiar about that voice that tickled her brain even as she drew a blank. Her need to know fought with her need to not get roped into anything by showing her face. She was surprised Robert hadn't barged in already and designated her as the welcoming committee. When the sound of the other door shutting reached her, it spurred Ava into standing and making a move.

The hallway was clear by the time she opened her classroom door and Ava straightened her outfit before walking over and knocking on the new teacher's door. She cursed the old frosted glass window obscuring her vision. If they had bothered updating it, she could have walked by and peeked in unseen. It took her a minute to realize that the door hadn't opened so she knocked again a little louder in case the person hadn't heard her.

"One minute," they called out, voice clearer now that she was closer, and Ava felt herself freeze. It had been a decade, but without the extra barrier of a concrete wall to muffle it, she swore she knew that voice even after all these years. The door opened as if in slow motion and before she could school her expression into something more neutral and less shocked, it was too late.

"Ava—"

"You?!" she blurted before her mouth could catch up to her brain. It hadn't been the only commentary running through Ava's mind, but it probably was the most pleasant.

"—hi."

Hi. That was all Grace fucking Jones could come up with after nearly a decade of space between them. It wasn't that Ava had never imagined what would happen if she and Grace were ever face-to-face again, but she hadn't expected it to be at work. She hadn't prepared herself for this scenario.

She wasn't ready.

Without saying another word, Ava pivoted on her heel and made a beeline back to her room. It wasn't until the classroom door was firmly shut behind her that Ava realized she was trapped.

Grace was here, back in Peach Blossom.

Grace was across the hall.

Ava should have taken a sabbatical.

Two

Grace had barely gotten her bearings when someone knocked on the door. She stared at it, wondering if Robert had forgotten something. He hadn't seemed like the type to knock and wait for a response. Grace knew she would probably be watched carefully given this was her first year of teaching. When the person knocked again, she shifted into gear. If she had known who she would come face-to-face with, she might have made a different decision or at least taken more deep breaths and sent up a silent prayer to whoever was listening.

Grace found herself looking down into familiar dark brown eyes for the first time in nearly a decade, and all the carefully rehearsed speeches she had prepared for this moment flew from her mind, leaving her with only one thought.

"Ava—"

"You?!"

"—hi."

That wasn't quite the welcome she had been expecting. She

had imagined this moment many times over the years even as life seemed to take them further apart. Grace had always been drawn to romance books and movies where the two main characters realized that rivalry was the best foreplay leading to love. Deep down in a place where she only recently started to acknowledge, she hoped that maybe that was her story. Maybe that was why when her ex-girlfriend, Emily, had mentioned marriage, Grace had hightailed it the other way. Realistically, she knew there were other reasons her and Emily's relationship hadn't worked out without the fact that they never quite had the same addictive intensity, even after so many years together, but Grace was a hopeless romantic. Or maybe just hopeless. She hadn't quite decided.

Still, she was left reeling by how things were playing out. She had been prepared for yelling and maybe a couple tears from herself. She had fantasized about a quick acknowledgment of how things had gone down before falling into the simple rhythm they'd had as kids and frantically making up for all the things they had missed as adults. However, in all her imagined scenarios and wishful musings, the one thing Grace hadn't thought would happen so soon was to see Ava's back once again as she turned and walked away. The door shutting behind her had a click of finality that seemed to echo down the hall. Grace's eyes burned as she fought against closing them and it wasn't until she heard footsteps coming down the hallway that she finally turned and walked back into her own room, shutting the door behind her.

She leaned against the door and stared out into the empty classroom. Nothing in her teaching manuals could have pre-

pared her for this. Her heart was still pounding even as she took
deep breaths. With shaky hands, she pushed off the door and
walked back over to her desk. Flopping down into the chair
seemed the best course of action, though it did nothing to give
her insight into what she should do next. Grace could walk over
to Ava's classroom and try to speak to her again, maybe even
squeeze out more than two words this time, but that might make
things worse. She had no idea what Ava was thinking, but if she
was even faintly similar to how she had been when they were
younger, confrontation now would only lead to more conflict.

The Ava of the past did not like to be surprised, good or
bad, and this was probably firmly in the bad category if Grace
was to go off her reaction. Ava hadn't said more than one
word, but that word conveyed a world of feeling, transporting
Grace back to their last conversation when anger had gotten
the best of both of them.

I should have reached out and told her I was coming back. Hindsight being what it was made that clear. Maybe it would have
made for a better reunion.

Or at the very least, a longer one. That had to be a world
record for the quickest *hi* and *bye*. Then again, Ava hadn't even
said bye. She had turned and left with her bright skirt wink-
ing out of sight with a snap. That closed door had sounded an
awful lot like *fuck you* and Grace could take the hint. Forcing
another meeting would not be the best move, so she settled
in and slowly unpacked her bag and gazed at her classroom.

The long tables from her time attending the school were
the same save the black stone top that was a change from the
blue. The room was still bright with a long row of windows

on one side letting light filter in, and even though a couple were open for a cool breeze, the faint scent of lemon cleaner still clung to the air. This was home for the next two years. It was that thought she clung to now. Maybe if she could focus on getting her room set up, she would be less likely to dwell on just how lonely this place felt already.

The excitement of coming home had dampened until she was questioning if signing that contract had been the best idea, after all. Grace stared at the laptop screen unseeingly. The agreement had come with a signing bonus she didn't need. She could easily give it back and be fine but that would leave the school without a science teacher. She knew small-town schools always had trouble with recruitment.

Her cell phone rang, pulling her out of her thoughts, and Grace welcomed the distraction. She connected the call without bothering to see who it was.

"This is Grace."

"Hey, kiddo. How's your first day?" Grace shouldn't have been surprised it was Nolan. Although he had come into her life when she was in high school, they had bonded less in a father–daughter way and more like a favored uncle. He had been the one person who didn't question Grace's career change and she was grateful for that after having gotten more than an earful from most of her friends and her mother.

Grace relaxed slightly as she continued connecting everything. "Not bad, though I don't think they consider this the first day since the students aren't here yet."

"Oh. Makes sense," he replied. "Well, is everyone being nice to you, at least?"

She chuckled. She knew he was as concerned as her mother about Grace leaving her university position and moving back to small-town Georgia, but somehow, he always managed to phrase that worry in a way that didn't raise her hackles. If she had been talking to her mother, even hinting at things not being 100-percent perfect would have gotten her a swift "I told you so" and probably a plane ticket.

"I've really only met the principal and he was nice. Gave me a tour of the school on the way to showing me my classroom. This place looks just like it did when I was a kid. I swear it even smells the same." It had been a little like walking into a time capsule if she were being honest.

She tapped on the keys before pausing. After her disastrous first run-in with Ava, she needed a second nonjudgmental opinion and Nolan was usually good at that. "Do you think I made a mistake coming back?"

He was quiet for a moment and Grace waited. She always appreciated that he took his time to respond to her questions rather than giving her a flippant answer. She might not like what he said, but at least she knew he wouldn't try to shame her. She loved her mom, but this was not a question Grace wanted to ask her.

"Well, I think you needed a change," he replied delicately. "I won't say this is a break, considering you're teaching high schoolers, but maybe this will help you decide what's next. You know, it's not a bad thing to not know what you want to do for the rest of your life. You're only old when you're dead."

Grace chuckled. It was a phrase he had repeated to her many times over the years, and she took it for the encouragement it was. This was just the start. She knew Ava was probably thinking back to the last time they spoke, so the best thing to do was give her time. Plus, Grace hadn't come here just for her. This was her home too.

"You're right. I know you are."

"Of course, I am, kiddo. And remember, we are only a plane ride away. You let us know and we will be there." Voices grew louder in the background. "Listen, give your mom and me a call tonight. We both want to make sure you're doing okay."

Grace knew he was probably being called away so she reassured him she would before disconnecting. It was good timing because no sooner had she put her phone down than the class speaker clicked on with Robert's voice calling for the teachers to head to the library for the staff meeting. Several deep breaths later, Grace felt ready to face everyone. This was going to be her life for the next two years and it was time to face it head-on.

Three

"So, I heard the new teacher used to go here."

Ava ground her teeth but said nothing as she took her seat. She hadn't managed to get anything done after being greeted by the still perfectly unblemished face that belonged to Grace fucking Jones. She hadn't seen the other woman in years outside of accidentally running across her profile online.

Ava hadn't been looking Grace up specifically. She had just been curious to see what their other classmates were up to and happened to see Grace tagged in a photo. It was normal to look up your former rival and hope they had gotten an unexpected visit from karma. Ava hadn't been able to help herself from clicking through a few more pictures. It wasn't until she had seen Grace with her arm around a woman Ava didn't recognize that she closed the profile. She hadn't been jealous. It was none of her business who Grace dated. If Ava occasionally ran across more pictures of her later, it was a coincidence and not because she was trying to keep up with Grace's life. She would die on that hill.

Grace had looked as shocked as Ava felt when the door opened. Her eyes had widened comically, and it made Ava wonder if there was something wrong beyond the fact that they were once again face-to-face after so many years. Grace's full lips had parted, and it had been her voice, soft with a hint of southern sweetness, that kicked Ava's brain into gear. She had blurted out one word before beating a hasty retreat to the safety of her classroom and shutting the door for an added barrier between her and the past she didn't need to remember.

"What do you think?" Brad continued, not clued into Ava's quiet panic. "I suppose if someone is from here and comes back, they're more likely to stick around."

That didn't make her feel any better. Why would Grace be here? Why would she want to stick around? Her mom didn't even live here anymore. As far as Ava knew, Grace hadn't come back to town once in the years after graduation. If she had come back, people would have spent days if not weeks talking about it.

"Are you listening to me?"

"No." Ava came up for air from her thoughts and glanced over at Brad. He was looking at her with a small frown. "I'm sorry. What did you say?"

"Are you alright? You look like you've seen a ghost and I do not have the time to be haunted this year."

"Haunted? What are you talking about?"

He waved a hand at her. "I'm talking about you staring out into space like you're possessed or something. You want to share with the class? Do I need to break out the smelling salts?"

Ava shook her head. "I'm not possessed, just... I know who the new teacher is."

Brad's frown deepened. "How? Were you holding out on me earlier?"

She shook her head. "No. I heard Robert in the hallway talking to someone and figured it was the new teacher, so I decided to be nice and go over to say hello." Ava was regretting that decision now. She hadn't even known what to say when the door opened. Grace was standing there looking like a tall glass of sweet iced tea and if not for the past slamming to the forefront of her memories, Ava would have been tempted to take a sip.

She really needed to date more if she was thinking of *her* that way. Clearly, it had been too damn long since Ava had been around someone who wasn't family, a colleague, or a friend, and it was affecting her sanity. Dating in a small town was difficult enough. Throw in the fact that she bowled from her same lane, and it made things damn near impossible even in a town as progressive and welcoming as Peach Blossom. Unless, like Brad, a person moved here with a partner, they weren't likely to find one outside of the internet and long-distance dating.

"Well, don't keep me in suspense," Brad cut in, interrupting her thoughts. "Who is it?"

She sighed. Going over her past wasn't the least bit appealing but now her past was in the classroom across the hall from her. Ava had no clue how to handle this.

Before she could say anything, movement at the doorway caught her attention and for the second time that day, Ava's gaze landed on Grace. The other woman seemed to glide in a way that Ava refused to admit she envied. Long legs were hidden under pressed slacks that matched the jacket adorning Grace's shoulders. Her long ink black hair fell straight over her shoulders, making Ava reach up a hand to finger her own curls. She never bothered to straighten her hair in the height of the Georgia heat, but clearly Grace had no such issues with humidity.

"Grace Jones."

"Like…like *the* model, Grace Jones?"

"No relation," Ava said, frowning at how easily that flowed off her tongue like no time had passed. It was something she and Grace used to joke about when they were younger.

Brad chuckled, only quieting when Robert started to speak.

"Welcome to our kickoff staff meeting for this upcoming year. I am happy to see so many familiar faces as we gear up for another great year of learning." He smiled wide as he looked around and Ava barely managed to keep her lips from curling in disgust. The man was fake with a capital *F*. "I am also excited to announce that we have a brand-new AP Chemistry teacher joining our ranks. Our very own, Grace Jones!"

His exclamation was met with a smattering of claps, but Ava's hands stayed firmly in her lap. How Grace managed to smile through such an awkward introduction, Ava would never understand. Her own introduction four years ago had been similarly awkward, and she had rushed to sit as soon as she were able. Grace though didn't seem to be suffering from any of the same issues as she waved like a pageant queen and gazed around.

"I'm looking forward to getting to know everyone," she said, voice carrying easily. Ava saw some of the other teachers straighten slightly as if invigorated by Grace's simple words. Instead, she crossed her arms and sat back. "This is my first year teaching high school, but I hope I can continue the successes you all have already started with the students."

Robert gestured for Grace to sit before he continued with his usual spiel. Ava tried to focus on his words, but all she could see was Grace moving down the aisle of chairs. There were a couple available, including one beside her, and Ava's pulse picked up when Grace continued to move closer. She squeezed her upper arms, muscles locking at the thought of having to sit beside Grace for the next couple of hours, only to feel as if her strings were cut when Grace stopped a couple chairs away and sat beside Janae, the school's art teacher.

"You alright over there?"

Brad's soft voice might as well have been a shout the way it startled Ava into jerking her eyes away from Grace. She fixed her gaze on Robert with a stiff nod. "Yeah, I'm fine. Why?"

"You were staring."

She didn't bother to reply to that comment. She hadn't been staring. *Right, and you're also not disappointed that Grace sat with someone else instead of you.* The thought was unnecessary. She didn't care who Grace sat with. What Grace Jones did with her time was none of Ava's concern. Not anymore.

"I was not." As far as comebacks went, it was weak. Thankfully, Robert spoke up again, drawing everyone's attention.

Ava tried to remain focused on his words, but it was harder to make her thoughts behave and they were inevitably drawn back to Grace. Out of anyone in the world, it had to be her that came back to teach. Even as Ava wanted to push Grace from her thoughts, she wanted to know why *here* and why *now*. A small part of her felt bad for their abrupt reintroduction, but what else was she supposed to do? How else was she supposed to act when confronted with the one former friend whose absence she felt the hardest? How was she supposed to act when she had been so easily left behind?

"Alright, everyone," Robert said with a clap of his hands rousing Ava from her musings. "We'll break for a longer lunch today. See you back in here at two. Don't be late."

Ava sighed as murmurs started up around her. She stayed seated for a moment, gathering her thoughts and trying to ignore other teachers who were making a beeline straight for Grace. She supposed she could forgive their excitement. It was somewhat novel to get some new blood in the teaching crowd and if it were anyone else, she too would be eager to get to know them. But she knew Grace. Or at least, she *had*. It might have been nearly a decade, but Ava was pretty sure she could pass over the meet-and-greet portion and skip to civil indifference. She would be helpful as far as teaching went, but they didn't need to interact more than that.

"We should go say hello."

"What?" Ava frowned up at Brad.

"I said, we should go say hi to Grace."

"Who is *we*?"

He rolled his eyes before prodding her into standing. "We as in you and me."

Ava batted his hands away even as she found herself being herded like cattle. "Let go of me. There is no need for me to go say hello when my classroom is across from hers. Plus, I already know her."

"Well, I don't," he replied with a smile too full of teeth to be genuine. "You can introduce us."

"No."

"Ava."

"No."

"I'll get Thomas to make that sandwich you like so much from his secret menu."

Ava paused and looked over her shoulder giving him a steady look. Brad's smile wasn't to be trusted, but she *was* hungry, and nothing tasted better than free food especially if it was his boyfriend making it. "Only if I get the love-of-my-life discount."

He snorted. "You usually get that anyway, but sure. Lunch is on me today."

"Fine," she finally agreed. "But we say hello, welcome to the shit show, and goodbye. No long-winded stories. I'm hungry and if we're late getting back—"

"Yes, yes, I know. Now, scoot your cute booty over there."

Ava slapped his hand away, but as much as she wanted to turn and walk the other way, she led him to where Grace was surrounded by other teachers. He would introduce himself and then they would leave.

In and out.

Easy.

Or, it would have been had she not gotten caught up thanks to Brad and his need to be welcoming. Today had started out so promising, but now Ava was wondering if she should have called out sick.

Four

Standing in front of the other teachers was enough to have Grace sweating under her jacket and regretting her outfit choices. If she had known most staff would show up in jeans and blouses, she would have done the same. Instead, she looked like she was about to conduct a business meeting. It left her off-kilter, and she couldn't find a seat fast enough.

There had been an empty chair next to Ava, and Grace had eyed it the whole time. At the last minute, it was the memory of Ava's back and the awkward reunion in her classroom doorway that had her slipping into a chair a few rows over.

Coward.

Her inner voice might have been an asshole, but it wasn't wrong. Confrontation wasn't her strong suit and this *thing* between them had her floundering. They hadn't left one another on the friendliest of terms, but Grace hadn't expected a welcome quite this chilly given that they had been friends and teammates before rivalry and some not-so-nice words drove them apart. She knew they should probably talk to make sure the school year went smoothly, but Grace had no idea how to even begin that conversation.

"Hey." A soft voice pulled her out of her thoughts and Grace quickly shook the offered hand. "I'm Janae."

"Grace," she said, kicking herself internally at being redundant after having just introduced herself to everyone. The other woman's smile was open and friendly though, so she rallied with a smile of her own. "Nice to meet you."

"You too," Janae replied. "It's nice to see another Black woman in here, especially teaching science."

Grace nodded, fully aware of how excited some people were when she interviewed for the job. Robert's face had lit up when she walked into the conference room two months ago. "I'm looking forward to it. It's going to be a big change though from being a teaching assistant and doing research at a university."

Janae's chuckle wasn't unkind as she nodded. "I came from teaching at a university too and it takes some time to get used to. It's nice being able to encourage younger students who might not have realized their future possibilities before college though. You might be able to inspire more future scientists if you play your cards right."

That was part of what had drawn Grace to choosing this position. She would miss her students, but she was looking forward to the challenge of teaching younger kids and showing them that learning about science could be fun. It might even help reignite her excitement for science, which had dimmed under the pressure she had been under at the university and with Emily.

"I hope so," she replied, before settling down as Robert continued talking. The conversation had helped take her mind off the awkwardness with Ava earlier, and it wasn't until they were dismissed for lunch, and she was fielding questions from some of the other teachers, that she was once again confronted with her past.

"Grace."

Ava's voice was calm and her gaze steady. The crowd seemed to part for her and even Janae moved away, leaving Grace alone with Ava and another teacher she didn't recognize.

"Hi, Ava." Grace counted it as a win that her voice seemed calm, even though on the inside she was anything but. "It's good to see you again."

"You as well." Ava turned and gestured at the man beside her. "Bradley wanted to come over and introduce himself."

The man leaned forward and offered his hand. His smile was wide, and Grace felt a little of her nervousness melt away in the face of it. "Bradley Parrish, but you can call me Brad. Great to meet you."

"You as well," Grace replied honestly. She could feel Ava's eyes on her, but she forced herself to keep her gaze on him. He was a tall guy with sand-hued skin and the type of naturally good looks that probably made him popular back in high school. "What subject do you teach?"

"PE, and I coach the debate team. I hear you are going to take us into the scientific future."

Grace chuckled and shook her head. "I don't know about that, but I am looking forward to doing some fun experiments with the students." When the room started to empty, she looked around before turning her attention back to Brad. "I suppose I should figure out what to do for lunch."

"Oh! Why don't you join Ava and me for lunch?" He glanced over at Ava with *something* sparkling in his mocha gaze. "We were about to head to my boyfriend's café to get a second wind, a couple more coffees, and some amazing sandwiches."

Grace looked over at Ava then, trying to read the expression on her face. A decade being gone meant she didn't know what the complicated eyebrow thrusts meant, but she was sure she was the last person Ava wanted to have lunch with.

"Seriously," Brad continued. "He makes all his bread in-house, and I'm not joking when I say you've never tasted paradise until you've had one of his sandwiches."

Ava snorted, drawing Grace's attention again. Just from the interaction they'd had so far, Grace was sure Ava didn't want to be anywhere near her. So, color her surprised when Ava spoke up in favor of it.

"You might as well give in now," she said, crossing her arms and looking off to the side. "Giving up isn't in Brad's vocabulary, and he's annoying when he starts whining."

Brad nodded, looking a lot like a bobblehead figurine. "She's right. I don't."

"Well…if you're sure—"

"We are. I'll drive."

Grace didn't get a chance to second-guess her decision as she was herded out of the building and toward a beat-up old Jeep. She climbed into the back seat and hoped she wasn't making a terrible mistake.

"So, what brought you back to town?" he asked as they

backed out of the parking lot and made their way down the street and onto the main road that ran straight to town.

"I helped put together a summer chemistry program in partnership with a couple of the high schools when I was finishing my PhD at Columbia and that's when I started thinking about teaching."

Brad whistled. "Wow. Cute and incredibly smart. How do you not have a ring on your finger already?"

"Um…" she trailed off.

"Really, Bradley?" Ava's interruption saved Grace from having to answer the question. "You don't have to answer that. Brad is bad about asking too many questions."

"And you don't ask enough," he shot back.

"I ask the questions that are needed, not the ones to satisfy my curiosity for gossip."

Brad's affronted gasp had Grace hiding a smile behind her hand. She didn't have any siblings, but she recalled being around Ava and her sisters when they were younger and how hilarious it was to be a spectator when they really got going. The conversation between Ava and Brad had that same familiar dynamic and was just as amusing. Brad kept glancing back with a gummy smile as he riled Ava up and Grace felt herself relax a little bit more.

Ava didn't glance back once, but Grace told herself it would take some time. She was starting off with a clean slate with Brad, so it was easy to fall into something fresh and new, but with Ava it was different. There was history there; history Grace knew they needed to address. For now though, she sat back and kept the easy smile on her face as they made their way into town.

It took some time to find a parking space, but Grace didn't mind the walk. She shimmied out of her jacket and unbuttoned the top of her blouse. The sun was high in the sky and the air sang with the shrill song of cicadas. This was the beat of summer she had missed when up north. Sure, she liked not having to drive and she would absolutely miss being able to essentially eat in a different culture every night, but it had also been too noisy, and she missed the stars. It was weird, but the moment she drove over the county line, it was like the years melted away and her body recognized this place as home.

"So, how does it feel to be back?"

Grace unbuttoned her cuffs and rolled up her sleeves, baring her lower arms to the heat of the sun. She caught Ava's eyes briefly before she looked away and started walking down the sidewalk. "It feels pretty good so far," she answered honestly. "It had been a while since I came back, and things have changed. But it also still feels the same, you know?"

Brad fell into step beside her with Ava leading the way. Grace couldn't help but smile as she saw a few familiar places that she had spent a lot of time in growing up. The old bookstore was still there, as was the family-owned pharmacy that she remembered getting suckers from every time her mom visited. A lot was still the same, but a lot had changed as well. There were more fast-food places on the way to Main Street and a Walmart that she hadn't remembered being there ten years ago. The old vet hospital had expanded and there was even a new car dealership.

"I can imagine," Brad said as they turned a corner. "The town I'm from is smaller than Peach Blossom, so for me this is a good mix. I lived in Atlanta for a while, but it wasn't really my scene. Helped me bag a cutie though."

Grace chuckled and turned her face up at the sun, not at all concerned with the fact that she could feel her makeup melting. This was home.

Soon enough, Ava turned and opened a door. The bell above the sign naming the place as T-Bird Diner hit the wood loudly, announcing their arrival. Grace followed and sighed at the blast of ice-cold air that met her. Inside, the sun streamed in from the large windows and there was a hum of activity as others enjoyed their lunches. Grace vaguely recognized a few faces from the group of teachers she had met and waved when they acknowledged her. When Ava steered them toward a booth and sat down, Grace hesitated, not knowing whether it would be better to sit across and fight the urge to stare or beside Ava and fight the urge to lean closer. In the end, she slid onto the seat across from her and hoped the food would be good enough to steal away her attention. No sooner had they sat down when a man walked over to their table.

He was a couple inches taller than Grace with skin the color of wet earth. He hadn't been smiling as he walked up, but when his gaze turned to Brad, something in his expression seemed to soften. Grace was pretty sure this was Thomas, the boyfriend she had been told about, and Brad's radiant smile pretty much confirmed it.

"Please don't tell me you two are causing trouble again." Thomas's voice was soft and deep, the type of voice that could talk you into beautiful dreams. Even Grace could appreciate the baritone flavor of it.

Brad shook his head, but his smile didn't wane. "No trouble today. Just making new friends." He gestured toward Grace. "This is Grace Jones, the new science teacher at the school. We decided to introduce her to your famous sandwiches before she made the mistake of going elsewhere for lunch."

Thomas snorted but turned to look at Grace. "It's good to meet you. Hopefully, these two don't scare you away from coming back in."

Grace smiled up at him. "I never shy away from good food." After he took their orders, he headed off to the back of the café, leaving Grace to wonder if this was when things got awkward again.

"So, he's cute," she threw out before giving Brad a thumbs-up. "Good job you."

Brad ducked his head, but his smile looked pleased. "I had next to nothing to do with it. He saved me from being stood up, fed me, and didn't complain when I kept coming back. He does have a brother, if you're interested." He looked her up and down before continuing, "He also has a sister, though I think she might be dating someone."

Grace snorted at his subtle yet obvious play. She had nothing to hide and didn't feel the need to keep her sexuality a secret. All it would take was one social media search anyway to see her choice of past partners. "Well, if she is ever single again, let me know."

Ava's expression didn't change, but she did stare at Grace a beat longer than before. Grace wondered if that was because she was surprised by Grace's response. Ava had dated men and women, if her social media was accurate, so Grace doubted there would be any conflict there.

"I did just get out of a relationship though, so probably won't be ready for dating anytime soon."

Brad nodded before switching gears to work-related questions that Grace appreciated. She could see them becoming good friends eventually, but for now Grace was happy enough to sit back and chat about the upcoming school year and try to pretend that she wasn't watching Ava more than was necessary.

Five

Grace sighed as she stared into her empty refrigerator and tried not to think about the sandwich that was no longer in there. Brad hadn't been lying about how great Thomas's sandwiches were. He had made her a pesto, mozzarella, and tomato panini that was so good she immediately ordered a second to take home for later. Grace had no shame when it came to good food. But maybe there was a little shame, considering she ate it before the night was over.

The conversation after they had gotten to the café had been stilted, with Brad carrying most of it, but it wasn't completely terrible. Ava had even looked her way a couple times with more than a blank stare. The smile she had when she first bit into her own sandwich was enough to leave Grace thinking about the days when Ava did nothing but smile. It was strange to realize how much had changed.

"God, I am pathetic," Grace groaned before shutting the

refrigerator. "Food first, then I can sit around questioning what is my life."

There wasn't much she could do about the lack of food other than take her ass to the grocery store. She hadn't dealt with small-town living since reluctantly leaving the first time at eighteen, secure in the knowledge that there was always somewhere to return. It had always appealed to her to come back to take a break and slow things down, but one thing or another had always pushed that desire back.

First, it was that she was interning overseas. Then, it was that her mother and stepfather had wanted her to join them for a season in Mexico. Even after thinking she might come back, she ended up starting her PhD program and didn't have much time off. When she did have free time, Emily had insisted on doing something more exciting than spending time in a small town in the middle-of-nowhere Georgia.

The old house Grace had grown up in had still been here though, and she was glad she had talked her mom into keeping it instead of selling it off or tearing it down. Since moving back, she had spent most of her time inside, organizing and reorganizing the rooms. She might have also spent some of the time rocking back and forth under a cold spray of water as she tried to talk herself out of an anxiety attack at having quit her research and changing the trajectory of her life, but that was to be expected.

Totally normal.

"Yeah, it's time to get out and about before I talk to *and* respond to myself."

The sun was high in the sky when Grace finally made her

way out of the house and the short walk to her car left her wiping sweat from her forehead. The heat was almost unbearable after spending so much time farther north and the humidity left her tank top sticking to her back. The air seemed to shimmer in front of her as she backed out of the driveway. It took a few moments for the air-conditioning in her car to kick in full blast, and it almost wasn't worth it since it took so little time to get to the family-owned grocery store in town. She could have driven a bit farther and gone to one of the chain supermarkets that had popped up since she left, but she wanted to fully get back into the community and part of that was shopping local. Plus, she wondered if it was still owned by Mrs. Patrick. She was eager to build back ties that had lapsed in her absence.

"Well, as I live and breathe. I heard you came back, but I didn't believe it until now."

Grace smiled and let herself be pulled into a tight hug. "Hey, Mama Patrick. How are you?"

The older woman hadn't changed aside from having more gray in her hair and a couple extra smile lines on her face. Grace was amazed at the height difference. Mrs. Dahlia Patrick might be shorter than her now, but she still felt larger than life. Kind brown eyes looked up at her and the familiar smile was like the warmest of hugs.

"Can't complain. I'm still here." Mrs. Patrick pulled her farther into the store, and Grace let herself look around, feeling something loosen inside her chest. When she was a kid, this had been a place she frequently stopped in after school or on the weekends, before she and her friends headed elsewhere to see what kind of trouble they could get into. "I am surprised to see you back though. I thought for sure you were out and gone from here for good."

"No way," Grace replied, wrapping an arm around Mrs. Patrick's shoulder. "I always would have come back here at some point in time. Y'all can't get rid of me that easily."

Mrs. Patrick swatted at her arm but chuckled. "Not about getting rid of you. Most of you youngins tend to grow up and move on. It's the way things go." Heat rushed in when the front doors opened again and someone else walked in. "Go on and get your things. But don't you even think of leaving without letting me know."

"Yes, ma'am." Spirits lifted, Grace grabbed a small basket and made her way through the aisles.

The produce was still as fresh as it had been years ago, and she knew it was grown locally. She got enough to hold her over for the next couple of days before making her way back to the front. There was a girl there in one of the three counters available who looked to be about high school–aged, but Mrs. Patrick was nowhere to be seen. Grace unloaded her items and gave the girl a small smile. Silence stretched between them for a moment only broken by the beep of the barcode reader before she decided to speak up.

"Hey, um…sorry, what's your name?" Grace asked, feeling awkward with saying *hey you* to someone she didn't know. The girl glanced up from where she was keying in Grace's items and gave her a weak smile.

"Tabitha."

"Tabitha," Grace repeated with a nod. "Is Mrs. Patrick in the back or…?"

Tabitha leaned back and looked at a small television on the counter beside her. "She's out front, talking to Ms. Ava."

Grace swallowed hard, her gaze drawn toward the door. It opened and Ava walked in, looking just as good as she had when Grace first laid eyes on her the day before. Thick curls were pulled back and piled high on her head, leaving Ava's shoulders bare. The thin-strapped top she wore was sunflower yellow and looked bright and cheerful against her deep brown skin. Another flowy skirt swirled around her, making Ava seem like she should be lounging on a beach somewhere with a glass of something equally colorful in her hand. After realizing she had been staring, Grace knew she was going to have to say something if only to not be rude.

"Hey, Ava."

Ava paused as she reached for a basket and, if not for being so tuned in to her, Grace might not have noticed the aborted motion. When she straightened, Ava's face was expressionless, but Mrs. Patrick was looking back and forth between the two of them with a small smirk on her face. That didn't bode well. Mrs. Patrick wasn't the biggest gossip in town, but she also wasn't the quietest, especially if she could fix something she thought was broken.

"Grace. It's good to see you again."

Was it? By the tone of her voice, Grace wasn't so sure. Not wanting to start anything or make things more awkward, she decided to not press and instead opted to get out of the store as quickly as possible with at least a portion of her threadbare dignity intact.

"You as well." Grace gathered her items and put them in the bags she had brought with her. When she glanced back up, Ava had moved on and was making her way down an aisle. Grace let out a breath and tried not to think too hard about the tension between them. Having lunch together had fooled her into thinking that maybe things would have warmed between the two of them. With anyone else from high school, Grace might have tried cracking a joke or asking them about what they had been up to since graduation. But then, she hadn't ended on bad terms with anyone else, which made a mountain of difference.

She had a break today, but tomorrow she would be right back at school with Ava across the hall. Sure, she could leave her door closed the whole time, but that would make it seem too obvious that she was avoiding her. Grace needed to come up with a plan that didn't consist of sitting back and waiting to see what would happen. That wasn't how she treated anything else in her life, so why was she doing it now?

"Well, that was interesting." Mrs. Patrick came back around the counter and patted Tabitha on the hand. "Go on and take your lunch, hun. There should be some things to unpack and set out when you get back."

Grace nodded at Tabitha before her attention was again pulled back to the awkwardness at hand.

"You know, there was a time when you two were thick as thieves," Mrs. Patrick said. "If we saw one of you, the other wasn't too far behind."

"Yeah," Grace replied, not knowing what to say. She fondly

remembered those days before the rivalry between them left them both worse for wear. So much time had passed, and so many things had changed.

They had changed.

"It was great to see you, Mrs. Patrick."

She smiled knowingly and patted Grace's hand like she had Tabitha's. "You too, baby. Don't be a stranger. You staying out in your old house?" Grace nodded. "We started doing a delivery service too so feel free to let me know if you want to set that up. Deliveries come every Monday, Wednesday, and Friday. Tabitha even got me set up online."

"Yes, ma'am. I'll let you know." Grace hefted the bag straps onto her shoulders and walked around the counter. She glanced around one last time, eyes landing on Ava as she came out of an aisle. Their gazes caught, but it was Grace who broke first. With a nod, she called out a final goodbye and made her way out of the store.

She could feel their gazes on her back as she tried not to look like she was making a quick escape. Clearly, she needed to rethink her strategy when it came to reacclimating to being around Ava because avoidance would never work. They were going to have to talk again sometime and the sooner they did, the sooner this awkward thing between them could be dealt with and overcome.

Hopefully.

After returning home and putting away her groceries, she tried to come up with a plan of attack. She had only been back in town consistently for a week and the whole time she had not seen hide nor hair of Ava. Now it seemed that bubble had popped. Tomorrow, she would be right back where she was yesterday and if she were anymore awkward, none of them would survive.

"Knock knock!" a voice rang out from the front of the house, startling her. Grace quickly made her way to the front door and her eyes widened when she saw her mother.

"Mom? What are you doing here?"

"What? Am I not allowed to come visit my one and only daughter?" Grace didn't know what to say to that as she moved and was captured in a quick hug. Her mom looked around, nose wrinkling. "I don't know why you insisted on keeping this old house the way it was. Wouldn't it have been better to tear it down and put up something more modern?"

The thought of someone coming in and demolishing the home she grew up in was like a hand squeezing around her heart. Grace couldn't understand why her mother even thought that was something she wanted. The house was the last piece of her dad she had left outside of a few watches and photo albums. Getting rid of it wasn't an option.

"No, Mom. Why would I—no. I like the house the way it is."

Millie Bradford was not known for keeping her thoughts to herself, but Grace was relieved when she didn't push for why the house had to stay the way it was. Instead, she stepped farther inside. "Well, at least you put up some new coats of paint. Maybe I could bring in some different furniture to really help brighten up the place."

Grace sighed and shook her head. She loved her mother, but

there were times when she wished she weren't so involved. "I plan on getting some new furniture eventually."

"Or," Millie continued, "Nolan has the furniture from the summer house in storage you could use. I'm sure he would love to know it was here instead of gathering dust."

"That really isn't necessary, Mom."

"Oh, it's fine, sweetie. It will be a welcome-home present from us." Before Grace could decline again, her mom was on the phone. It would be pointless to fight now and pushing would only devolve into a guilt trip that Grace didn't have the spoons to deal with. She shook her head and walked back into the kitchen, hunger making itself known again.

She grabbed some bread, intent on making some easy sandwiches. Nothing would beat the ones she'd had from Thomas's café, but it would at least hold her over for now until she felt up to making something more substantial. By the time her mom finished her phone call and wandered into the kitchen, Grace was chewing on her second sandwich and felt with it enough to deal with whatever had really brought her mom to the town.

"Now," Millie said, setting her purse on the counter. "Tell me everything. How was your first day?"

Grace shrugged. "It was fine. The principal showed me my class and introduced me to the other teachers. I had lunch with a couple of them yesterday."

"Oh, good. I'm glad you're making friends. I was so worried about you coming back here with all this." She waved her hand around. "Most people move away and stay away once they see how much good there is out there. I know your father would have been so proud to see you branch out after everything that happened."

"There's good here too, Mom," Grace pushed back. "I think I am going to really like being back here for the next couple years."

Millie nodded, though her expression said she didn't agree. "Well, remember your plan. Two years teaching here and then on to bigger and better. I'm sure Nolan has some contacts who would love to meet you. He talks so highly of—" Her words were cut off when her phone rang again, and Millie held up a finger before she connected the call.

Grace snorted softly when her mom turned and walked back out of the kitchen, no doubt on the phone with one of the women who made up her social group of wives whose husbands were all in business together. Grace was still shocked that her mom had showed up in-person to begin with. After Grace's father's death, Millie had always talked about getting out and starting somewhere new away from the painful memories. It wasn't until Grace's senior year that the desire became a reality regardless of her desire to finish out high school with her friends.

And Ava.

With another sigh, she thought over her list of things to do tomorrow. Ava was still a big unchecked box on that list, but she doubted her mother would have anything helpful to add. To her, the town and the people in it were a thing of the past. Grace wasn't quite convinced, but until she had a plan, she wasn't quite sure how or even if she wanted to make this place part of her long-term future.

Six

"Hey, bestie."

Ava groaned. "Absolutely not." She picked up some papers, wondering how long she needed to stare at them before they made sense. "I should have taken this year off to work on my book without teenage drama and gossipy coworkers around to scare my muse away."

"Nah, you would have missed us too much." Brad laughed when Ava fixed him with a glare. "What? You know I'm right."

"I know no such thing," she denied before opening the top right drawer in her desk and shoving the papers inside. Ever since the lunch she hadn't asked for, her mind had been preoccupied by things she'd rather not think about. Namely, Grace and the fact that not only was she annoyingly attractive, but also she dated women. Openly. If it were anyone else, Ava would have had to rethink her no-sleeping-with-people-she-worked-with rule. As it was, she was wondering why the universe had decided to be so cruel. A knock on the door sent her pulse racing, but when she looked up, it was only Alyssa, one of the other English teachers whom she had worked with since joining the school. "Hey, Alyssa. What's up?"

Alyssa pushed a box through the doorway. "Office asked me to drop off your books when I went to pick up mine."

"Oh, thanks!" Ava had worn jeans today for that very reason. She was expecting a few more boxes to be delivered and she didn't feel like getting caught up in her skirts while she moved around. She grunted as she lifted the box and turned to put it on one of the tables.

"So, how are things with the new girl?" Alyssa asked, pitching her voice low. Ava heard Brad making shushing noises behind her and sighed. She had hoped to get through the day without having to talk about Grace. Running into her yesterday had been awkward enough and Mrs. Patrick was no doubt spreading word about just how awkward it was. She loved the older woman but being the talk of the town was not something Ava enjoyed.

When Brad said nothing, Ava finally turned around and let her expression settle into a mask of indifference. Clearly, she was going to have to figure out how to navigate talking about Grace before the year really began. Students could smell conflict a mile away and would ruthlessly exploit that to their gain. She didn't need any of them trying to sow discord amongst the teachers. There was enough drama with the students without the teachers being dragged into it.

"They seem to be going fine," Ava replied finally when it was clear Brad was going to leave her hanging. "I saw her earlier bringing her own books in."

Alyssa nodded. "Seems she's settling in, then."

"Seems so."

"We got to know her a little a couple days ago when she ate lunch with us," Brad chimed in. He leaned on one of the desks and folded his arms. "She seems sweet. Maybe a little anxious about the start of the school year."

Ava wanted to roll her eyes at that one. Grace didn't get anxious. The woman always had nerves of fucking steel and never choked under pressure. Ava couldn't remember a time when Grace appeared anxious about anything. That word was probably nowhere in her vocabulary. "She seemed ready for the school year to me."

Alyssa cocked an eyebrow up at Ava's words. "Oh? So, she hasn't come over here and asked you about anything at all?"

"Nope," Ava replied, popping the last *p* before turning her attention back to the box. "I'm sure she has it all under control."

To Ava, there was nothing more to discuss. She had seen Grace earlier that morning. She had come in a few minutes after Ava and this time had ditched the suit and was in well-fitting jeans and a loose, flowy forest green blouse. Ava had tried not to look like she was staring, but Grace had caught her eye and paused before nodding her head in greeting. Ava knew she would look like an ass if she didn't return it, so she did the same. This time, Grace had kept her door open, giving Ava a clear line of sight to her desk when she stood in front of her board.

It had taken Ava a few moments to realize that she was still standing in front of the whiteboard and gazing across the hallway into Grace's room. She made a strategic decision then to leave her door open as well. They were colleagues after all, and Grace *was* new. She wouldn't begrudge the other woman having questions as she settled in. Still, it had left her feeling off-kilter the longer time passed between the two of them with Grace not coming over and reaching out. Ava wasn't even sure why the hell it mattered to her. She didn't want to talk to Grace anyway.

"You all heading back to Thomas's for lunch again today?"

"Probably," Brad replied, including Ava in that with a sweep of his hand. "Unless Ava wants to go elsewhere."

She shrugged and straightened. "The café is fine with me. The closer it gets to the start of the new year, the less of an appetite I have anyway."

Alyssa nodded. "I know what you mean. I put a couple new books on the list this year, and I'm hoping I made a good choice, otherwise..." she trailed off with a slicing motion on her neck. "Luckily, I'm married to the librarian otherwise I don't know if I would be up to speed on what kids like to read these days. Pretty sure they wouldn't be happy with me reading them a book on colors and shapes."

Brad laughed and Ava chuckled along at the thought of Alyssa reading her toddler's books aloud to her junior and senior students. When Alyssa fixed blue eyes on her, Ava swallowed hard.

"So, a little birdy told me that you and newbie were quite the pair back in the day."

She wanted to wrinkle her nose in disgust at how eager Alyssa was to discuss matters Ava thought were best left in the past, but she knew she had to keep up her appearance of being unbothered if she wanted to keep herself out of the school's rumor mill. The best approach was probably a direct one without adding too much detail.

"Grace and I were on the bowling team together."

"I didn't realize you two were on the team together." Brad gave her a considering look.

"Yes, well, it was a long time ago," she said simply, hoping the bitterness she felt at how their camaraderie had ended didn't carry over into her tone. "As far as I know, the team only lasted another year after I graduated."

"Huh," Alyssa said, giving her a once-over. Ava let her look her fill. She had nothing to hide. The intercom clicking on drew all their attention, and Ava grimaced at the static overhead before Robert's voice came on.

"Teachers, our staff meeting today will start an hour earlier than originally planned. Please be on time and ready to work. That is all."

This time, Ava didn't hide her annoyance. It was echoed on Brad's and Alyssa's faces, so she knew she wasn't alone in her feelings. Movement by the door caught her attention.

"Sorry to interrupt."

Alyssa whirled around faster than Ava had ever seen her move. When Ava saw who was in the doorway, she begrudgingly understood Alyssa's excitement. "Oh, you aren't interrupting anything. In fact, we were just talking about y—"

"Bowling," Ava cut in. "We were talking about bowling. Did you need something?"

Grace looked at her for a beat before she gestured behind her. "I got a strange email, and I was wondering if you wouldn't mind taking a look at it." She glanced between the three of them. "Or any of you. I didn't want to ignore it if it was important."

Alyssa jumped up, walking quickly over to Grace and linking an arm with hers. "I'll help you with that. It's probably a little phishing exercise IT sent out to test if you were a security risk. They do that every so often to see how many people they can catch and force into extra training." Brad nodded in agreement, but Ava stayed quiet as she watched them walk out.

Silence fell over the room after they left, and Ava tried to pretend it was because they were both thinking about safe topics like the upcoming staff meeting or global warming. She should have known not to get her hopes up by now. That was always a good way to have them come crashing back down to earth.

"Okay, you have been acting weird for the past couple days. What gives?"

"I don't know what you're talking about."

Brad's hand came down in front of Ava halting her from taking the books out of the box. She sighed before glaring up at him. There was still so much to get done and the last thing she needed to deal with was a meddlesome friend.

"Brad, seriously. I have work to do."

"And I will let you get back to doing it," he replied, giving her hope anew before slamming it to the ground again. "After you tell me what the hell is going on with you. Every time Grace is around, you start acting all weird."

"We've been around her like twice."

"Still weird," he pointed out. "You might as well spill it

now because you know I am not going to rest until I figure out what is going on."

Ava set the book in her hand down, feeling slightly better at the loud thump it let out. "You can be a real pain in the ass sometimes, you know that right?"

"Oh, no. We are not talking about my issues right now," he countered before walking over and shutting the classroom door. He leaned back on it and crossed his arms. "Now. We are alone. Tell me everything."

She groaned before looking toward the windows. The day was perfect with hardly a cloud in the sky and yet Ava could feel her mood sinking like a ship in a storm. "Fine. Grace and I have…history."

Brad rolled his eyes. "Anyone with two eyes and a sensitivity to drama could tell that. Give me more."

"There isn't more to give," Ava insisted even as she internally winced at her own lie. There was a lot more to give, but she didn't see the point in bringing it up now. It was over and done with. They had both grown up and moved on. "We were good friends as kids, and we grew apart when she switched schools. It happens all the time. It's just weird to see her now because we haven't talked in years."

He slowly lowered his arms. "Okay. I can understand that, but I still feel like there is a lot you're leaving out. Did you two ever…you know…date?"

Did we? It was a question that had come up in Ava's mind the first couple years after they had gone their separate ways, and she still didn't have a definitive answer. By the time she had noticed something strange and new building between them, things had already spiraled too far out of control, leaving them on opposite sides of a line she hadn't been aware was being drawn. When she thought about it, Ava wondered if Grace's mom knew something was up. It would have explained why she always seemed on edge when Ava was around.

"No," she said finally. In the end, they had never talked about that night. Things had been so overwhelmingly hectic after that, it had gotten buried and then forcefully forgotten. "We kissed once, but that was it."

Brad's eyebrows raised. "Oh really?"

This time it was Ava who was left rolling her eyes at his tone. "We were young. Lots of girls kiss their friends."

"That is such a cop-out and you know it."

"It doesn't matter. We grew up and moved on," she insisted. "It was ten years ago. I'm sure she doesn't even remember it."

And, if Ava found herself wondering if Grace did remember that kiss they shared so long ago, that was nobody's business but her own.

"Is having her across the hall going to cause a problem?"

Ava frowned. "Having who across the hall?" He blinked at her with a "bitch, you tried it" look on his face. She sucked her teeth but gave in if only so they could move on. "No, there won't be any problems."

"Are you sure? Because you have been acting off since she got here and as far as I know, she's the only thing new."

Ava didn't want to concede that he may have a point about that. Having Grace across the hall wasn't ideal. Hell, having her in the town at all was so far from ideal that Ava didn't even know how to handle it. But she knew admitting that would mean having Brad up her ass, asking if she were okay every five seconds. She didn't need the headache. And really, she was a grown-ass adult. She dealt with people she didn't like all the time. She was southern. Being civil was practically built into her DNA.

"You know how you get when you don't like someone," he said before she could speak up.

"What the fuck is that supposed to mean?"

"You know exactly what that means. You hide indifference easily, but dislike shows all over your face." Brad smiled but it did nothing to combat the truth in his words. Ava knew she wasn't always able to hide when she wasn't about someone. Still, she didn't have a choice here. If Grace went to Robert with any issues, Ava doubted he would see her side of things.

"Besides, maybe Grace being here will restart your friendship. Ten years is a long time and people change. This could be the start of something wonderful and new."

Ava wrinkled her nose. "Your boundless optimism is nauseating at times, but fine," she said quickly before he said anything more. "I will do my best to go into this year with an open mind. Besides, soon we will all be too damn busy to have issues."

She didn't believe that, but Ava knew if this awkwardness that seemed to linger was going to abate, she needed to give things a try. Perhaps leaving the past behind them would work out.

Seven

Grace smiled and waved when Alyssa walked out of her classroom. She wondered if she was headed back over to Ava's. She wanted to follow, but that probably would go over as well as being invited to lunch had. Plus, she did have a lot to do. The email issue had been solved finally. Grace hadn't quite been prepared to answer some of the questions Alyssa asked so nonchalantly, but she thought she had handled it adequately.

"Ava told me you two were on the bowling team together."

It had been a question completely out of left field.

"We were for a couple years, yes."

Alyssa's blue eyes had glittered then as she fixed Grace with a wide smile. "That is so random. I didn't even know bowling was considered a sport."

Grace felt a string of irritation thread through her. It wasn't the first time she'd heard that. Emily had initially teased her about it, but after Grace had won a couple tournaments, she had laid off the jokes and even accompanied Grace to a few events out of state.

"I think Ava does bowl in a league on the weekends. You two should team back up."

As much as Grace would like that, she had known Ava wouldn't appreciate her randomly showing up. Still, maybe Grace could figure out a way to accidentally on purpose show up. She had quit her old league when she left New York and she did miss it. There was something about the balls smashing the pins that was very therapeutic.

"Now that I think about it, I do remember Ava trying to get a bowling team started here at the school a couple years ago."

Grace hadn't been able to keep herself from latching on to that. "She did?"

Alyssa had nodded before shrugging. "Yeah. Nothing came of it though. Robert is a tight-ass when it comes to money and clubs. He probably saw it as useless." She leaned up then. "You should be good to go now."

Grace had nodded before thanking Alyssa for helping her out. She was grateful, but now she had even more to think about. Robert had mentioned his desire for Grace to think about sponsoring an extracurricular activity during her interview and she had happily thrown out some ideas about a science club. But Alyssa might have just given Grace something to help her bridge the gap with Ava. Before she could overthink it, Grace left her classroom and headed to the office. She was running on vague ideas of what to say by the time she made it to the front office and was welcomed back to the principal's open door.

"Ms. Jones, I didn't realize we had a meeting scheduled today." Robert stood when she walked in and reached out a hand. She shook it with a quick smile before sitting in the offered seat across from his desk. "Are you settling in well?"

She nodded. "I am. Everyone has been very helpful."

"Glad to hear it." He clapped his hands before taking his seat again and looking at her expectantly. "So, what can I do for you?"

"Well, I remember you asking about potentially sponsoring a club this year and I had an idea I wanted to run by you." At his nod of agreement, she continued. "I'm not sure if you know but there used to be a bowling team here at Peach Blossom."

He scratched his chin and looked up at the ceiling. "I vaguely remember Ms. Williams mention something about that. I also recall it only lasting a couple years before being dissolved."

Grace nodded. "I heard, but I think it would be a good idea if we thought about reinstating it."

Robert frowned slightly, and Grace's pulse picked up. She knew she needed to make her case and make it fast before he blew her off completely. "I think Ava, I mean Ms. Williams, might know if there is enough interest, and we could use it as a learning opportunity for the students."

His frown didn't lessen, but Robert slowly nodded, and his gaze shifted to somewhere over Grace's shoulder. "We have been toying with adding an additional girl's sport to balance the offerings out."

Grace nodded with him in encouragement. She didn't know the first thing about starting a school team, but she figured the seed had been planted at least, with Ava's initial push and now Grace's. Surely, both of them wouldn't be completely ignored.

"You make a good point," Robert said finally. "Can you do some initial research about leagues and what we would need to do to get this idea of yours off the ground?"

Grace frowned. This wasn't her idea. Not the way he was implying. "I'm sure Ms. Williams probably started looking over the necessary steps when she brought it up previously. I can meet with her and see what might need to be done and get back to you?"

Robert stood up, prompting Grace to stand as well. He reached out his hand with a smile and Grace quickly did the same, shaking his hand. When he withdrew, he fixed his suit jacket and she considered herself effectively dismissed. Grace had thought that being in a high school would be completely different, but the principal acted like some of the professors she had worked with.

"I like your initiative, Grace," he said before walking around his desk. He gestured to the door, and she turned, following his lead. "That will serve you and the students well around here. We need teachers who are more than willing to go that step further to provide the students with a host of experiences. Keep up the good work."

Now Grace did feel dismissed. She wanted to believe the words but something about the way he said them felt like little more than lip service. With a sigh, she prepared herself to partake in some fruitless research that would probably be promptly ignored just like it no doubt had been when Ava brought it to him. With a tight smile, Grace nodded to Robert and thanked him for his time before making her way back to her class.

Things were quiet, though she knew next week all that would change. Anxiety bubbled in her as she thought about walking into class on Monday and seeing a room of kids staring back at her. It was the same anxiety she had at the start of each semester, but it was made worse by the fact that this classroom would be her own, to make of it what she would. The thought of messing up was terrifying.

Grace glanced over at Ava's classroom, but the other woman was nowhere to be seen and she didn't want to risk sticking her head through the doorway without a game plan for what to say once she had Ava's attention. Instead, she walked into her own classroom and sat down at her desk with a sigh. The computer screen in front of her was dark like her mood.

No.

She sat up straighter and thought about how much she and Ava had enjoyed bowling together when they were kids, before stats started to mean more to them. It hadn't been the only thing to bring them together, but if Alyssa was right and Ava still enjoyed it as much as she had before, Grace had to try to use that opening to her advantage. She couldn't chicken out of this. Not if she wanted to find her way back into Ava's circle and solve this tangled web of a mess between them.

With a nod, she turned her laptop back on and moused over to the search bar. Talking to Ava about things crossed her mind, but Grace wanted to have as much information as possible at her fingertips before she crossed that bridge.

Determined, she got to work sifting through facts until she

felt the sting of not blinking enough. A knock had her fingers freezing in the air and she turned to see Ava standing in the doorway. She was wearing jeans, with a bright tie-dye-pattern top. Her curls were piled on top of her head with a rainbow headband finishing off the look. The whole thing should have clashed, but she effortlessly made it work. Grace envied that. She spent so much time each night sifting through outfits, hoping they would turn out right.

"Ava, hi." Grace internally kicked herself. One of these days, she would get her shit together and figure out a way to say hello that didn't make her sound like an awkward teenager. "Is everything okay?"

Ava took a couple steps into the room before gesturing behind her. "The staff meeting is about to start, and I thought I would come see if you had left already."

A quick glance at the clock let Grace know she had been lost in her research for nearly the whole hour. "Oh, wow, I didn't realize time had gone by that quickly."

"What were you looking at?" Ava asked. "I called your name a couple times, but you didn't respond."

Grace looked at her screen before shutting the laptop with a click. She wasn't ready to tell Ava about her conversation with Robert or the information she had found. She needed more time to feel comfortable with approaching Ava and hopefully working with her to convince Robert that a bowling team was a good idea. She had to be strategic and play her cards right.

"Oh, nothing. Just some last-minute ideas for experiments." She stood and tried to look calm and collected. Ava had sought her out directly. That had to mean something, right? Unless it meant nothing. The possibilities were almost enough to have Grace tripping over her feet. "Are you… I mean, do you…"

Ava cocked an eyebrow when she trailed off. Grace had presented scientific research in front of a room of faculty on only two hours of sleep and half a can of Red Bull, yet somehow being in front of Ava had her struggling to voice a coherent thought.

"Should we go?" Grace finally got out, feeling proud of finally finishing a sentence. She took a step toward the door, happy to find Ava following closely. Grace paused at the door and gestured for Ava to go through first.

"Since when are you so polite?" Ava asked with a soft snort.

"I've always been polite." The look she got in return had Grace smothering her own snort behind laughter. "I have. Mom would have had my head if I weren't."

Ava nodded before looking ahead. "Your mom always was weirdly strict about that."

"She still is."

They made their way down the hallway, pausing when other teachers stepped out of their classrooms. Ava called out hellos and Grace followed her lead, occasionally reintroducing herself until they made it to the library. When they entered, Grace saw Brad waving at them and she pointed him out before following Ava to where he was saving two chairs for them.

This time, Grace found herself seated beside Ava like she had wanted to be before, and she figured this was a good first step at reigniting their friendship. She knew they still needed to talk to air everything out, but it didn't have to happen today. They had the entire school year to get to know one another again and resolve their past. Fresh starts didn't come every day, and Grace didn't want to rock the tentative peace she could see them slipping into. When Robert walked in, she turned her attention to him.

"Welcome back, teachers. I have a couple of announcements before we get into our main topics for today." He looked around, gaze landing on Grace. She felt a frisson of unease slide up her spine.

"First, the teacher parking lot will be expanding. The last two rows will be blocked off as construction takes place so, please try to park as far from there as possible. I would encourage you to utilize carpools until the expansion is completed."

Ava leaned over to whisper to her. "They have been talking about doing that for three years and just broke ground a few weeks ago. That tells you how slow things tend to move around here."

Grace ducked her head with a smile. "So, requests are met with glacial speeds. Got it." She was warmed at Ava's soft chuckle. She mentally braced herself for what that meant for her earlier request. If it took three years to get to something as needed as parking, Grace figured she wouldn't hear anything about the bowling team for the entire two years she was at the school.

It never occurred to her that she would be wrong.

"Second, as you all know, we have been looking into additional extracurriculars to get students interested in new opportunities for building their experiences ahead of college applications." Grace saw a few teachers nodding in agreement.

"Well, one of our very own has come to me with an excellent plan for a low-cost way to do that."

"Huh, I'm surprised he didn't just allot more money to the football team," Ava whispered. She was leaning toward Brad, but her voice was pitched just loud enough for Grace to hear her words as well. It shouldn't have surprised Grace to hear that football was still king at the school. It was the same when they were younger. No matter how few games the team won in a season, anytime they needed something, magically there was more money in the budget to give them.

When Robert turned his gaze toward Grace again, the sliver of unease turned into a sinking sense of dread. Robert smiled her way, but she didn't feel any warmth. "Our newest addition has taken the initiative to come to me with a wonderful idea that I am fully behind. This school year, we will be adding bowling to our list of sports available to students."

If the floor had opened and swallowed her whole, Grace would have found that preferrable. Instead, Robert continued talking as if he hadn't just dropped a live grenade. All she could focus on was the way Ava froze beside her. Grace saw her eyes widen even as her lips flattened in a line.

"I think this is a wonderful activity to add new skills while encouraging students to think outside the box when it comes to options." Robert gestured toward her, and Grace wanted nothing more than to disappear. "The new team will be coached by our town's own super bowler, Grace Jones, with Ava Williams as her assistant. Let's all congratulate them for taking on this amazing opportunity."

Claps blanketed the room as Grace tried not to show just how sick she felt. Alyssa and Brad were looking at her with clear bewilderment, but all Grace could see was Ava and the fire of anger blazing in her eyes.

Eight

"That asshole. I can't believe she did that."

The sound of the refrigerator door slamming shut did nothing to lessen Ava's fury. Every time she thought about Grace turning to her with that same ridiculous wide-eyed stare, she wanted to hit something. And don't get her started on Robert and his smug grin. There was now no doubt in Ava's mind that the man clearly had it out for her.

"And the audacity to call me an assistant coach. For an idea that was mine to begin with. Has he lost his damn mind?"

She turned around, banging a bowl of cherry plums down on the counter. Every part of her was heated as she remembered Grace's staccato mutterings. Ava hadn't stayed around to try to make sense of what she was trying to say. The desire to start screaming had been damn near overpowering. At the first chance, Ava made her escape.

So, here she was. Heated as hell and hungry. She hadn't packed anything to eat, having planned to go with Brad to

Thomas's café, but she knew he would want to talk, and even worse, Grace might try to join. Thomas didn't deserve to have his table flipped, so Ava decided to remove herself from the equation.

"What are you doing here?"

Ava rolled her eyes at the inane question. "I live here." She ripped the stem from the fruit in her hand before popping it into her mouth and chewing furiously, being careful not to crack a tooth on the pit. When an empty bowl was sat on the counter in front of her, she reluctantly acknowledged the gesture with a soft thanks before spitting the seed into it. Her younger sister, Vini, walked around the kitchen island and gifted Ava with a look that wasn't needed.

"Why are you home?" Ava countered. "Aren't you supposed to be at work?"

Vini shrugged before flopping down on a stool and leaning her elbows on the counter. "Decided to have a bit of an extended lunch today before getting started on the next car. It's hot out there and I'm waiting for that new AC unit to be delivered. Clarence told me he'd ring me when he's in town."

Their deliveries were usually brought by Clarence, and he was nice enough to give people notice so they could get other things done instead of waiting around for a package.

"Do you plan on sharing or am I going to have to buy more of those?"

Ava frowned and looked down. She had only meant to have a couple cherry plums, but the bowl was halfway gone. With a grimace, she pushed it across the counter. "Have at it. I need to eat something more substantial anyway." Vini nodded, not needing to be told twice. She grabbed a couple of fruits, eyes still locked on Ava.

"So, what has you in such a shit mood?"

"Nothing."

Ava saw Vini's eyebrows raise before she turned around and opened the refrigerator again. She had gone grocery shopping yesterday, but nothing looked good. With a sigh of defeat, she closed the door and resolved herself to eat ramen. She didn't have all day to waste staring into the fridge in the hopes that it would tell her how to handle things. She had thought herself ready to start over with Grace. They had gotten through their first lunch together with only a few awkward silences, but overall, it hadn't been absolutely terrible. Aside from Ava barely being able to keep herself from staring. But this new mess had her kicking that plan to the curb and stomping on it for good measure.

"Right," Vini replied, voice tinged with disbelief. "Why not try that again, but this time with a little honesty."

Ava rolled her eyes again before ducking down to grab a saucepan. "It's work stuff."

"Work stuff doesn't normally piss you off like this." She knew Vini was right, but Ava stayed quiet as she went through the motions of fixing lunch. It wasn't until she was done and leaning over the counter, about to take her first bite, that Vini spoke up again.

"Does your shit mood have anything to do with Grace being back in town?"

Ava froze with a forkful of noodles near her mouth. She shouldn't have been surprised. Vini was always up on the town gossip and now that Grace had been back for nearly a week, everyone probably knew. Ava put her fork back down with a sigh.

"Fine. What have you heard?"

Vini shrugged. "Mrs. P mentioned running into you two and how you both were awkward as fuck."

"I doubt she said it like that."

"You'd be surprised what comes out of that lady's mouth when she gets going," Vini replied with a grin. "Regardless, she was keen to mention how neither of you two would look at one another for longer than a second, though she wasn't sure why and how it was such a shame to see two former best friends acting so removed from one another. That last part was pretty much a direct quote."

Ava took a bite of her food to give herself some time to figure out how to explain the shit show that was having Grace across the hall from her. Everything sounded bitter and childish, never mind that was how she really felt. It was like the universe was screaming at Ava that being around Grace was the worst idea in the history of bad ideas.

"You never did tell us why you and Grace stopped being friends," Vini pointed out. She thrust a cherry stem at Ava. "One minute she was always over here and then the next you never wanted to hear her name again."

Ava waved off Vini's words. That was a total exaggeration of what had happened.

Kind of.

True, she hadn't wanted to talk about Grace, but she hadn't been a bitch about it. Had she? "There was nothing to tell," she replied finally. "We grew apart. It happens."

Vini's eyebrows were trying to talk to her, but Ava didn't want to hear it. That was the story she had stuck with for the past ten years and that was the only one that mattered. "Besides, I'm pissed off about what happened today, not past shit."

"For a teacher, you have a potty mouth."

"Do you want to fucking hear about it or not?" Vini waved her hand, imploring Ava to go on. "So, get this. You know how I've been on Robert's ass about restarting the bowling team? And you know how he's blown me off, talking about how we don't have enough money in the budget even though the football team miraculously found more money last year?"

Vini nodded. "I don't know why you're still hung up on that though. Everyone knows the football team gets whatever they want no matter if they win games or not."

"That's not the point," Ava growled out before taking a deep breath. "The point is, I've been raising the idea for years and not once did he even pretend like he was considering it. Well, guess who apparently brought it up to him?"

"Um..."

"And guess what he actually decided to approve?" Ava continued, feeling vindicated when Vini's eyes widened slightly. For her that meant she was shocked to hell and that reaction added fuel to Ava's indignant fire. "That's right. Grace Jones comes back for a week, wiggles her magical fucking fingers, and suddenly we now have money in the budget for a bowling team days before school starts."

Vini pursed her lips for a moment, not saying anything and giving Ava time to take a few more rage-filled bites. The fact that it was Grace who somehow managed to get Robert to give in to the idea Ava had been voicing for the past three years was enough to nearly send her over the edge. No matter how many plans she had presented, Robert had always given her the same answer. *No.* And then maybe a *hell no* for good measure. Not to her face, but with how often he dismissed her, it certainly felt that way.

"Not only does he announce that we suddenly have money for this," Ava continued, anger building again, "Grace is going to be the coach. And guess who he decided to stick as her assistant."

"Well—"

"*Me* as *her* assistant when it was my fucking idea to begin with. Can you believe this shit?" Ava finished her rant and looked down at her bowl. She was only half done but already she had lost her appetite. "I can't even finish this."

Vini reached out with grabby hands. "Don't waste good food. Give it here." Ava handed the bowl over with a sigh. She looked down at her watch, groaning when she realized she should get back. Time was ticking and she only had a few days left to prepare before the students returned. She needed a game plan for how to handle dealing with Grace.

"So, are you going to do it?"

"Do what?"

"Be her assistant coach?" Vini waved the fork at Ava. "You've been wanting this bowling team for a while and now it's here. Are you going to walk away from it or join?"

Ava frowned before worrying her lip. "I don't have much of a choice. Walking away won't stop this from happening. Practically everyone knows I wanted to start a bowling team and now that Robert announced it in front of the whole damn staff, if it gets out that I turned it down, people are going to start talking."

"Fair enough." Vini's slurps were the only sounds while Ava tried to formulate a possible way out. No matter what idea she came up with, they all seemed to end the same way: tongues wagging and rumors flying. It was too early in the school year for that. Four years of calm and now everything was ruined by the one person Ava had thought she would never have to deal with again.

There was a lot to hate about Grace Jones. Being stuck with her now was one of them.

Nine

Thanks to Robert's announcement, some teachers had wanted to join Grace for lunch and talk about how she was settling in, but Grace had waved them off, citing a need to finish preparing for the start of school. Really, she had wanted to escape Ava's look of anger. Even Brad's smile had dimmed as he looked back and forth between them, and Grace knew that she had managed to royally fuck things up without even trying.

She had tried to speak with Robert and fix this mess, but he simply praised her again for her forward-thinking before leaving to no doubt start more wars between the others. Grace was quickly realizing that his smiles and words of platitude were nothing more than a cover for him being a demon of chaos. She resolved herself not to bring any shiny new ideas to him until after she had already talked things through with her colleagues. There was only so much damage control she could do before people stopped trusting her.

Now it was Saturday and unlike back in New York where

she always had something to do or someone to see, Grace had a whole day and not much to do with it. She had been cleaning the house in the evenings to keep from unwittingly running into Ava in town so now all that was left was to wait for the furniture. Nolan had called her last night and let Grace know it would be delivered sometime today, but an exact time hadn't been hammered down. That meant she was left to wait all day until she heard something, or someone showed up at her door. When her cell rang, she jumped at it, hoping it was the movers.

Or Ava calling to tell her she understood Grace wasn't at fault for Robert's announcement. Really, only one of those was even remotely possible.

"Hello?"

"Gracie poo. How are you?"

Grace sighed and shook her head. She wondered if she should just get used to being continuously wrong. "Why do you insist on calling me that?"

The giggle on the other end of the phone had her lips twitching. "Because I know you hate it. I can imagine your nose wrinkling from here and it fills me with such joy." Grace rolled her eyes, even though Jessica couldn't see it. "How are things going down there? Have you roped any cows?"

Grace snorted. "You have the weirdest ideas about the South. I don't own any cows and you know it."

Grace and Jessica had met in undergrad and instantly hit it off, even though they could not have been more different. Where Grace tended to make a plan and then another plan for her plan before she made a move, Jessica floated along on whichever breeze blew the hardest. It drove Grace up a wall at how little Jessica seemed to plot out her life, but there were times when Jessica's penchant for being up in the air meant she could see things Grace couldn't. Jessica Miller kept Grace from spiraling down into panic when her blueprints went awry, and Grace helped Jessica realize she could plan things and still live a spontaneous life.

"Where are you this month? Backpacking through the Swiss Alps?"

"Not a chance, you know I hate snow," Jessica replied with a laugh. "I am currently sitting at the cutest little café in Stuttgart, Germany. You should totally have come and joined me."

"What took you to Germany? I thought you were planning to go teach in Thailand for a year."

"Mom is over here filming a commercial, so I figured I'd visit for a bit. I was actually thinking that maybe I would drop in on you and see if southerners are actually hospitable or if you are all just massive assholes who have everybody fooled."

Grace's laughter felt good, and she felt herself relaxing in a way only Jessica could get her to do. Before answering, she hit the video button. When the screen swiped on, Grace smiled wide at seeing her friend after three months of only texts and phone calls.

"Oh, we are assholes, but you'll never know," Grace replied. Jessica laughed again, her eyes crinkling up in the familiar way they always did. The sun made her tawny skin glow and her hair fell in tightly coiled waves over her shoulders. "Where are the parents? I'm sure they were happy that you decided to drop in on them."

Jessica waved a hand. "They're around somewhere. I needed

another coffee and to answer some emails about my next contract, so I ducked in here. I thought Europe was all cold and dreary, but it is hot as Satan's ball sack out here."

Grace gagged at that descriptor before shaking her head. The only type of balls she liked to think about were bowling balls. "You have such a way with words."

"Don't I?" Jessica replied with a wink. She leaned forward, gaze going serious as she stared at Grace through the screen. "Now, tell me everything. How is being back home? Is everyone being nice to you? Do I need to throw hands?"

Probably. Having Jessica come rescue her from the situation Grace had unexpectedly found herself in was incredibly tempting, as was canceling her contract and booking the first flight out to Germany.

"Everyone is being perfectly nice," she replied instead. "I'm nervous about the start of school on Monday, but it should be fine. I even have furniture being delivered sometime today."

"Oh, wow. So, you really do plan on staying for two years?"

Grace nodded. "If things go well, I'm not opposed to staying longer. It's not like I have anything to go back to in New York." She walked over and dropped onto the couch. "You saw Emily's announcement, right? Her engagement."

Jessica slowly nodded, her smile dimming slightly. "I did. That was way too fast. I mean, I know stereotypes and U-Hauls and all that, but still."

Grace agreed, but she figured it didn't matter what she thought, considering she'd been the one to call it quits after turning down the job offer from Emily's uncle to work at his

pharmaceutical company. The fight they'd had that night after
she declined had been the beginning of the end.

"Well, her loss," Jessica replied with finality. "Anyway, I
give it six months before she is knocking on your door."

Grace wasn't so sure about that. They hadn't exactly parted
amicably. Plus, Grace wouldn't agree to trying again. The more
space she had, the more she realized they were simply not com-
patible. If she were being honest with herself, Grace had sort
of known that from the start.

"But enough about her," Jessica said, switching things up.
"I want to know if you've met up with Ava. Last time we
talked, you mentioned hoping to rekindle that flame. How's
that going?"

Grace knew exactly which conversation Jessica was talking
about, and she was regretting everything that led to that point.
It had been a moment of weakness when she was sitting alone
on her living room floor, nursing a half-empty bottle of wine
and a bubble of nostalgia for how easy things had been back
in the day. Still, there was nothing to report other than the
fact she was now further in the doghouse than she had been
before she came to town.

"There is no flame. In fact, what we have is whatever is the
complete opposite of a flame."

"Oh? That bad? You never did tell me why your friendship
fizzled out in the first place," Jessica replied with sympathy
clear in her tone.

Grace sighed and leaned her head back on the couch cushion. Although she had mentioned Ava many times over the

years, she had never really touched on why their relationship went south.

"I'm not sure either," she admitted finally. "We were good friends and teammates until like senior year. But after mom switched me to private school, things changed."

Even though she and Ava had promised each other things would remain the same, neither kept it. First, it was the distance between them when Grace moved with her mom to Nolan's house an hour away. Then it was their summer schedules being so different that they barely got to hang out before they started their final year of high school. Finally, it was facing off on the lanes. Something that had been a fun rivalry before had started to take on a different meaning until at last things broke apart in a way Grace had never imagined.

"We kissed," Grace admitted quietly as if taking confessional. A kiss.

An innocent, ill-timed, wonderful kiss heralded the end of their friendship. The kiss itself had been the simplest of pecks and yet it confirmed everything Grace had felt. But in that awareness, their friendship had imploded, leaving her to finish senior year adrift without the constant of Ava by her side. When she had gotten her acceptance to Vanderbilt with a welcome to their bowling team, she had jumped at the chance to get away even as she clung to the thought of things going back to the way they had once been.

Jessica's eyes widened. "Was it a bad kiss?"

"No! I mean, I don't think so?" It hadn't seemed bad at the time. Ava had even smiled at her. The memory of that warm smile hardened her resolve. "No, it wasn't a bad kiss. It was sweet. It was when I finally admitted to myself I liked girls. Specifically, one girl."

"Did she not feel the same?"

Grace shrugged. "I thought she did. I know Ava's had girlfriends since then, so I guess she just didn't like me that way, especially after what happened."

Jessica's frown broke briefly when a barista sat a cup in front of her. She thanked him before turning back to her phone. "What do you mean? What happened after the kiss?"

"My school's bowling team beat hers in our state championship." It had been an intense match with the final scores being determined by Grace and Ava. In the end, Grace had squeaked by when Ava's form collapsed, leaving her with two pins up and no way to spare it out. She had taken the single and Grace's team had taken the trophy. It hadn't seemed like the type of thing that would have broken their friendship, and yet it had. When they had shaken hands after the match was over, the look in Ava's eyes had been one Grace had never seen aimed at her before, and when her phone calls and texts went unanswered, she knew something had gone horribly wrong.

Jessica's whistle pulled Grace out of the past. "Sounds to me like she was a sore loser."

Grace frowned and shook her head. Ava had never been a sore loser in any of their other games. She and Grace had had a friendly rivalry with one another practically since they met. It was that rivalry that had always pushed Grace to aim higher. It had taken her years to fully admit to herself why, although she was pretty sure it had been obvious to anyone who bothered to pay attention. Grace hadn't cared about anyone else when it came to scores or points. Most of the time, she was in it to show off for Ava.

Having the attention of those fierce brown eyes had been thrilling to the point that she sought it out again and again until one day it was all gone, having slipped between her fingers before she even fully grasped it.

"Ava never cared before," she insisted, wanting to set the record straight. "But everything fell apart after that and then the summer before college, Mom and Nolan took me abroad. By the time I got back, Ava had already left. I didn't even get to say goodbye."

That had hurt, as had the pitying looks Ava's sister Vini and their parents gave Grace. They had given her a card that Grace took with her to college, making sure it was kept safe throughout the years. Even now, it was behind lock and key in her safe where she kept all her other valuables whether they were expensive, sentimental, or both. When she had found out Mrs. Williams died, Grace came back to town briefly for the funeral but out of respect for Ava, she stayed in the back and out of sight. Thankfully, no one had noticed her, and she hadn't stayed for longer than a day.

"Well, maybe now is your second chance."

Grace snorted, glad for the slight change that allowed her to fight back the burn in her eyes. "Doubtful after what happened a few days ago." Remembering the whole thing was enough to make Grace ill. "I brought up the idea of restarting the school's bowling team, like Ava wanted, but instead of giving me time to talk to her about it, the principal announced in front of everyone that he decided to add the sport thanks to me."

"But why would that—"

"Ava had been asking for permission to start the team for years, but he always told her no."

Jessica's silence was very telling.

"And what was worse, because of course it gets worse, he names me as the head coach and Ava as the assistant." Grace put her free hand over her face. "She probably thinks I stole her idea."

"Yeah, babe, you're a bit fucked thanks to him," Jessica replied. Grace groaned out a sarcastic thanks at her astute take on the situation. "But listen, all this seems like a massive breakdown in communication. You two were kids then so it is to be expected, but you're both adults now. Talk to her. Explain the situation."

Grace dropped her hand. She knew Jessica was right, but confrontation was not Grace's forte. She could argue science with the best of them, but when it came to feelings, she always froze and never knew what to say or how to say it.

"I know you're right, but—"

"No buts," Jessica cut in. "No excuses. If she has been at that school for years, then she probably knows the principal is an ass. Apologize and then thank the universe for putting you two together again."

"Why would I do that?"

Jessica's smile turned sly. "Because now you have an excuse to get together with Ava one-on-one and figure out if that kiss you two shared was a fluke or if there really could be something there. Clearly, you didn't want to propose to Emily for a reason. Maybe that reason is her."

Hope fluttered anew in Grace's chest even as she told herself not to get overly excited. One innocent kiss as teens didn't mean they could find love together as adults. Still, they would be working together so the least Grace could do is apologize.

"I don't know about all that, but I will apologize to her on Monday. Hopefully, she doesn't decide to say no to coaching with me."

"Babe, put on that outfit I bought you when I was in Paris and I guarantee she will be all about you and forget any animosity. I have to go. Mom and Pop are calling. Love you! Invite me to the wedding. Bye!"

Jessica disconnected the call before Grace could reply. She chuckled and shook her head before letting her hands drop into her lap. Grace had two days before school started and she would be face-to-face with Ava again. She needed to come up with a solid game plan…and probably a contingency or two.

Ten

Ava leaned back in her chair with a heavy sigh. The first day of school was always a tough one filled with starts and stops and not much learning. There were a few students she could already tell she would need to look out for, but overall, they seemed like a good bunch. Only having four classes and one study hall to monitor would come in handy when she needed to grade. Ava hoped that her schedule wouldn't change, especially with the added mess of having to assist Grace with coaching a team she hadn't asked for.

Or rather, she had, but not like this.

"Knock knock, bestie."

"I swear to God," she replied, groaning as she lifted her head back up. The school day had only just ended and here she was having to deal with yet another annoyance. Brad didn't bother waiting to be invited in. He walked over to the desk closest to her and collapsed down, his long legs jutting into the aisle.

"I'm exhausted already." His smile hadn't slipped, but Ava could see the exhaustion underneath.

"You and me both," she replied, knowing exactly how he felt. It was always the same those first couple weeks, not that it got much easier as the school year went along. Down times were few and far between, especially when factoring in grading and sponsoring sports and after-school activities. "I still haven't gotten all my books in for the kids, even though I ordered them back in—you know what. It's too early in the year to be complaining already. I refuse."

Brad chuckled before leaning his head back and stretching his arms with a soft groan. Ava knew when she got home, the first thing she planned to do was take a relaxing soak in the tub. That is, if one of her sisters weren't hogging it. If they knew what was good for them, they would be far out of sight by the time she pulled in the driveway.

"So, have you checked how the newbie did on her first day?"

"No, and I won't be. How she did is none of my business." Brad's snort had her frowning. "What? You think I should be the one to have to fall to my knees and go grovel at Ms. Goose's golden fucking shoes?"

He rolled his eyes. "Not what I said, but okay. It's interesting that I mention her and the first thing you think about is getting on your knees." Brad's smile morphed into a self-satisfied grin. "Is there something else we should talk about?"

"Absolutely not," Ava hissed, ignoring the tiniest part of her that wondered just how that would look. It didn't matter. She didn't think about Grace that way, and even if she had, it wouldn't be her on her knees, that's for damn sure. "And that is inappropriate to be talking about at work."

"Uh-huh," he replied, tone one of complete disbelief. "Tell

that to someone who isn't familiar with what goes on in your pervy little head."

A knock on the door drew her attention, and she barely managed to keep from scowling when she saw who it was.

Today was quickly becoming one for the birds.

"Hey, Ava. Is it okay if we talk for a moment?"

If not for Brad's wagging eyebrows and the knowledge that Robert would no doubt sack her if he found out she strangled his golden goose, she would have. Instead, she pasted a grim smile on her face and waved Grace in.

"I'll leave you two to talk," Brad said, desk screeching slightly as he stood.

Grace's eyes widened. "Oh, you don't have to. If I interrupted—"

"You didn't," Ava replied in a clipped tone. Grace seemed to pause at that before she took another step in, stuffing her hands in the pockets of her slacks. Ava wished she hadn't done that because it drew attention to how well they fit around her form. *Legs for damn days*, she thought angrily to herself. Being angry didn't stop her from noticing the woman Grace had grown into and it pissed her off even more.

Brad nodded. "We were just lamenting how exhausted we were already, even though it's only day one. How did you fare on your first day? Ready to run away screaming?"

Grace's smile was wide, and she chuckled softly. The sound of it floated through the air and Ava would have found it pleasing if not for how fiercely she clung to her anger.

"It was the same and yet completely different from teaching at a university. The students seem great though. Is it normal to have such small class sizes these days?"

"How many do you have?" Ava asked before she could stop herself. Her speaking seemed to catch Grace off-guard, though she recovered quickly, shooting her a small smile that Ava refused to find cute.

"I have about fifteen in each class except for Honors Chemistry. There's almost thirty in that one. It seemed like such a big jump so I wondered if I should go to the administration to make sure my class rolls were correct."

Brad shrugged. "They'll check them over when you send them in for the week. The first two weeks are usually a bit flexible, especially for the juniors and seniors as they finalize their schedules."

Grace nodded along to his words, though she continued to glance over at Ava. "That makes sense."

"Right, well I am going to head out," Brad said, his smile widening when he saw Ava's look of panic at being left alone with Grace. "You two play nice."

They were alone. Faint sounds of people laughing and talking filtered into the room, making the tension between them even more painfully obvious. Ava wished she had anything else to keep her occupied, but her gaze was drawn to where Grace stood in the middle of the room. Her blouse was loose again and white. *Of course, she could wear white and not worry about it getting dirty.* The last time Ava wore a white shirt to school, she somehow ended up with half a handprint on her arm and pen ink on her collar. She never made that mistake again.

"So," Grace started, making Ava jerk her eyes back up. Long kohl-dark lashes brushed Grace's cheeks and Ava wondered, as she had when they were teens, just how Grace managed to skip past the ravages that were teen acne.

It was one more thing to hate about her.

"So…" Ava parroted, not giving an inch.

Grace shifted one hand out of her pocket and rubbed the back of her neck. Gold bracelets dangled, glinting in the afternoon light that trickled in from the windows. "I think I owe you an apology."

"You *think*?"

"Yes, but not for what you think."

Ava narrowed her eyes. "Bold of you to assume you know what I think."

Grace sighed, and Ava felt a sense of accomplishment at making her just as frustrated as she was. Served Grace right for coming in and throwing her weight around like she knew every damn thing.

"I didn't come to fight with you, Ava. Honestly, I came because there has been a huge misunderstanding, and I wanted to not only clear it up, but see what we can do, what I can do, to remedy it."

Ava frowned, suspicion rising in her like the crest of a wave. She crossed her arms and looked Grace up and down, trying to figure out her angle. "Go on."

Grace lifted her other hand out of her pocket, and both dropped down by her sides. "I'm sorry. It's true I did go to Robert to talk about a bowling team, but only because Alyssa said you had been trying to start one," she finished quickly before

Ava could say anything to cut her off. It didn't dampen Ava's suspicion, but she did pause to think about Grace's words.

"Why?"

Grace shrugged. "Because I remember how much fun we had bowling together, and I thought…" She glanced up from underneath her lashes. "I hoped that maybe if both of us expressed interest, he'd approve it. I didn't ask him to make me coach or even suggest it. I even emphasized that it was your idea and I supported it."

Ava gripped her elbows tighter. Inside, some small part of her wanted to believe that Grace was telling the truth. Grace didn't have anything to gain from lying, but people lied for no reason all the time.

"Then why didn't you come to me before asking him to announce it?"

"I did *not* ask him to announce anything," Grace insisted. "Honestly, when you told me how long it took to get the parking fixed, I assumed it would be the same for this. He even asked me to do some research and get back to him, so I thought, well, there goes that. If I had any idea that he would jump straight to saying yes and announcing it was my idea when it wasn't, I would have come to you in a heartbeat."

Ava slowly dropped her arms. Grace seemed sincere and while Ava was open to accepting the apology, she still wasn't happy with the results of Grace's meddling. True, Robert had blown her off for the past couple years about starting the team, but Ava had encouraged a few of the students to join the youth league at Terry's. Some of them had even taken her up on it and bowled weekly. She had been doing just fine without Grace's interference.

"I swear to you, I didn't ask him for any of this," Grace insisted. "And if me stepping down so you can be made head coach—"

"No."

Grace's eyes widened. As much as it rankled Ava's pride at having her suggestion only taken seriously because of Grace's interjection, she had to admit that she was finally getting what she wanted.

Sort of.

"If you step down, Robert will probably roll back his acceptance and I'll be right back at square one." Ava fixed Grace with a cool look. "I accept your apology, but if we're going to do this, we're doing it my way."

Grace raised her hands in surrender before nodding. "Fair enough. So, how do you want to handle it?"

How, indeed. Ava was probably going to regret this. She had been willing to give Grace a try before. She was more hesitant now, but it was only the first day of school. She had to figure out a way to get through the entire year and that meant playing nice no matter how much she wanted to resort to pettiness.

"First off," she replied, counting on her fingers, "I am not your assistant coach. I have done the research for this, and I have had budgets and plans prepared for the past two years in the hope that Robert said yes. I will share them with you so you can check my math and then we will present them to him."

Grace agreed readily enough, and Ava almost smirked at

how easy that was. It had taken her months to plan all that out and while she was not a numbers person, she knew she was on the ball with the costs. The school truly didn't have a lot of money, so she had kept to a shoestring budget.

"Second, we go into this as co-coaches. I get that you got this out of the slush pile, and for that… I might eventually be grateful, but it's still fucked up and while I forgive, I do not forget." She raised her eyebrows at Grace, trying to convey just how serious she was about that. If holding grudges was a superpower, she was fucking Superman.

With a nod and a small smile, Grace held out her hand. "That sounds perfect to me."

Perfect was not the word Ava would have used, but for now it would have to do. She closed the space between the two of them and reached out to grasp Grace's hand. While her heart wanted to focus on how soft and warm Grace's grip was, the rest of her was tuned in to just how close they stood. The space between them was charged and even the air seemed different. Ava took a deep breath and forced her mind back to her plans. With a smile, she shook Grace's hand firmly.

"Well then, let's get this over with."

Grace knotted her eyebrows as she looked down at Ava. "Get what over with?"

Ava walked back to her desk without answering. She might have said she forgave her, but it felt good to know she had Grace's attention. She pulled out her folder that contained all the plans she had put together for the bowling team. If Grace was truly on board with doing things Ava's way, then she should pass this test with flying colors. If not, Ava would know she was full of shit and spend the rest of the school year ignoring Grace's existence.

"We're going to let Robert know about the change of plans for the team." Ava walked back over to Grace and looked up at her with a determined expression. "I had already drawn up plans for this year like I do every year. Ready to present them?"

Grace blinked quickly. "Are you going to let me look over them first?"

Ava smirked. "What? Don't you trust me…co-coach?" Ava felt a tendril of satisfaction curl through her when Grace sighed before giving in. She decided to be nice and handed the folder to her. "If we're lucky, we can catch him before he leaves for the day."

Grace scanned the first page before looking up. "You really did have this all planned out, huh?"

Irritation had Ava clenching her jaw. Why the hell would she have tried to start a team if she hadn't planned for it? She didn't get to reply before Grace closed the folder and nodded.

"Lead the way, fearless leader." Grace's smile was more of a smirk, but instead of rising to the bait, Ava nodded sharply before making her way out of the classroom. The sound of Grace's heels left her patience worse for wear, but Ava stayed quiet as they made their way down the hall toward Robert's office. When they entered, the look on his face made Ava want to cackle.

Hadn't been prepared for this had you, asshole?

"Good afternoon, ladies. To what do I owe this pleasure?"

Ava took the lead. She didn't want him to butt in about anything until he heard her terms. If Grace didn't back her up, Ava refused to be held responsible for her actions or any property damage from her ripping his office apart.

"We have plans for you to review regarding the bowling team, including comments from the district athletic director."

Robert's expression didn't change, but Ava could see a slight tightening around his mouth that filled her with malicious glee. She knew he was counting on them not having contacted the director already, but Ava was nothing if not thorough. Grace slid the folder across Robert's desk. She was quiet, but Ava felt bolstered by her presence. As Robert read over the information, Ava couldn't help glancing at Grace. Her reassuring smile left Ava perturbed at the warmth that bloomed in her chest.

"And you've run these numbers by—"

"By this year's budget? Yes," Ava replied, interrupting him. He glanced at her over the papers before going back to reading. The silence was thick with anticipation and Ava could hardly stay still. This was further than she had ever really gotten with her bowling team proposal and even though she was sure she had covered all bases, she also knew Robert was a jerk who got off on saying no. When he finally placed the folder down, she was ready to have to defend her plans to the death if necessary.

"Well," he started, clasping his hands, "it certainly does look like all the information is here. I, of course, will have to request final approval before I can give you a definitive answer."

"That's fine." Ava knew from her discussions with the athletic director that if her calculations were right, they should be good to go.

"There is also another matter regarding the team that we needed to talk about." Grace glanced at Ava before continuing, "Given that this was Ava's plan originally, I think it only fair to name us co-coaches and give us equal say."

Robert's smile noticeably slipped, and Ava was surprised it didn't drop completely. "I understand. However, I do believe your opinions should carry more weight given your prominence in the sport. Surely, you see how that would have more pull."

"Regardless, I wouldn't feel comfortable making the majority of the decisions when it was not my idea to form the team originally." Grace's smile turned sharp, and Ava swallowed hard. That was the smile of someone who knew they had won. "Surely, you understand."

Goddamn that's hot.

It wasn't the first time she had seen one of her colleagues stand up to Robert and his bullshit, but it was hot as hell watching Grace do it on Ava's behalf. She turned her attention to Robert before she got caught staring. His answering scowl was vindication enough that Ava had him right where she wanted.

"Fine," he huffed out before leaning back in his chair. "That means you are both equally responsible for ensuring the team produces results."

Ava fought hard not to roll her eyes. Did he really think that they would start a team and not try to win? This wasn't a passing fancy for her. She had put in the work to even figure out if her plan was viable. She wasn't about to sabotage it.

"You get one shot at this, to show me the school's budget is being used wisely. Six months. If you can't prove you two can lead a team to victory, I will remove funding and put it toward something worthwhile."

Ava frowned and when she glanced over, she saw a similar look on Grace's face. "That is only one season," Grace replied. "How can we possibly pro—"

"If you don't think it's possible, then we can just scrap this plan altogether and move on."

Ava ground her teeth together at how ridiculous this farce was.

Six months.

One season.

How the hell were they going to train a winning team in so little time? *He's setting us up to fail.* The truth of it hit her like a train and Ava almost let her polite mask slip. That was exactly what he wanted. Robert didn't have any intention of giving them a fair shot. If Grace had gone along with things, maybe he wouldn't have given this ultimatum, but now they would never know.

It was clear from Grace's expression that she thought the whole thing was bogus, but she gazed at Ava as if to ask what they should do. Ava refused to back down. She had given up a lot over the years, and finally she wanted something for herself.

"Fine. Six months."

Eleven

One week.

That was how long it took for Grace to wonder if she had made a terrible mistake.

She had thought teaching high schoolers would be easier than university students, but she was realizing how wrong her assumption was. The class sizes might be smaller, but the personalities were larger than life. Somehow in the mad shuffle that was the last decade, she had forgotten just how dramatic high school life could be. And it was only the first week! How the hell was she supposed to do this for the next two years?

She leaned back against the whiteboard. Her feet ached and her legs felt as weak as a newborn colt's. She had a smudge of marker on her palm, and she would probably be arrested for driving under the influence of dry erase fumes if she tried to drive home now. Still, she had survived, and no one broke out in tears.

Though she herself had come pretty close.

A quick glance at the wall clock had her groaning. She only had thirty minutes before she had to meet up with Ava to finish the fliers they needed to hang around the school. Robert had approved the plans she and Ava presented, though his previous smiles were nowhere to be seen. The change in his persona plus the ridiculous ultimatum he had issued cemented her realization that the man was not to be trusted. She had dealt with similar personalities at the university so she knew how to handle him without being obvious in her pushback. It was a dance she despised, but she could hoedown with the best of them. Plus, seeing Ava's smile of unrepentant glee when he agreed had made it worth it.

And there lay another problem. Although Ava had said she forgave Grace's faux pas, the tentative working relationship was still just that. Tentative. Outside of preparing things for tryouts and practices, she and Ava hadn't talked much at all. It wasn't that Grace didn't want to; it was just that she was trying hard not to overstep this time. It left her in a tunnel of confusion about what was too much and what was not enough.

"Well, look who survived her first week."

Grace snorted softly before pushing away from the board. It was a relief to have Brad actively seeking her out. She knew Ava was her own person but being accepted by him seemed to be a big step in getting her and Ava's future relationship on track.

"Is this what survival feels like? Seriously?" she joked back. "I feel like someone chewed me up and spit me back out. Repeatedly."

Brad's laughter perked her up, and he glanced at the board. "What does all this mean?"

Grace gave a sheepish smile. "It means that I'm in trouble. It was way too easy for them to get me off track and down a tangent about hydrogen peroxide and how it reacts with blood. I'm not sure if I should be impressed or worried by the students' fascination."

"I don't know, I might have paid more attention in chemistry class if it were brought up when we were in school," Ava chimed in from the doorway. Grace hadn't noticed her come in, but at the sight of her now, her pulse jumped a beat.

"I didn't realize you were already doing experiments."

"I wasn't," Grace replied. She stood a little taller and hoped that her exhaustion wasn't clear on her face. She had sweat out her thin layer of foundation by third period and only her break was able to save her face from sliding onto her shirt. She was wondering if it was worth it to just forgo makeup completely. "Well, I talked about some of the ones we might do, but I had to get the experiments approved before the start of school so I'm not sure if I could add any others."

Ava shrugged. "I wouldn't know."

Brad chimed in, giving Grace a gentle smile. "Plus, Robert is a bit of a hard-ass, so he would probably reject changes now. It's better to ask for forgiveness than permission with him."

Grace nodded. She was quickly learning that dealing with him required her to play chess and not checkers.

"So, what are your plans for the rest of the afternoon?" Brad asked.

Ava spoke up before Grace could answer. "We have to put

up fliers for bowling team tryouts. There's only two weeks before the regular season starts so everything is being kicked into overdrive." She looked over at Grace with a smirk. "No rest for the wicked and all that."

Hearing Ava mention wickedness with that smirk did something to Grace that was unneeded if she were planning to keep everything strictly professional. She forced herself to smile back and hoped her less than innocent thoughts weren't being projected onto her face.

"Are you coaching the debate team this year?" Ava asked Brad.

Grace was momentarily blindsided when she realized they were having a normal conversation. There were no undercurrents of awkwardness and none of the tension that had persisted for most of last week. Was this what it would be like to be accepted into Ava's circle again? She hoped so. Grace hadn't realized how much she missed the camaraderie of discussing work and life with other people. Last week had been a solitary existence and not one she wanted to repeat.

"What about you?"

"Me what?" Grace blinked, quickly realizing she had missed some of the conversation. Brad watched her with sharp eyes and an almost knowing expression. It was a look that had alarm bells ringing in Grace's mind. "Sorry, I think I missed a bit from exhaustion."

Playing it off seemed to work with Ava who nodded like she understood. Brad's expression gentled, but he still looked at Grace like he knew something she didn't. What, she couldn't be sure, but resolved herself to ask about. Later. When Ava wasn't standing in front of her looking like the best kind of distraction.

"I was asking what you planned on doing after you put those signs up."

"Probably just head home and figure out what to eat." She knew eventually she would have a full plate with papers to grade, so Grace planned on enjoying as much afterwork free time as she could for now. "What about you guys?"

Brad wrapped an arm around Ava's shoulders. "I am trying to convince this little ball of sunshine to come over for dinner tonight and have a few drinks to celebrate a successful first week. You up for joining?"

Was she up for it? She wanted to say absolutely. Brad was inviting her, sure, but was it an offhand comment since the subject had already been brought up or did he actually want her to come? And what about Ava? He had said he was still trying to convince her to come. Maybe she knew he was going to invite Grace and she wanted to see what Grace said before going. What if Ava said no because Grace was going? Too many questions and not enough answers left her momentarily frozen while she watched Ava wiggle out of Brad's grip.

"I told you I'd come but only if you let me cook something," Ava specified once she had managed to slap his arm away. She straightened her blouse and glared at Brad for a moment before turning to Grace. "Usually Thomas cooks, but I don't want him to feel like he needs to cook when he gets home too."

Grace nodded slowly. Ava's words made sense and Grace hoped that truly was the only reason Ava was hesitating. "Makes sense. I don't mind making something as well."

Ava raised an eyebrow at her. "Oh? So, you're telling me you're no longer the girl who burns water?"

"That was one time!"

"Twice. In one week."

Brad put his hand over his mouth, but Grace could tell by the jiggle of his shoulders that he was laughing. Beneath a layer of indignation, she was preening at having a teasing conversation with Ava even if it was at her own expense.

"We were kids," she pointed out, refusing to fully admit Ava might be right. "All of us had moments where we stumbled on the road to adulthood."

Ava put her hands on her hips and pursed her lips. "Burnt. Water."

"I couldn't do research if I burned everything," Grace replied, refusing to let it go. "Plus, there were plenty of times where I had to feed myself that didn't include just going to the university cafeteria. I am a fully functioning adult." *Sometimes.*

Ava's gaze slid slowly down. Grace widened her eyes as she tracked the motion. Her limbs slowly started to tingle as if her skin could feel everywhere Ava's eyes touched. When she locked eyes with Grace again, there was *something* there. Something she desperately wanted to figure out.

"Adult, sure. The fully functioning aspect has yet to be seen." Ava's smile took some of the sting out of her words and left Grace feeling a little light-headed. "Then again, are any of us really fully functioning?"

"In this economy?" Brad scoffed. "Anyhoo, you know if Thomas wants to do something, he's going to do it. Your best bet is coming over and trying to convince him to put down the pans yourself."

Ava rolled her eyes but agreed before looking back at Grace. "You could ride with me over to Brad and Thomas's once we finish putting everything up. If you want."

Grace very much wanted, but she also needed to be sure. "Are you sure? I don't want to intrude."

Brad waved her concerns away. "Thomas is the main one inviting people over, so I know he would be thrilled. Plus, he mentioned regretting not being able to talk with you much when we got lunch last week."

Knowing that Thomas wanted her over was enough to sway Grace. She had been content to go home and gravitate to the spot on the couch that had quickly become her favorite while watching reruns of *The L Word*, but being able to spend more time with Ava, and of course Brad, was a better use of her time no matter how much she liked looking at Bette Porter.

"I'd be happy to come, then," Grace replied. "But I'm with Ava. At least tell me if there's something I can bring so Thomas isn't doing everything."

Brad argued with her about bringing anything, and it made something in Grace loosen. Ava was still looking at her, expression one she couldn't parse, but just having that attention was more than she had hoped. When Ava noticed her looking, her lips twitched as if she wanted to smile, and Grace would have given anything to turn that little betrayal of motion into a full-fledged grin.

"Fine, I'll text Thomas and tell him you two want to take over making dinner, but I guarantee you he will shut that down quick. Food is his love language." Brad shook his head, but he was all smiles. Of course, he was. He had an attractive partner who wanted to feed him delicious things. If Grace tried to cook more than the basics she had mastered, the person who ate it would probably assume she was trying to poison them. Logically, she understood recipes. You add a little of this and a little of that to create something delicious. It was just that somehow her results were usually less than edible.

Surprisingly, thinking about how lucky Brad and Thomas were didn't make her miss Emily. That ship had sailed. No, she missed what could have been if she had a partner who fit her the way the two of them seemed to fit one another. Before she could stop herself, Grace looked at Ava and let herself imagine how things might have been.

Twelve

Why Ava thought this was a good idea, she would never know. She had been fine working with Grace to correct the bullshit Robert tried to pull, and Grace had been doing everything right so far. Ava was still wary, but Brad had already chastised her once about either moving on from the mess of the past or laying it all out on the table and talking about it.

The idea of talking about feelings had her gagging and desperate to run the other way.

Footsteps coming up behind her had her tensing before she turned around. Grace was steadily loping toward her, stride wide and easy like she had never had to deal with gravity a day in her life. This new fashionable adult was also throwing her for a loop. Ava couldn't deny that Grace had always been good to look at, but when people talked about a glow-up, Grace's picture was no doubt front and center. It was distracting. The past between them should have been enough to have Ava's libido stopped in its tracks, but of course Ava's life couldn't be that simple.

The universe saw fit to torture her.

Ava swallowed hard and tried to look like she wasn't wondering if Grace had on a matching set under her clothes. "You all done?"

Grace nodded and held up a flier. "I only have this one left and I figured I would just leave it in my class and see if anyone is interested in trying out. What about you?"

"Same. I plan on dropping this one off at the bowling alley on the way to Thomas and Brad's. I can wait for you to grab your things if you want."

Grace's smile was radiant. "Are you sure? I don't mind driving myself."

Ava waved her off. She was trying to be nice here. "It's fine. Plus, you should have a celebratory drink for surviving your first week."

Grace nodded before hurrying back down the corridor in the direction of their classrooms. Ava watched her go and felt a jolt of something when Grace turned to look back at her over her shoulder before turning the corner. Being left alone with her thoughts was a supremely bad idea, so Ava whipped out her cell and quickly dialed her older sister Dani's number. Talking to Brad about this would only lead to madness, she was sure. He would no doubt tell her to break out the video tapes and relive that past kiss in Technicolor.

"This better be important. I'm on my break."

"You're not even working today."

"When you have a kid, you have to schedule breaks," Dani

shot back. Ava would have refuted that, but she had babysat her nephew enough to know Dani was speaking the truth.

"Fair enough. I need some sisterly advice."

"And you called me?"

Ava looked to the heavens and prayed for patience before replying, "You are my sister, aren't you?"

Dani's snort was unnecessary, but she conceded. "Last I was told. What's the problem?"

Ava switched the phone to her other hand and looked around to make sure no one else was close enough to overhear. "So, you know how Grace is back? Well, we're coaching the bowling team together."

"I didn't know we had a bowling team again. When did this happen?"

"It hasn't yet," Ava replied. "We're holding tryouts and then have to deci—that's not what I wanted to talk about. Not exactly. The problem is Grace." And the way she looked too damn good to be so off-limits.

Dani sighed and the sounds of low murmurs filtered over the phone line. "Didn't she just get back to town? Don't tell me you made her your enemy already?"

"That's not what I'm saying."

"You couldn't even give the poor girl time to unpack her shit before you attacked. I know you two had a falling out back in high school, but holding grudges isn't good for you." Ava frowned at the accusation that she had done something and not the other way around. She couldn't get a word in edgewise with Dani rambling on. "And really, you two were attached at the goddamn hip when you were kids, so I don't know why you won't just put the petty away and embrace adulthood."

"If you would shut the fuck up and let me talk, I could tell you what's really going on. Jesus."

"Don't take the Lord's name in vain."

Ava closed her eyes and tried to find some semblance of calm. Clearly, this was a bad idea but hanging up now would make it even worse.

"Listen, will you? Damn. We aren't fighting. We're getting along just fine." Ava had been biting her tongue whenever she felt the need to throw in a snarky comment. It wasn't easy. She had forgiven, but she hadn't lied when she said she never forgot. If there was one thing she and her sisters had in common, it was their ability to hold grudges.

"So, what's the problem then?" Dani asked. Before Ava could answer, Grace came around the corner. "Could it be that you still li—"

"Thanks, Dani. Bye." Ava hung up the phone and pasted a smile on her face as Grace approached with her satchel on her shoulder. "All set?"

"Yeah. Was that your sister Dani? I haven't seen her in forever. How's she doing?" Grace asked before falling in step with Ava and following her out of the building.

"She's good. A pain in my ass, but most older sisters are."

They made it to Ava's car and out onto the street while Ava absentmindedly chatted about Dani and Vini and what they had been getting into for the past few years. Grace's long legs barely seemed to fit into Ava's Prius, but she didn't say anything like Brad did whenever he rode with her.

"And now that Vini's taken over the shop, Dad has slowed way down and usually attends Jordan's events at school if Dani can't make it. We like to call him the classroom mom because half the time when there is a call for volunteers, he answers it."

Grace's chuckle was soft as she looked over at Ava. The sun illuminated her russet skin with an almost ethereal glow. It was like she was brushed with flecks of gold that caught the light and reflected it in patterns that begged to be worshipped. Ava gripped the steering wheel tightly to remind herself that her focus should be on the road and not the woman seated beside her. She changed subjects in hopes that it would keep her focused.

"So, we need to come up with a game plan for how the first few practices will go. I'm assuming we might have some naturally gifted bowlers trying out, but I doubt they will all be bowling three hundreds on the first try."

Grace nodded. "True."

Ava flipped her turn signal on and made a quick right. "We should probably work on their stamina and get them used to the game. Bowling is fun with friends, but if they aren't playing for real, most people tend to take their time."

"I guess. Though a bad form means that no matter how much stamina, the results will be inconsistent."

"Without stamina though, it doesn't matter if their form is perfect," Ava countered as she turned onto Brad and Thomas's street. She agreed with Grace that form was important, but she couldn't help but push back. It was almost habit to see Grace go one way and her decide to go the other. She wondered if

Grace had picked up on it as well. As she eased the car into Brad and Thomas's driveway, they continued their debate.

"The kids aren't going to just luck into a good technique," Grace pointed out as she unbuckled her seat belt. "Plus, we don't need them going online and doing random research themselves only to try something outside of their skill level."

Ava rolled her eyes and turned the car off. "I think they are smarter than that."

"We weren't."

"Maybe you weren't," she shot back, smirking at Grace's disgruntled expression. The air was still hot and sticky as they left the car and walked up to the porch. Ava rang the door-bell and glanced back at Grace. The slight frown on her face had Ava fighting laughter.

"Uh-oh. What happened?" Brad asked when he opened the door. He looked between the two of them before crossing his arms and giving Ava a look. "What did you do to her?"

"The fact that y'all think I'm the one doing anything is starting to get old." Ava shook her head and brushed by him when he took a step back and let them in the house. "We were just having a discussion. No big deal."

"Which do you think should come first—stamina or tech-nique?" Grace asked as she stepped into the house.

Brad raised his eyebrows as he looked at them. "Well, that depends. What is the stamina and technique needed for?" When he waggled his eyebrows, Ava almost slapped him on the arm. She didn't need any additional reasons to think about stamina or technique outside of bowling when it came to

Grace. That direction would only lead to the type of madness that required multiple double-A batteries and a locked door.

Grace coughed before she shook her head. "Bowling. We're talking about bowling." Brad dropped his arms, disappointment written all over his face.

"Oh. How boring. I'm not a bowler so I have no idea."

"Helpful, Brad."

He waved Ava's comment away before gesturing for them to follow him into the kitchen. "Why don't you just make a list of basics to cover and focus on those for the first few practices?"

It was Ava's turn to be surprised and when she looked over at Grace, she could tell the other woman felt the same. "That is a surprisingly good plan."

He shrugged. "I have them sometimes. Not that most people listen."

Grace nodded at Ava in agreement. "That might just work. See, first argument solved. We're coaching together already."

Ava snorted but she couldn't help the small smile that she hid by turning her head as she followed Brad. It was a small win in the larger war that was making their team successful for the season, but Ava was happy to enjoy it for the night.

Thirteen

Grace's relief was palpable as she looked over the curious faces staring back at her. The turnout was more than she had expected. She hadn't mentioned anything to Ava, but she had been concerned that all their planning and preparation would go to waste if they didn't have enough interest in the bowling team. After the way things had started between them, Grace felt it had been best to keep those concerns to herself.

"Welcome to bowling tryouts," Ava said, voice pitched loud enough to be heard over the crash of pins. They were at Terry's Alley, occupying the last four lanes.

"We're excited to see so many interested in joining the team. I'm Ava Williams, but feel free to call me Coach Ava, and Ms. Grace Jones is my co-coach."

"Call me Coach Grace," Grace added in helpfully, giving smiles all around and an extra wide one when she saw Tabitha. A girl Grace didn't recognize held her hand up. She stood when Ava called on her but turned to address Grace.

"Is it true you won the US Women's Open like four times in a row?"

Grace couldn't hide her surprise. Most people didn't even know there were local bowling leagues, let alone national. "Yes." Her answer was short, but it caused a ripple to go through the group. Those who had been quiet now sat up and whispered as they glanced at Grace.

Beside her, Ava cleared her throat and tried to get them back on task. "We will have you each bowl three games, and then—"

"So, are you a pro bowler?" another girl asked, interrupting Ava's instructions.

Grace nodded before glancing over at Ava. "I am. But I think w—"

"Do you get money when you win tournaments?"

"What's your highest score?"

"Have you ever bowled a three hundred?"

Questions started coming like a flood with one adding more momentum to the next until Grace wasn't sure how to get them back to the task at hand. When she looked over at Ava, her expression had gone from excited to nearly blank. The only thing that let Grace know she was about to lose her cool was the ever so slight twitch at the edge of her lips as they pressed against one another in a flat line. Grace had to do something to save this.

"Maybe we should save the questions for af—"

"We all know Coach Grace is our local celebrity, but that won't help us on the lanes." Ava's voice was loud and firm, and her words dropped over them like a bag of wet cement. Some might have thought being referred to as a local celebrity was a good thing, but the way Ava said it dissuaded Grace of that. Her tone had been biting and almost taunting in its sarcasm. Grace almost dropped her smile, but miraculously kept it pinned on her face.

Ava managed to finish explaining the process for tryouts, but all Grace could do was keep the brittle smile on her face until she felt that she could trust her mouth not to say something rude. Somehow, she managed to rouse herself enough to oversee two lanes of students, helping them find balls and going through the instructions for taking turns. It seemed self-explanatory, but Grace knew from experience that there always came a time when someone got confused and bowled out of turn.

The repetitive sounds of balls being released, and pins being tumbled soothed her annoyance, and after a couple hours, Grace found herself at ease as she observed the students and made notes. Some of them asked her for pointers and she made sure to call out helpful tips for everyone's benefit. Before she knew it, tryouts had come to an end and the last of the students were making their way back to the counter to turn in their shoes.

"So, that went fairly well," Ava said from somewhere behind her. Grace didn't turn around. Maybe it was petty, but she was still stinging from Ava's earlier words. "I suppose we should talk about how things went and grab the scores."

"Suppose so." Not waiting to see if Ava was following, Grace made her way to the counter. She waited patiently before asking the attendant for the printout of the scores. When she felt a presence come up beside her, she knew instinctively it was Ava. She shifted over slightly and crossed her arms, going against everything in her that wanted to be closer. Grace was aware she probably looked like a petulant child, but she didn't care.

"What's your problem?"

"I'm not the one with the problem." That wasn't 100 percent correct. Grace had a few problems, but this one was not of her making.

"Sure, seems like you have a problem," Ava replied. Her tone dug at something in Grace and if she had feathers, they probably would have ruffled up in indignation.

Grace looked over at her. "I wasn't the one who snapped at the students because they were asking questions." She knew she had hit the mark when Ava's eyes narrowed. Grace had apologized and given in to most of Ava's wishes concerning the team. But she refused to spend the entire season fending off passive aggressive cheap shots thrown in her direction. Especially when she'd done nothing to deserve it.

Ava scoffed and crossed her own arms. "I'm sure you were just loving them too. Never mind the questions had fuck all to do with tryouts. But I suppose you can't ever turn down a time to show off."

"I was answering their questions and trying to turn the conversation around to get back on track. If I had wanted to show off, I would have brought my damn trophies."

Ava dropped her arms and took a step closer. The air between them was charged enough to almost see the particles whirling around before crashing together. It made the hair on Grace's arms stand up and she felt something like a thrill run through her. She and Emily had argued, of course, but never had their disagreements felt like this. It was the same feeling Grace had always gotten when facing off against Ava on the lanes or the moment they both got a test back and hadn't yet flipped the papers over to reveal their grades.

"So, you admit it. You were showing off."

"I don't have to. My records speak for themselves." Grace relaxed her stance, dropping her arms down by her sides. Ava's scowl had her quirking her lips up in a small smirk that she knew would get under Ava's skin. This was the fire that had often burned between them before the roof came crashing down. "If you need a refresher, I could get you on the lanes and take you down memory lane."

"You are such a fu—" Ava's sentence was cut short by the return of the attendant and Grace let her smirk morph into what she hoped was an innocent-looking smile. She knew she shouldn't keep score, but she couldn't help but think that if it came down to it, this round went to her. She and Ava both reached for the papers at once and when their fingers brushed, an electric shock left Grace short of breath. If not for the way Ava paused and looked at her, eyes wide with something simmering just below the surface, Grace would have questioned if she were the only one who felt it.

But when Ava pulled away, expression shuttering faster than Grace could blink, she sighed with the knowledge that this would be another one of those things they didn't talk about. The tension from before, electric and energizing, was still there, beckoning Grace to fall into its temptation. Even high-profile bowling tournaments never keyed her up like the barbed wire–laced jabs that Ava could dish out without breaking a sweat.

"I'm glad you guys are bringing back the bowling team," the attendant said, giving the two of them a crooked smile. "Terry will be happy to see more kids enjoying the lanes that's for sure. Might even bring some energy back to this place."

"Thanks, Jeb," Ava replied before taking a step back from the counter. "Tell Terry I said hey and I'll see him on Saturday bright and early."

Grace nodded before following Ava back to the now-empty lanes. They didn't speak as they gathered their things. As much as she wanted to throw a few balls and sink into the repetitive motions to clear her mind and reset, she knew that they wouldn't be able to get much discussion done with the noise.

Ava paused outside the door and sighed. "We should sit down and go over these."

Grace's heart stuttered before picking up its normal rhythm. "Are you hungry? We could talk about things over dinner. Maybe at Thomas's?" Grace nearly kicked herself after she spoke. She hadn't been trying to, but it sounded like she was proposing a date. "Or you could come over to mine. I could make us some dinner while we—"

"Didn't we just have this conversation about you and your lack of cooking skills?" Grace's mouth shut with a click, and she felt her cheeks heat. Before she could respond, Ava did something unexpected.

She apologized.

"I'm sorry. That wasn't very nice." She sighed and pulled on an errant coil that fell over her forehead. It was a habit she often had done when they were younger, and Grace knew it meant she was uncomfortable. "Is this how the entire season is going to go? You snipping at me and me snipping back? I don't think I have the energy."

Grace swallowed hard before answering. "I don't want it to." The admission was clearly not what Ava expected given her widened eyes. "Maybe we should just talk things out and get everything into the open so we can start fresh."

Ava's eyes shifted back and forth as she looked up at Grace, but finally she nodded. "Probably for the best. Alright, lead the way. Daylight's burning, and I'm hungry enough to eat whatever you come up with."

She snorted, but Grace walked over to her car. "I can cook a decent meal you know."

Ava raised her eyebrows. "Well, thank fuck for that. I wasn't looking forward to having to call the fire department tonight. But just in case, maybe I should watch any pots of water to make sure they don't burn away with the heat still on."

"That was one time!" Grace exclaimed. She wanted to be mad, but it was impossible with the sound of Ava's laughter floating on the breeze.

Fourteen

Ava wasn't sure what she was expecting when she got to Grace's house, but it wasn't to walk into a time capsule. The living room walls had been updated to a cool gray and some of the furniture was unfamiliar, but the bulk of it was the same as it had been the last time she was there more than ten years ago.

"Wow."

Grace glanced over her shoulder before continuing through the living room and into the kitchen. "What?"

Ava shook her head and thought carefully about what to say that wouldn't be rude. She wasn't lying when she said she didn't have the energy to fight with Grace at every turn. As entertaining as it was to wind Grace up, she could only maintain that for so long. Then again, the little smirk that Grace favored her with before biting back had been hot as hell. It wasn't that she didn't know that Grace had teeth, but they came out so rarely that it was fun to push until they made their appearance. Her blood had been singing when thinking about facing Grace out on the lanes, and she still regretted not pulling them to a lane to work some of that tension out in a way that was familiar and safer for her sanity.

"Nothing. It's just nice to see that you didn't strip it completely and change it to some modern boring canvas." Ava looked around as she followed Grace into the kitchen. The waning sunlight streamed through the large windows, bathing the kitchen in reds and deep oranges. Some of the beams slid over Grace, showcasing the luster of her hair and setting her skin aflame. Ava had to force herself to look away before she got caught staring. "So many places that have sprung up in town lately have zero personality."

Grace nodded before opening the refrigerator door and leaning inside. "Yeah, I passed by a ton of new construction when I drove down here a couple weeks ago." She straightened up, pulling a casserole dish out before shutting the door. "There was even a new subdivision being built down on McClaren Drive. I can't imagine people want to live this far out, but I suppose things change."

That was an understatement. Things certainly had changed, and she and Grace were prime examples of that. Even the conversation they were having now was underlaid with latent awkwardness as if neither one of them truly knew what to discuss. They had grown up, but between the two of them was a big chasm of nothingness that Ava didn't know the best way to traverse. With Brad or her sisters, she could just blurt out what she thought was the problem and they could duke it out until they were all satisfied with the outcome or too exhausted to continue. But she didn't know if that would work with Grace or further damage the already brittle peace they had been stoking before the blowup of today.

"I suppose change is inevitable," she said finally. Grace glanced over her shoulder at her, expression unreadable, before she leaned down and put the dish in the oven. Ava wrinkled her nose. "Aren't you supposed to preheat the oven before putting the food in it?"

Grace straightened up and turned around. Her lips were split again in that damningly attractive smirk that did nothing for Ava's focus. "You have your ways and I have mine." She walked over to the island and leaned down, propping herself up on her elbows and gifting Ava with a penetrating stare. "Now. Are we going to talk about why you insist on making things difficult?"

"Excuse me?" That was not how she expected the conversation to start. "I'm making things difficult?"

"Yes." Grace's one-word answer almost had Ava wishing there were a table she could flip, and her next words didn't dampen that desire in the least bit. "I know we didn't end things on the best note, but I don't understand why you hate me so much."

Ava stood up and leaned over the counter. "First of all, saying we didn't end things on the best note is a goddamn understatement and you know it." Anger bubbled in her words as Ava thought about that last encounter that had sealed the end of their friendship. It hadn't been the only thing to put a strain on their relationship, but it had certainly been the thing that snapped the thinning cord of their friendship. "You know what you did."

"I know I kissed you and you kissed me back," Grace stated plainly. "Then you effectively disappeared and refused to return my calls and emails."

Ava scoffed as she looked at Grace in disbelief. "I kissed you back because I was surprised. You kissed me first to make a point."

"And what point was that? That I liked you?"

"No, that you were better than me."

Grace's eyes widened almost comically. "That doesn't even make sense. Why would I kiss you to prove I was better than you?"

Ava narrowed her eyes and tried to ignore how badly her heart wanted to latch on to the idea that Grace really did kiss her for no reason other than she had liked her back then. But it didn't make sense. Before the kiss, there had been no indication that Grace felt anything for her other than camaraderie and friendship. She didn't believe that Grace was clueless about her actions, not with the way her little friends had acted after.

"I don't know how your brain works, but whatever. It doesn't matter anymore," Ava replied, waving her hand and retaking her seat at the island. She pulled the score papers from the bowling alley out of her purse and set them on the counter between them. "All that matters is that we make this team successful so that it continues next year, and we can make Robert choke on it. We don't need to be friends to do that."

Grace stared at her for a beat longer and Ava sat still, letting her drink her fill. This was important, and if they needed to hash out unimportant past events to make this work, she was happy to do it. Well, that was a lie. She wasn't happy about it, but she would do it if it was the only choice left, even if she knew it wouldn't do anything other than frustrate her even more.

"You're right. We don't need to be friends to do that, but I think we need to talk about it at the very least instead of us doing whatever this is," Grace said finally.

"Then why don't you just admit to it, apologize and we can move on."

"Because I don't know what I'm apologizing for." Ava's disbelief must have been clear as a summer day on her face because Grace's eyes narrowed and she crossed her arms. "Fine, I apologize if I surprised you with the kiss."

Her words sounded sincere, but the hurt deep down Ava had felt back then was still there coating her thoughts. "And leaving? Do you apologize for that?"

"Leaving?" Grace frowned. "What are you talking about? You're the one who walked away from me."

Ava wanted to eat her words, but they bubbled out of her before she could get a handle on them. "No, you left me to hold our team together and traded us in for expensive equipment and snottier friends. You say you had no motive and yet you—"

"I didn't have a choice, Ava," Grace cut in. "Mom told me we were moving and put me in St. Mary's before I could argue. I would have stayed if I could."

The kiss between them had played over and over in her mind, but not as much as the thought of walking back into the school and on to the team alone. It was that memory that had her clamming up and forcing her emotions back down.

"Like I said, we don't have to be friends," she said finally, not knowing how to give voice to her deeper thoughts. Grace's deep sigh pulled at Ava, and she looked up at her from beneath her lashes. Grace's head was turned as she gazed out the window. Ava's gaze swept over her, taking in every change that she hadn't been there to see. A pearl of regret revealed itself then as she thought about how things could have been. Would they still be best friends? Was the kiss a one-off; something that was done with little thought of consequence and then to never be repeated? Or would they have done it again? There was so much left unknown, and it irked her that she couldn't simply let it be.

"Maybe we can just start again. Start off with a fresh slate," Grace said finally, voice soft and almost too low for Ava to hear.

"Do you really think we can just act like we don't know each other and start again?" When Grace turned to look back at her, Ava pursed her lips but doggedly continued on. "Seriously."

"Why not? We haven't seen each other for a decade. That's enough time to effectively act like we are strangers."

It seemed like a ridiculous notion, but there was something seductive about it.

"Fine," Ava agreed. She felt ridiculous, but if they were going to do this, she had to go all-in. Before she could second-guess herself, she stuck her hand out. "Hi. I'm Ava Williams."

Grace blinked quickly before her lips split in a wide grin like the sun finally peeking out from behind the clouds after a hard summer rain. She reached out and shook Ava's hand. The warmth of it spread over Ava and she squeezed softly. "Hey,

Ava. I'm Grace Jones." She cocked her eyebrow and gave Ava a crooked smile. "No relation."

The words made something unnecessary flutter in Ava's chest, but she stuffed the feeling down. This was for the good of the team. Grace being attractive was unimportant. They had a job to do, and it was time to concentrate on that.

It was too damn hot. That was all Ava could think about as she made her way into Terry's. The results of bowling try-outs had already been announced after she and Grace spent two days arguing about it. Surprisingly, treating one another like they had just met and were coming together for the first time had been working out. There had still been some half-hearted jabs back and forth as they tried to settle on the ten members of the team, but if Ava were being honest, it was almost like foreplay.

Grace had changed, that much was clear. She had always been funny, but now it was tinged with a dry wit that had Ava snorting to keep herself from full-blown laughter. They had eaten dinner together Tuesday night while they went over the scores as well as the state requirements for the team. With the papers spread out on the table between them, they had finally made the decisions and chopped the names down to those they wanted on the team. It had sucked to tell the other girls that they hadn't made the cut, but it had to be done.

Cool air rushed out, beckoning her through the open doors, and Ava stepped in with no hesitation. Her eyes adjusted to the lack of light compared to the harsh afternoon sun, and she smiled at Jeb before walking over to the where Grace's tall frame stood head and shoulders above the students. The smile she was graced with when she got close enough to hear their conversations was enough to have Ava giving her traitorous heart a talking to. There was no reason for it to beat faster or slower just because Grace smiled her way. She was an adult, not a lovesick teen.

"It's great to see you all back," Ava called out. She had stayed behind to print out the forms they needed to hand out, outlining the rules and costs associated with joining the team.

Grace reached out, and Ava passed her some of the forms. Their fingers brushed, but this time she was ready. There was still a tingle of electricity when their skin met, but she was able to keep herself from jerking away or letting out a sound betraying how that small touch felt to her. She turned to the students closest to her and passed out each packet of forms.

"You'll see the schedule for games on the first page as well as the locations. Unfortunately, we'll be traveling away for most of these as the locations were chosen before our team was decided on. Those of you who don't have a car are more than welcome to ride with Coach Grace or me." Ava nodded at Grace before continuing, "Please have your parents fill out the next forms. If you don't have sports physicals on file with the office, you'll need to get those by the end of this week, otherwise you won't be able to bowl in our first match."

Grace said some encouraging words before telling them they were free to leave or enjoy a couple games at the alley for free. Most of the girls went to grab shoes, and Ava felt encouraged for the first time in a long while. This was finally happening. She had been pushing for this team for so long and now it was finally coming together. She glanced over at Grace where she was talking with a couple of the girls as they picked out balls to use.

Ava knew she should have thanked Grace a while ago. As much as it still irked her, without Grace's interference, the team would not exist. She was so lost in thought Ava didn't realize she was no longer alone until a deep voice spoke up from beside her. She jumped slightly before turning to the newcomer. He was a tall man with a long face, sun-reddened skin, and piercing gray eyes. His gaze was aimed in Grace's direction before he looked down at Ava.

"Excuse me. I needed to speak to Grace."

Ava cocked an eyebrow before gesturing over to Grace. "Well, she's over there so…" She trailed off, not sure why he was asking her to speak to Grace. She wasn't Grace's keeper. When he nodded and moved around her, Ava's eyes followed, unsure of who he was or why he was here in the first place.

"Coach Ava?"

One of the students calling her name took her attention away from the unfamiliar man, and she turned away before she could see how Grace reacted. After helping Tabitha and a couple others find their own balls to bowl with, Ava was on her way back to their designated lanes when she was stopped by Terry.

"Why is he in here?" he asked, brown eyes cutting over to where the mystery man was still chatting with Grace. She was smiling widely and openly, which did a little to put Ava at ease. Clearly, she knew who the man was.

"No idea. I don't even know who he is."

Terry grimaced, and his dark brown eyes were full of concern. "You don't remember him? He was the bowling coach from that private school Grace went to. They bowled against you guys for the district championship."

"What?" Ava whipped her gaze back to the man and Grace, who had now been joined by a few of the players on the team. When the man leaned down, hitting a classic bowling pose, Ava felt a knot of unease form in her stomach. "Why is he here if he coaches another team?"

"Last I heard, he wasn't coaching anymore," Terry replied. His attention turned when another person came up to the counter, and Ava stepped away so he could attend to them. She slowly made her way back to the lanes they were occupying. As she walked up, she caught the last snippet of what the man was saying.

"...would love to have dinner and catch up."

"We've got the lanes for the next two hours," Ava said, interrupting them. She was annoyed by the man's smile that matched Grace's own grin, and she was sure her expression probably reflected that. Brad was right that she was good at keeping a neutral face with someone she didn't care for but was shit at not telegraphing when she actively disliked someone. Right now, this man was firmly in the realm of dislike. "Apologies, I never got your name."

The man's smile didn't change but something shifted behind his eyes that made Ava drop him further down into the dislike column in her mind. Grace didn't seem to notice anything was amiss as she took a step toward Ava and gestured to him.

"This is Grant Thompson. He was my bowling coach at

St. Mary's." She switched hands, gesturing to Ava. "Ava and I are co-coaches for the team."

Grant nodded and took a step forward, holding out his hand. For a moment, Ava thought about smacking it away, but in the end, she gave in to good manners, shaking his hand quickly and firmly before dropping it. She rubbed her hand against her skirt and twisted her lips up in a smile that felt more like a grimace.

"It's great to meet you, Ava," he said, though she didn't return the sentiment. "You did look familiar when I came in. Did you bowl in high school?"

"Yes." When she didn't say anything more, Grace gave her a look before jumping in.

"Ava was the best bowler on the team back in high school. I almost didn't want to leave just so we could bowl senior year together."

That was news to Ava, and she couldn't stop herself from glancing at Grace in surprise. "You never told me that." Grace had said she didn't want to switch schools, but Ava remained unconvinced.

Grace rolled her eyes. "I'm pretty sure I did, but you probably weren't listening."

"So, you went pro as well then?" Grant asked, reminding Ava that he was there. She could have happily ignored him for the foreseeable future, but she was trying to start over with Grace, which meant being civil to the people she brought around no matter how little Ava cared for them.

"No," she said, more to keep her answer from sounding so blunt. "I worked during college and didn't have time. But now I get to help lead the next generation of bowlers so they can."

Grant nodded. "Well, it's good to see people still interested in it. I'm sure Grace will enjoy imparting her professional touch to round them out. Listen, I have to head out, but let me know about dinner."

"Absolutely. It's great to see you, Coach Grant."

Ava didn't feel that in the slightest, but she kept her smile pasted to her face as he and Grace hugged, not dropping it until he was gone. She looked back at the doors through which he had just left. "What was that all about?"

"What was what all about?"

Ava sucked her teeth before deciding to let it go. Grant was none of her concern as long as he wasn't bothering her team. The day had been going too well to let it go to shit now.

"Never mind. Are the girls ready? I don't want to go over our two hours. Terry would probably let us stay longer, but I don't want to take advantage of his good graces."

Grace's dark brown gaze assessed her for a moment before she finally spoke. "They should be ready." She looked like she wanted to say more, but Ava was relieved when all she did was walk over to the kiosk and begin entering in names.

They had somehow achieved a fragile peace, and maintaining it was crucial. Anything that threatened the team's success had to fall to the wayside.

Fifteen

Nerves Grace didn't even know existed were singing as she walked into the alley with the team. This was only a practice game with a team from the small private school a few miles outside of town, but it was still the first official game. They hadn't even gotten their jerseys in yet and here they were about to hit the lanes. Thankfully, Terry had known someone who could get matching T-shirts in for them. The look on the girls' faces when they put them on was one Grace wished she had captured on camera. She had been excited at being able to coach the team, but she hadn't thought about how good it would make her feel. That alone was enough to make her abrupt career switch worth it.

"Oh, good, we got here at the same time."

Ava buzzed with energy as she stepped up beside Grace. The other team members came in behind her and gave the two of them nervous smiles before they went to get shoes and find the lanes. Grace recognized a few parents thanks to the team meeting earlier in the week. She was happy they decided to join and knew the girls would appreciate the support. First games were always nerve-racking, especially when you were part of an inaugural team. She and Ava had both been in rare agreement to not mention Robert's ultimatum about this season. The girls would already be under enough pressure. They didn't need to know that this might be the one and only shot the team had to exist.

Grace glanced down at Ava. She had forgone her usual colorful outfit and instead was in a pair of form-fitting jeans and a matching team shirt. Her curls were in two puffs at the top of her head with a few shorter coils framing her heart-shaped face and Grace nearly lost her breath. Even dressed down, Ava was gorgeous, and it was taking everything in Grace to keep ignoring that fact for the sake of the fragile peace they had lucked into. Curious brown eyes looked up at her.

"You good?"

"I am so good." That didn't come out exactly as planned, but it was out there now, and Grace had no regrets when Ava chuckled in response.

"I'm sure you are," she replied with a twinkle in her eye that hadn't been there before. Grace had the ridiculous urge to lean down and taste her amusement from Ava's lips, but with a twitch of her own, she fought against it and instead gestured for them to join the team.

They had chosen the girls who would be bowling in this team match, and after a pep talk, they got started. The scores and outcome wouldn't count for anything when it came to the regular season, but it would get them used to the style of play. Stamina was important when bowling as was choosing the right starting lineup and substitutes. The vibes needed to be immaculate to keep everyone's energy up as they bowled their frames.

As each girl lined up, Grace and Ava would occasionally speak on her approach and follow through as they made notes. Grace had been coached for a few years before going pro, and she tried to think back to the advice she had been given then. Ava had even taken it a step further, showing clips of other bowlers during practices and encouraging them to take what they learned and make it their own. The sage advice had Grace wondering why Ava never thought to take her bowling career further.

When there was a brief lull in game play, Grace spoke softly to the girls, giving them tips for the next games when it came to using the oil pattern on the lane as well as modifying their arm swings. A few of them had power but lacked the control needed to truly utilize it. It was something Grace had also struggled with in the beginning. It had taken weeks of practice and the knowledge that Ava would kick her butt before Grace finally found her control and tapped into her strength consistently.

Ava had always made bowling look like an art form. Grace likened it to an enchanting performance. Ava bowled like a dance that only she could hear the music for. Her approach had always been measured and controlled with not a movement wasted as she took her steps. Her swing was precise and smooth, and the ball had always seemed to glide away as if propelled by an invisible force as it swung a clear arc before meeting the pins. It was like magic, and Grace had been entranced from the first moment until the very last.

"Great job, Tabitha!" Ava's praise snapped Grace out of her thoughts of the past. She rallied, giving Tabitha a high five when she came back to take a seat. Grace refocused her attention where it needed to be, on the game ahead.

When the final frame was done and the scores were tallied, the girls were all smiles and dutifully gave the other team handshakes for a game well done. Ava's grin was radiant as she gave a round of high fives.

After the match, Grace passed out a couple pizzas before sidling over to Ava.

"So, how does it feel to coach your first win?"

Ava's smile was wide and nearly took Grace's breath away. "Feels pretty good. Almost as good as bowling my own win." She looked away but Grace was still locked in her thrall. "I know I gave you a hard time when all this started, but I am grateful."

Grace swallowed hard. Ava's voice was pitched lower, so it didn't carry beyond the two of them, but the sincerity in it was doing things to Grace that didn't need to happen when they were surrounded by other people.

"I'm sure Robert would have eventually given in. You're not the type to give up so easily, after all."

Ava snorted. "Is that your nice way of calling me stubborn?"

"Determined," Grace insisted. "I wouldn't call you stubborn. That's rude, remember?"

Ava's soft laughter had her cheeks warming, and Grace knew that if anyone paid them close enough attention, her feelings—those traitorous things that she had thought long gone—were clear as glass on her face. The candle of her feelings lit so long ago had been left simmering, not a full-on flame but never fully extinguished. It explained so much and yet left her with even more questions, namely what the hell she should do now. Realizing that she still had feelings for Ava didn't give her the faintest clue for what to do with them.

"Always so polite." Ava turned her face up to Grace, her eyes crinkling in clear delight, and all Grace could think about was reaching down to taste the happiness from her lips. She had to get away before she did something ridiculous, like listen to the voice in her head telling her that going for a repeat of their first kiss was a great idea. When a familiar voice called out, she turned quickly, sending up a silent blessing as thanks for the interruption.

Brad and Thomas walked toward them both carrying a box. "A little birdie told us you guys won your first game, so we brought a gift."

"You didn't have to," Ava replied but she moved so they could set the boxes down as the team crowded around with curious chatters. When the boxes were opened to reveal rows of cupcakes, the cheer let out was even louder than the one after winning the game and Grace laughed. No matter how old you got, cupcakes were always something worth celebrating.

Thomas pulled the box flaps down before stepping away as eager hands descended. His smile was small, but Grace knew he was probably pleased by how eager even some of the parents were to get a cupcake.

"Of course, we had to," Brad said from a few feet away.

Grace listened in even as she reached for one of the remaining cupcakes. She bit into it, savoring the buttercream icing with a soft groan.

"Thomas, is there anything you can't make?" she asked from behind her hand. His smile widened.

"Not really."

The matter-of-fact response made her laugh again, but she conceded that he had the food to back it up.

"Brad wanted to invite you guys back to ours tonight for dinner and drinks." Thomas looked over the pizza and cupcakes before his smile turned rueful. "Well, maybe just drinks. Seems you guys already had dinner and dessert."

Grace nodded. "I probably won't be able to fit anything else in my stomach, but drinks would be great. I didn't have any plans for the evening anyway."

"What about you, bestie?" Brad asked, nudging Ava with his shoulder. She pushed him back.

"Stop calling me that." It was cute enough to have Grace hiding a snicker behind taking another bite of her cupcake. "I have to check to make sure Dani doesn't have a shift, but if not, then yeah. I'll come by too."

Brad clapped his hands, a gleeful look on his face. "Perfect. It's a double date then."

At the word *date*, Grace inhaled sharply before doubling over as a crumb tumbled down the wrong hole. A hand smacked her back as she coughed. When she could draw in a breath without feeling like she was choking, she straightened up and was startled to see Brad's face wearing an expression that said he knew exactly where her thoughts were.

"You okay?" The worry in Ava's voice was echoed in the faces that had turned to pay attention to Grace's struggle. She waved them all off and gave them a thumbs-up.

"Yeah. Cupcake went down the wrong hole. I'm good." She wasn't really, but they didn't need to know that. She took another bite of her cupcake and hoped the subject could move on so she could recover her calm. Thankfully, after the cupcakes, most of the girls and their parents said their goodbyes. When only Grace, Ava, Brad, and Thomas were left, they made their way out after delivering the few remaining cupcakes to Terry and his staff as a thank-you.

"Do you remember how to get to our place?" Brad called out from where he was standing by his Jeep. "You can ride with us if you need to."

Grace waved him off. "I remember. I'll see you there."

Thomas nodded before beckoning Brad into the car, and Grace followed their lead, unlocking her door and sliding into the seat. She tried not to let her thoughts wander as she backed out of the parking space and followed the Jeep's taillights to the house. Grace pulled her car in behind them and quickly got out. She pulled at the collar of her T-shirt as the evening heat reached her again and quickly followed Brad and Thomas inside, with Ava in the rear. Grace could feel the heat of her at her back and rather than make her uncomfortable, it had her shivering.

It wasn't until they were settled in the living room, Grace and Ava sharing the larger couch with Brad and Thomas settled close on the love seat, that Grace felt herself relax. She had plenty of friends back in New York, but this—sitting around with a breeze blowing in from the window as well as the soft chirps of summer bugs—called to her in a way the city never had. She settled back against the couch, slouching down until she could rest her head against the cushion.

"You look like you're about to pass out," Brad said with a chuckle. Grace knew her smile looked dopey, but she couldn't help it. She was in a good mood.

"I might," she conceded before taking a sip of the drink Brad had made for her. The tequila hit just right and paired perfectly with the sweet tart touch of mango. It was refreshing on a warm night and left her feeling a pleasant buzz beneath her skin. "Today was a good day."

From beside her, Ava agreed. "It was. The girls did so well."

"They did, didn't they?" Grace hummed as she turned her head to look at Ava. The little smile on her face was so damn cute, and only force of will kept Grace from saying that aloud. Instead, she lifted her glass toward Ava. "Couldn't have done it without you, coach."

Ava lifted her own glass of wine before clinking it with Grace's. "Likewise. We made a good duo."

"Damn right, you did," Brad spoke up, raising his glass as well before settling back against the arm Thomas had thrown over his shoulders. "I'm glad that hard-ass principal of ours finally approved the team. Sometimes I think he just enjoys saying no because he can."

"Probably," Grace agreed. She tried not to let the green-eyed monster of jealousy creep in as she watched Brad and Thomas settle against one another as she lamented the amount of space still between her and Ava. "We had a few people like that in our administration too. I swear they rejected proposals like it was something they got off to."

Ava's snort was soft as she turned to lean against the armrest. She bent her knees and leaned them against the back of the couch, leaving only an inch or two between her feet and Grace's thigh. It was a space that Grace wanted to breach, but instead she switched her drink to her other hand to keep from reaching out. She knew Ava would not appreciate being manhandled and Grace was not trying to set their relationship back now that it was finally going in a positive direction.

"So, Grace. How are you enjoying being back home? Thomas told me you stop by to grab food every couple days."

Brad's question was appreciated so she could focus on something else. "It's been great, though outside of working, the team, or grabbing food, I don't get out much." Ava's chuckle wasn't unkind as she spoke up.

"You get a lot of takeout, huh? I thought you said you could cook."

Grace narrowed her eyes but found herself enjoying the teasing. "I can cook. I cooked for you."

"You made lasagna."

"And you ate two plates of it," Grace shot back, her grin showing teeth. Ava leaned forward, her legs slowly straightening until her toes slid under Grace's thigh. For her part, Grace didn't change her expression, instead lifting her legs slightly to welcome Ava's feet.

"I didn't say it wasn't good," Ava replied before leaning back against the armrest again. She drained her glass but made no other move to readjust her position, leaving her feet under

Grace. It was so reminiscent of the way they used to effort-lessly fall into one another's space that, for a moment, the past and present meshed in Grace's vision until she had to quickly blink it away.

When Brad mentioned getting them a second round of drinks, Grace didn't think about turning him down. She was going to need as much liquid courage as possible to get through the night without doing something foolish.

Sixteen

Consciousness came slowly as Ava fought against thick waves of sleep. The angle of the sun was all wrong as blood rushed through her veins, enhancing the furious pounding in her skull. She yawned as feeling returned to her body, but when the bed shifted Ava realized she wasn't alone. She froze as an arm squeezed her waist, pulling her back against a body behind her.

Oh, no. Please tell me I didn't.

Her thoughts were frantic as she tried to pull together the pieces of last night after the drinks started flowing. The last thing she remembered was arguing with Grace about something ridiculous as Brad and Thomas laughed. Now that she was a little more awake, she recognized the curtains and walls as their guest room where she usually crashed when she had too much to drink. What she wasn't sure of was why there was another person beside her. No. Not another person. Grace. There was no one else it could have been.

Ava swallowed against the invisible wad of cotton in her

mouth and slowly tried to move away. She didn't get far before she was pulled back again like a rag doll. When two soft mounds pressed against her back, she couldn't stop her quick draw of breath. They were at least wearing shirts, but she knew from the feeling of the fabric that her jeans had been tossed sometime during the night. All she could feel was smooth skin pressed against hers. When lips brushed against her cloth-covered shoulder, she shivered. A hitching breath against her back had Ava freezing. She wasn't ready for Grace to wake up. She didn't have her story straight.

Minutes passed with no other change, and slowly the arm around her waist grew heavier as Grace relaxed again. Ava bit her lip as she tried to keep her breathing even and calm. Her skin tingled everywhere they touched. Even with the fabric separating them, she could feel Grace's heat as it tried to entice her back into sleep. It was more than a little tempting. Everything was soft and lush with an ethereal quality thanks to the wash of morning light coming in from the window.

This was not expected. Ava knew she found Grace attractive. She wasn't delusional. If Grace had been anyone else, Ava would have made her interest known from the jump. But this was Grace. Despite resolving to start over, Ava knew that it could only last so long. One day, they were going to have to make some decisions, especially if Grace was home for good.

Unless Ava left.

Leaving wasn't something Ava had spoken about with anyone, not even Brad. Things were more settled now than they had been when she first moved back home. Dani's job was going well, and Vini had fully taken over the family business, freeing their father up to retire and heal. Ava could think about the future without worrying about her family and that left her pondering her own. When the arm around her waist squeezed again, Ava couldn't help the soft groan that spilt from her lips. It had been a long time since she was wrapped in anyone's arms, and she couldn't deny that it felt amazing. Still, this wasn't right. They couldn't do this.

She couldn't do this.

Ava managed to wiggle out of Grace's embrace. When she slid from the bed and stood beside it, she couldn't stop herself from gazing down where Grace lay sleeping. She still had her shirt on as well, but she had pulled her hair back at some point, leaving her face free. Ava's eyes caressed the slope of her cheek and the elegant line of her neck before zeroing in on the hand that was outstretched as if reaching out for her. The temptation to go back and burrow in the deceptively strong arms that had held her so securely was almost incapacitating. It was only the sound of someone moving around outside the door that kept her from doing just that.

Ava crept silently across the room and opened the door slowly until she could slip out. She released the breath she had been holding before she realized that she still didn't have pants on. When a pair of shorts were thrust in her direction, she almost let out a yell of fright. Thomas looked at her, lips quirked up in a small smirk. Ava snatched the pair of shorts from his hand and put them on hastily.

"Sometimes you are as bad as Brad."

He snorted. "If I were Brad, I would have busted into the

room by now and demanded to know everything. You're lucky I sent him to get breakfast instead."

"Never mind. You're the best and I love you." She followed him down the hallway, the floors occasionally letting out a creak or groan, showing their age. "And nothing happened." *I think.*

Thomas glanced over his shoulder but didn't comment. "How did you sleep?"

His question was simple yet Ava had no idea how to answer it. Truthfully, she slept better than she had in ages. Whether that was because of the drinks, the thrill of the previous day, or the warmth of the body behind her was anyone's guess. Waking up in Grace's arms had been a pleasant shock and she could feel the phantom touch of those lips against her shoulder every time she moved.

Still, she figured a little honesty was fine as long as she didn't speak on exactly how she woke up. "Pretty good minus the horrible alcohol morning breath. Mind if I duck in the bathroom and clean up a bit?"

Thomas gave her a look like he wanted to call her on the unspoken fact that she hadn't gone to sleep or woken up alone, but blessedly he waved her toward the guest bathroom before heading toward the living room. Ava blew out a breath before walking in and locking the door behind her. She needed another moment to get herself together. She grabbed the extra toothbrush she had left last time she stayed over and quickly set to brush the lingering hint of wine from her tongue. After splashing water on her face, she felt more equipped to handle the morning, which was just in time to be reminded of why she was freaking out in the first place.

A knock on the door came, and she opened it before thinking about who might be on the other side. Grace stood there, her shirt askew and no pants to be seen. She was groggily rubbing an eye with a fist and looking like an overgrown sleepy kitten. She had taken her hair out of her ponytail and now it fell over her shoulders, wrecking the calm Ava had worked so hard to build.

"Sorry," Grace said, her voice still sleep-deep and pitched lower than usual. "Thomas said Brad is back with food."

"Okay," Ava croaked as she dutifully kept her eyes on Grace's face and not on the miles of skin bared to her gaze. "I'll be there in a second."

Grace nodded before wandering back in the direction of the bedroom. Ava didn't fight the urge to lean her head out the doorway, gaze raking over the curves of Grace's ass before she and it disappeared back into the bedroom. She slowly closed the door again and counted to ten before making her way toward the living room. Brad looked up at her when she entered.

"There she is. I'm surprised you're moving after the way you inhaled that last glass of wine."

"I hate you both," Ava hissed quietly as she sat back on the couch. "Why didn't you stop me?"

Thomas snorted. "I tried. You told me you were a grown-ass woman before trying to wrestle the bottle from me."

"It was actually kind of cute," Brad chimed in with an amused smile. Ava hid her face in her hands as she shook her head.

"It's like I'm not an adult." She heard the floorboards in

the hallway creak and had just enough time to brace herself before Grace came around the corner. She still looked half-awake, but at least she had her jeans on from yesterday. When she sat on the couch, she was closer to Ava than they had been last night when they first got to the house. Ava could feel her warmth seep into her side and tried not to shift away. It would have been in vain anyway. Her body didn't want to move away from Grace.

"Is that bacon?"

Brad's bark of laughter seemed to startle her, and Ava couldn't stop the twitch of her lips as she looked at Grace's confused expression. Taking pity on her, Ava grabbed a slice of bacon and handed it to her.

"Here. Maybe this will help you wake up."

She tried her best not to stare as Grace gripped the strip of bacon like it held all the answers to life. Her eyelids fluttered as she took a bite, and Ava swallowed hard against the burst of hunger that shot through her. It had nothing to do with the food and everything to do with the half-asleep woman sitting beside her, munching on bacon and completely unaware of just how appetizing she was. Turning away took effort but Ava managed to do it, letting her eyes drift back to the food that Brad had spread on the table and ignoring the feeling of other eyes on her. She knew she was being obvious, and no doubt she would have to deal with Brad commenting on it sometime soon. She hoped he would have enough sense not to say a damn thing right now.

"You look like you're starving." She shot her eyes up at Brad's knowing tone. His smirk belied the supposedly innocent words and Ava curled her lip up in annoyance. "You should probably grab a plate and get started before you try to eat one of us."

She narrowed her eyes at him before reaching for the outstretched plate and filling it with a generous portion of eggs, bacon, and toast. Grace grabbed a plate as well, murmuring a soft thanks as she loaded up and set to eating. Ava supposed she should be thankful that Grace was not a morning person, otherwise she might wonder why Ava was staring at Brad like she wanted to eviscerate him. The food soon overtook her concentration, and Ava's stomach appreciated it and the coffee that she slowly sipped between bites.

"So, what do you two have planned for today?"

That was a safe question. Ava had a plan to act like nothing strange had occurred at all last night and hope that everything blew over without needing to acknowledge it. She would finish eating, grab her shit, and make a hasty retreat.

"Well, actually I invited Vini over this morning," Brad replied. Ava looked up in alarm.

"You invited my sister? Why?" She narrowed her eyes, wondering what game he was playing right now. If this was Brad's way of trying to embarrass her, she would find a way to make his disappearance look like an accident.

"She's coming by to look at the Jeep," Thomas explained. "It started making strange noises yesterday, and I don't need Brad getting stranded on the side of the road with his crappy sense of direction."

"Hey!" Brad exclaimed in protest. "I can find my way back to town, no problem."

Thomas raised a single eyebrow and gave him a look. "Last time you went on a little bike ride I found you headed toward the next town over."

"Well—"

"In the rain."

"—okay then." Ava snorted at Brad's chastised expression. "It's not like I do it on purpose."

Thomas patted his knee. "We know, and we'll never hold it against you." The doorbell rang, drawing his attention. "That'll be Vini."

Ava nodded and watched as he left. When she felt a warmth at her side, Ava turned and was surprised to see Grace's face leaning closer to her. Ava's breath caught and her gaze was drawn to Grace's lips. They were full and looked amazingly kissable. A light sheen on them had Ava's mouth watering as she imagined tasting the sweetness of where the maple-smoked bacon had brushed her lips. This hunger wasn't new, but the intensity of it nearly had her heart beating out of her chest. It was as if the whole world stopped. When she finally lifted her eyes, the heat in Grace's eyes was unanticipated.

Where Grace's gaze had previously been unfocused and fuzzy, now there was a sharpness that left Ava feeling on full display. Ava breathed slowly, and with each second that passed, gravity had her swaying closer to those sinful lips. It didn't matter that Brad was still in the room, probably watching everything with a shit-eating grin on his face. The only thing that mattered was finding out if Grace's lips were as soft as they appeared. If not for Vini's loud greeting as she entered the living room, Ava wasn't sure what would have happened next.

"Aw, y'all didn't have to order breakfast just for me."

Ava stared down at her plate and attempted to get her lungs to expand and contract normally. When she looked up, Brad's smirk was the least of her worries. Beside her, Grace's gaze was still locked on her, and Ava wasn't sure how much she could take before she lost what little was left of her cool. She didn't need this shit so early in the morning.

"Hey, sis." Ava's voice was blessedly even, and she shifted over, giving Vini space to sit on the couch. This put her closer to Grace and her tantalizing heat, but there wasn't anything she could do. If she got up and made Vini sit between them, it would be obvious that there was a problem. She had to play it cool. "I'm surprised to see you up this early."

Vini snorted. "It's noon."

Chastised, Ava hit back with a weak response before rededicating herself to drowning in eggs and bacon. The conversation thankfully moved on, and before long, the food was demolished and they were all leaning back in their seats, contentment clear on their faces. It was then Vini turned to Grace.

"You're Grace Jones, right? I recognized you from some of Ava's old pictures." She leaned over, shaking Grace's hand. "Wow, you grew up pretty."

"Jesus, Vini," Ava hissed. Grace's laughter sent a bolt of jealousy through Ava. It was ridiculous and unwarranted to want to be the only one who triggered that sound.

Grace's smile was radiant as she nodded to Vini. "Thanks. You're pretty cute yourself. How old are you now? Twenty-three?"

"Twenty-two. I'll be twenty-three in a few months though,

so good guess." Ava shot Vini a look that was promptly ignored as Vini threw her arm over Ava's shoulder. "So, how is my big sister treating you? She's not giving you any trouble is she?"

Grace shook her head as she laughed and looked at Ava. Amusement danced in her gaze. "No. She's been great actually."

"You two are coaching the bowling team, right? Lots of long nights sitting close tog—"

Ava elbowed Vini, enjoying the soft sound of pain she made in response. Her smile was sharp when she addressed her sister. "Don't you need to look at Brad's Jeep? You should probably get started on that."

Vini rolled her eyes but stood up, rubbing her side. If not for the fact that she was being a little shit, Ava might have felt bad about elbowing her so hard. "Yeah, yeah. I'm going." Brad and Thomas stood up as well, and Ava felt a moment of panic at being left alone with Grace, which was ridiculous. She didn't need to be supervised by anyone and certainly not the two fools who were looking at her with matching mischievous grins.

Vini paused in the doorway. "It was good to meet you again, Grace. I vaguely remember seeing you a few years ago at our mom's funeral. I'm sure it meant a lot to Ava to have you there. Let me know if you ever need service done on your car. The first one is my treat."

Vini waved like she hadn't just dropped a bomb in Ava's lap before leaving, but Ava only had eyes for Grace as questions bounced through her mind.

Seventeen

Grace froze as large brown eyes looked up at her in clear confusion. She had thought no one noticed her when she chanced a return for Mrs. Williams funeral, so to now find out she had been witnessed by someone, and Ava's baby sister no less, was a shock.

"Grace? What is she talking about?"

She didn't know how to respond to Ava's softly uttered question. She had never expected it to come up, but now she was realizing how foolish she had been to think that no one had seen her. Once again, her lack of a spine had led to her having to come up with something before Ava got the wrong idea and things went sideways.

"I heard about your mom," she started gently, not wanting to prod at old wounds. "I wanted to come and pay my respects, but I didn't want you to feel you had to see me when you were grieving."

Ava narrowed her eyes. "Seriously? I didn't have it in me then to feel anything but pain."

"I know," Grace insisted. "But with the way we ended things, I didn't want to add to that pain even by accident. When my dad died, I was nothing but a ball of feelings and every little thing set me off. I didn't want to accidentally hurt you." That, and she didn't think having a reunion at a funeral was the best idea, regardless of who it was, but definitely not for Ava's mom. Darlene Williams had been a source of comfort for Grace for so many years, especially after losing her own dad so abruptly due to a drunk driver. The way Millie showcased her grief after had left Grace floundering until Darlene offered comfort in a way that sheltered Grace from the worst of it and gave her time to process the fact that her dad was gone. She hadn't wanted to do anything that would tarnish that. So, despite the fact that it cut her up inside to see Ava's tear-streaked face, Grace had said a silent prayer and left before she could be noticed.

Or apparently not if the youngest Williams sister had caught sight of her long enough to remember what she looked like.

Grace wanted to say anything to just get the conversation over and move past it, but the reminder of how content she had felt waking up with Ava cocooned in her arms was something she wanted, no, needed to have in her life again. Leaving clearly hadn't done their relationship any favors, and she refused to make the same mistakes. She was older and wiser when it came to relationships. It was time to prove it.

"Listen, if I had thought for a second that my presence would have been helpful instead of hurtful, I would have walked up to you immediately and lent you whatever strength I had," Grace said, hoping the sincerity in her voice was clear.

"I went back and forth on whether or not I should stop by and offer my condolences. But, Ava, when we last spoke, you told me you never wanted to see me again and when you never responded to any of my texts or emails, I figured that was that."

Ava turned away, leaving Grace unsure of where to go without being able to see her face. A cough from across the table made her jerk with the realization that she had forgotten Thomas was in the room. Grace looked at him helplessly, not sure whether to apologize or beg him to give her a sign for what to do next. His gaze was calm, and though Grace didn't know him very well, she could have sworn there was a glint of something like understanding within his dark brown eyes.

"Would you like me to leave?" he asked. Grace wanted to say no, but she waited for Ava to speak up. When no answer was forthcoming, Grace stood slowly.

"No," she replied with an air of finality. "I should probably go. Thank you for inviting me over last night. It was really great." She nodded to Thomas and glanced at Ava who hadn't moved from her position, her face still obscured. Thomas stood as well.

"Let me walk you out."

Grace nodded and followed him to the doorway leading to the front hall. She paused and glanced over her shoulder one last time, but Ava had shifted her gaze now to the table in front of her. The few curls framing her face kept Grace from gleaning any information from her expression and she sighed before leaving the room. In the hallway, Thomas was holding her bag. He handed it to her after she toed on her shoes.

"Give her some time," he said softly.

Grace shrugged. "That's all I have going for me really." At this point, all she had was time to see if this relationship could be salvaged or if the past was too much for them to overcome.

Sunday had been a miserable day. Grace had spent most of it in the house trying to distract herself by tackling her to-do list and knocking things out one by one until she found herself taskless by the early evening. Unfortunately, there were no streets to wander down where she didn't run the risk of bumping into Ava and having to deal with watching her turn and walk the other way. Part of her angrily wondered why she was even bothering. Clearly, Ava had made up her mind about Grace and that was that.

It was probably time for Grace to admit that her chasing the past was a foolish endeavor. She and Ava had changed, and it wasn't together. With a sigh, Grace decided she would do her best teaching the next two years while she really considered what she wanted next.

When the school bell rang, Grace pasted a brittle smile on her face. Mondays were thankfully easy in the mornings since she only had two study hall periods to supervise. It gave her more time to figure out her strategy for getting through this afternoon's bowling practice.

"Alright, y'all, you might not have anything to work on, but keep it down so we don't disturb the other classes. Reading a book is fine, as is being on your phone as long as it is set on vibrate." Grace walked along the path that separated the classroom in two. "If you don't want to do anything, taking a nap is always the next best thing."

Some of the students chuckled as she hung a right and made her way to the space between the windows and the tables. The sun was obstructed by clouds mirroring Grace's mood. She could smell rain on the breeze as it blew in through the open windows. Normally, Grace loved a good summer storm as long as it didn't come with the threat of funnel clouds, but today it just further soured her mood.

She walked back to the front of the room and sat at her desk. Most of the students were sitting in groups, with a few of them taking advantage of the time to catch a couple more minutes of sleep. Grace spent her time reviewing lesson plans for her later classes and trying not to let Ava consume her thoughts. When the bell rang, the students got up and eagerly made their way out the door as a new set of students came in.

Grace couldn't blame them. Her bad mood was probably wafting at them from all directions. Still, she was under no illusions that next period would be any better, and it wasn't. Thankfully, when the last bell of the day rang, Grace was finally left alone with her thoughts.

She collapsed into her chair and leaned her head back to rest on the whiteboard. Teaching high school students was proving just as tricky, if not more so, than her college students. Most of them were there because they had to be, but she could see a few students who really had the bug for science, and she hoped they would reach out with more questions when it came time to think about college. Grace glanced across the hallway in time to see Ava walk over to her board. She was wearing a bright yellow sundress that made her skin glow, and her hair was free flowing, the coils bouncing slightly as she wiped down the board. Seconds passed like minutes as Grace sat frozen in place, hoping that Ava would turn her head and look. When she finally did, she froze as well, her hand still poised on the eraser.

Time stood still as they stared across the hallway, and for a moment Grace remembered the feeling of having Ava in her arms. She had woken up groggily that morning, but it had only taken her a few seconds to realize that she wasn't dreaming. Ava really was curled up in her hold, her back radiating the most tempting heat. Grace had found herself leaning down and brushing her lips over Ava's shoulder before she got a grip. The warmth had lulled her back into a half-hearted doze until she felt Ava stir and move away. She hadn't been able to stop her hand from reaching out on top of the covers even as she kept her eyes closed and pretended to still be asleep.

It had taken everything in her to knock on that bathroom door. The sight of Ava, hair slightly misshapen with the sheen of sleep still in her gaze had given Grace material to dream about even without the memory of their rushed kisses while the alcohol had still dulled their common sense. Ava hadn't said anything about those kisses when she woke up. That made Grace even more glad that she had put a stop to things before they had gone too far.

Now though, there was even more between them that seemed to block the way to a smooth transition of their relationship. She didn't know what Ava remembered of Friday night, and she wasn't particularly excited to bring it up, given Ava's reaction to finding out about Grace's presence at her mother's funeral. Shaking herself from the morose mood she had fallen into, Grace broke their gazes and turned back to her laptop. This wasn't something she could do on her own, and if Ava was determined not to bring it up, then fine. Grace had a job to do. She couldn't let her entire life back home revolve around Ava and her mood. That wasn't fair to herself.

When she dared to look up again, Ava was gone, and Grace sighed as she focused on getting things done for the next hour before she headed over to Terry's and forced herself to act like nothing was wrong all over again.

"Coach Grace!"

The shout knocked her out of the self-inflicted funk.

Grace glanced around, trying not to look like she was searching for someone, but she paused when she found the person she was hoping to see. Ava was standing at the counter talking with Terry, and she looked happier than she had when their gazes had met across the hallway hours before. Even with the weight of tension between them, Grace couldn't deny the pull that always seemed to radiate from somewhere in her chest and left her burning with the need to get closer. It said a lot that she couldn't tell whether that need was for something physical, emotional, or both. This was a dangerous game she was playing. With each day she spent so close to Ava, she seemed to grow greedier for more of her presence.

With a heavy sigh, she set her bag down before saying a few words to the girls and coaxed them into putting their names in so they could begin practice. Regardless of what was going on between the two of them, she and Ava agreed that the most important thing was making sure the team was a success. That meant putting its needs ahead of their own.

"Guess what," Ava said as she walked up to them. The smile on her face was wide, and Grace pasted a semi-smile on her own face.

"What?"

Ava looked like a kid who realized Christmas had come early. "I talked to Terry, and your equipment should be here by Wednesday. That means we'll have everything ready before our final preseason match."

The girls cheered, and even Grace's smile was more genuine as she soaked in their excitement. High fives were exchanged all around, and she posted up a few of her own before her gaze was once again caught by Ava. The smile on her face dipped slightly before she seemed to come to the same realization as Grace about what it meant to save face. This was a happy time for the team, and they didn't need to dampen that with their drama. It was even more important for Ava especially, after having fought to get the team started for the past few years.

Six months would be gone before they knew it, so it was time to buckle down and make things happen. If they were lucky, they would make it through regionals on their way to state championships. It was a dream, but one that Grace was happy to nurture instead of focusing on the way Ava always seemed to draw her attention when she walked into a room.

"Alright," Grace said, clapping her hands together to get everyone's attention. "Now that we know we're going to have our gear soon, we should probably get started so we have an idea of what to do with it. Don't you think?"

The girls nodded, and even Ava murmured a soft agreement. Grace could do this. She could co-coach the team with

Ava and protect her already fragile heart. It wouldn't be easy, but it was something she needed to do, if only for herself.

She had decided to come home, and now it was truly time to blend the past and the present into something new that she could feel proud of going forward. Grace's smile felt more genuine as she looked over at Ava. She had a plan, and now it was time to implement it.

Eighteen

Ava watched Grace as she knelt to help one of the students with her form. It was quickly becoming one of Ava's favorite pastimes, watching Grace do just about anything. She even found herself rapt while Grace rattled off names of things she only vaguely remembered from taking basic chemistry in college. But here on the lanes, watching took on a quality like no other as her nostalgia from the past blended with the present. She almost couldn't believe this was all happening in real time. Never had Ava imagined that Grace would come back and that together they would be working toward the same goal. If she were honest, she hadn't thought Grace would ever come back to Peach Blossom at all.

At first, the thought of never having to see Grace again was something that gave her comfort after the harsh way they ended things. But later, when the realization that the person she had called friend for so many years had really and truly gone, Ava felt nothing but regret. It was that regret she had turned into a weapon designed to keep her away from the feelings Grace's presence now unearthed.

Brad had given her shit when he heard that Grace had left his house the other morning. Ava hadn't known what to do. The double whammy of knowing Grace had come back to Peach Blossom and attended her mother's funeral left Ava with a brain full of static. Grace's expression had been so earnest and hopeful, but Ava hadn't known what to say. She'd had questions, namely, why. But it had seemed too callous to ask, which left her with silence and a mouth frozen with indecision.

At the base of it all, Ava had felt a sense of overwhelming gratefulness. She had been overcome with a swell of bittersweet happiness that even with the time and distance spread out between them like the widest river, Grace had still come. Ava's silence had no doubt been hurtful, and for that she felt tremendous guilt. It had been hard to open her mouth when fighting back the tears that had threatened to spill down her cheeks.

She had spent the rest of the weekend wondering if she should just show up to Grace's place and apologize. But then she hadn't been sure if chasing after her was the best response either. Truthfully, she felt ashamed about her reactions thus far to Grace's new presence in her life. She knew that something needed to change, and she was self-aware enough to know the something was her. This time, it would have to be Ava reaching out. As Brad had so eloquently put it, it was time for Ava to get her head out of her ass. Grace had done her part. She had come back and continuously reached out an olive branch of peace to figure a way forward between the two of them. It was time to swallow her damn pride and make things right before Ava had to mourn the loss of a friendship once again.

When Grace stepped back, letting the team practice without her interference, Ava knew it was her chance to speak without little ears listening in. "Looks like they are getting the hang of things."

Grace didn't look at her, but she did nod in acknowledgment of Ava's words. "They are. A couple of them I think are really going to be standout players this year."

"That's great." The enthusiasm in Ava's voice wasn't faked. She truly was excited to see how the girls grew and developed in their games. Even if they didn't make it all the way to the top, she wanted them to enjoy themselves and feel proud of the progress they made. "I wonder if any of them will think about playing in college. There are quite a few universities out there now that have bowling teams."

This time, Grace did look over at her, and Ava's breath caught at the small smile on her face. "Yeah. I know I enjoyed it. I had hoped that you and I would meet out on the lanes again."

Ava felt a flare of pain at the thought. She hadn't bowled on a college team because she hadn't gotten into her first choice. That rejection had hit her hard and left her self-confidence hanging on by a thread. The school she ended up attending had still been high up on her list, but it hadn't had a bowling team and she never joined the local league. She swallowed hard and pushed the unwanted memory away. As her dad always said, things happened for a reason. Not bowling allowed her to focus more on school and her classes, which led her to graduate with honors. It had been a particularly wonderful thing, as her family was there, whole and together, to celebrate the achievement with her. It had been one of the last wonderful memories before everything turned to shit.

"Yeah," she breathed out finally. It was time to focus on the present instead of getting lost in the what-ifs of days gone by. "It's weird how things came full circle, isn't it?"

Grace nodded. "It is." She didn't say anything else, and after looking at her profile for a few more moments, Ava turned and watched over the team.

After the two hours had passed, Ava and Grace called the team back together to talk and give suggestions. Ava was proud of their focus. When she was their age, she distinctly remembered goofing off from time to time. Grace hadn't been any better. At times, they had to take seats as far away from one another as possible because there was just no way they could be next to one another and pay attention.

"I sent a video out for you all to watch. Try to view it before our next practice so you have the basics for taking care of your equipment." The students let out whoops of excitement at the reminder that they would soon have their own balls and shoes to practice and compete in. "Any questions?"

When none were forthcoming, Grace dismissed them, slapping a few high fives as most of the team members left to return their balls and shoes before heading out. Before she could follow, Grace offered to go get the scores. Ava nodded, turning her head and watching Grace make her way to the front counter.

"Coach Ava?"

She swiftly looked away before she got caught staring. Tabitha was looking at her, nervousness in her gaze. Ava frowned slightly, wondering what the girl had to be nervous about. "Yes?"

Tabitha glanced at some of her other teammates as they walked by before seemingly gathering her courage. Ava grew even more apprehensive, not quite sure what was coming. Teenagers often surprised her. You couldn't always guess what was about to roll off their tongues and whether it was something that would leave you hunched over with laughter or crying alone in the shower.

"Well, we happened to notice…" She trailed off and glanced at her teammates again before the rest of her thoughts came out in a rush. "We noticed you and Coach Grace always seem to smile when the other isn't looking. And we just wondered if you two were together. Like, *together* together."

Ava had never had a student comment on her being romantically involved with another teacher. She had thought she was being sneaky with her glances Grace's way, but clearly, she was no match for the observational abilities of nosy-ass teens. If she could figure out the best way to harness that for her lessons to keep them on task, she could sell her knowledge at a premium and retire early to an island somewhere.

"That's kind of an inappropriate question," she replied delicately. Ava felt she had good rapport with the students and didn't want Tabitha to feel too awkward for having asked something completely out of left field.

"I'm sorry," Tabitha backtracked quickly. "We all think it's great that you two like each other."

"No." When Tabitha's eyes widened, Ava quickly clarified

while looking at the other lingering students in turn. "Coach Grace and I are not together. We're just colleagues."

"And friends," one of the other girls added.

Ava wasn't sure if they could be considered friends just yet, and she knew that was largely her fault.

"Yes. And friends."

Soon, Ava thought to herself. They clearly needed to have a long discussion to not only dispel this rumor before it really got going, but also to truly clear the air. When she saw the girls look behind her, she turned and saw Grace standing there with a confused expression. Ava wasn't sure if she had heard any of the conversation, but it wasn't something she felt they could discuss in front of the team. They needed to talk alone.

"Great, you're back." She sent Grace a reassuring smile and was bolstered when Grace gave her a small grin in return. Ava saw a few of the girls glance back and forth between her and Grace as they grabbed their bags to leave, but she knew calling them out would just draw more attention to their assumptions. It wasn't until the last of them had passed through the sliding doors that Ava turned to Grace.

"Can we talk?" Grace's eyebrows rose but she nodded, and they walked over to a set of tables by the small food section. Most of the other tables were unoccupied, giving them some privacy. "Don't be alarmed, but the team asked me a question, and I think we should probably figure out a way to squash it."

Grace frowned, and Ava's fingers twitched with the need to straighten out the little forehead wrinkle between her eyes. She balled her hand into a fist to stifle that desire and pushed on.

"It's nothing bad... I think."

"That doesn't relieve me in the slightest," Grace replied. "Are they all quitting?"

Ava shook her head. "No, nothing like that. They asked me if we were dating."

"We who?"

"We, us. As in, you and me."

Grace's eyes widened and she crossed her arms. "Why would they think that? Why would they even ask that? Is that a normal question for high schoolers to ask their teachers?"

Ava snorted. "You would be surprised at some of the questions I have gotten from students over the years. But this is the first time I have ever been asked if I was dating a colleague." She watched Grace, studying her reactions. Ava wasn't sure what she was expecting, but it wasn't for Grace to slowly smile and shake her head.

"True. I guess I shouldn't be surprised either since I have had some of my past university students ask me if I were dating someone before." At Ava's raised brow, she quickly explained. "Because of my research, I often worked closely with colleagues late into the evening. Someone unfamiliar with that would probably assume something similar."

That was news to Ava. She slowly was starting to realize that despite their shared past, she didn't really know much about who Grace was now and what she had been doing for the past decade. It was something she wanted to remedy.

"Oh, really? What research were you doing?"

Grace opened her mouth before quickly snapping it shut as her eyes widened. She paused before asking a question of her own. "You really want to know?"

Ava fought her desire to shrug and nodded instead. "I wouldn't have asked if I wasn't interested." She couldn't maintain the earnest eye contact though and eventually turned away. "Also, maybe I want to apologize."

"Maybe?"

Ava looked back at Grace and was relieved to see her smiling openly. Something warm fluttered in Ava's chest and she had to duck her head down again to keep from smiling dopily in response. Her reactions to Grace were starting to become a real problem, but one she had no idea how or if she wanted to remedy.

"Fine. I definitely want to apologize," she said with a shake of her head. "I didn't want you to leave on Saturday. I just didn't know how to handle…everything."

"I can imagine. I know how close you and your mother were," Grace conceded.

That was true but not the entirety of the reason for her garbled feelings. She had thought Grace hadn't cared and to find out that she was wrong had taken some time to have the spoons to handle. There was more she wanted to say. More she wanted to divulge, but now was not the time and Grace probably didn't want to wear Ava's emotional vomit all over her shoes.

"We were," Ava conceded. She had been close to her mother, especially right at the end. Watching her waste away as the cancer ravaged her body had been one of the toughest things Ava had ever had to deal with. There were still some days when she reached for her phone to call her mom only to have the memory of her being gone slam into her face-first, leaving her gasping desperately for breath.

"But I do appreciate you coming to the funeral."

Grace was quiet as their gazes locked. Ava didn't have the strength or desire to look away. Not when it felt so important that she didn't. They were on the cusp of something vitally important. She could feel it down to the marrow in her bones, and as she stared into Grace's deep brown gaze, another memory slowly slid to the forefront of her mind. Frantic kisses under the cover of darkness.

"Shit."

Her gasped word broke through the magic that had them bound, and Grace blinked quickly before glancing around them as if looking for something. "What? What happened?"

Ava wasn't completely sure, but she swore she could feel the impression of lips pressed against hers. "Friday night."

Grace frowned, not looking like she understood where Ava was going with this. Ava wasn't sure if that made the memory better or worse. The kiss floating in her head was not the same innocent peck she remembered from their childhood. Truthfully, it wouldn't be the first time she had imagined kissing Grace, but the depth of the memory was nothing like her transparent dreams.

"I kissed you." Ava watched Grace carefully, her eyes widening when Grace's expression shifted. *She knew.* Ava was sure of it. That was a guilty look if ever she saw one. But if Grace knew, why hadn't she said anything?

"Well, it was more like we kissed each other?" Grace said, making it sound like a question.

"I am so sorry."

Grace choked on a laugh before shaking her head. "You're

apologizing twice in one day?" Ava snorted but chuckled at Grace's words. "There's nothing to apologize for."

Grace was insistent, but Ava still felt horrible. She had put them in an awkward position. The kiss years ago could be chocked up to youthful indiscretions, but they were adults now. There were consequences to their actions that would affect more than just them. "Still. I can't just be a bitch and then kiss you. That's a bit rude."

"Yeah, kind of," she conceded. "But it wasn't a bad kiss, and you fell asleep quickly after that. We can just chock it up to one too many glasses and leave it at that."

That should have made Ava happy, that Grace just wanted to move on from the whole thing, but it didn't. She didn't want to just rug-sweep another kiss between the two of them, but what else could she do? Clearly, Grace wanted to move past the whole thing and that was probably for the best. Clean slate.

"That sounds great."

It sounded horrible, but Ava would just have to deal with it. That final kiss on her shoulder when she woke up was clearly just a fluke. She had let the students' assumptions get to her.

They were co-coaches and maybe eventually friends again. Nothing more, nothing less.

Nineteen

Grace's attention was shot. She had been looking over the same paper for the past ten minutes and none of it was making sense, even though she was the one who had created the questions. Even two days later, the conversation between her and Ava was still running through her mind.

When Ava had brought up their recent kiss, Grace had been quick to let her off the hook. She had been racking her brain for ways to bring it up between them, but when Ava had apologized for it, looking achingly sincere, all she could do was wave away the concern and act like it was no big deal. She wanted things to go back to the tentatively hopeful friendship that they had started building before that night, and waving it away had seemed to be the best way to do that. However, for a moment, after she mentioned just pretending like nothing had ever happened, Ava's expression looked almost disappointed. The downturn of her lips and her shaky smile after had haunted Grace for the past couple days. She had thought she was doing a good thing by letting them off the hook for a kiss that had been initiated by both, liquid courage or not, but now she wasn't so sure.

"Knock knock."

"Hey, Janae." Grace welcomed the distraction from her spiraling thoughts. She set the homework paper down and glanced at her clock. "Oh, it's lunch already. When did that happen?"

Janae chuckled as she pulled a chair over to Grace's desk. Even though she worked across the building, they had taken to having lunch together every couple days. Grace reached under her desk and pulled out her bag. She had gone to Thomas's café the day before and gotten a second sandwich to bring in. They were quickly becoming the best part of her days, if she didn't include the time she got to spend with Ava.

"You seemed hard at work interpreting whatever was on that paper."

Grace looked back at the homework when Janae gestured toward it. "Just some work I gave to the students. I'm starting to regret it already since I don't have anyone I can pay to help me grade them."

"I don't envy some of the teachers when it comes to how much work they have to assign." Janae pulled out a Tupperware container and the next few minutes were silent as they both took bites of their food. They didn't have a ton of time, and Grace always made sure to eat everything she brought. She was not a nice person when hungry.

"So, how is coaching going? You and Ava getting along any better?"

Grace had tentatively started opening up to Janae about some of her initial struggles. It helped that although Ava and Janae knew one another, they didn't cross paths much in nor outside of school. It gave Grace a little space and a person to talk with who might be able to give a fresh perspective about things.

"Maybe," she answered slowly. She hadn't told Janae about the kissing incident, and she didn't think she would. Somehow, that seemed like maybe too much information to divulge. "The good of the team is most important to both of us."

Janae shook her head. "I can't believe Robert gave you only six months."

"You're telling me." Grace felt that familiar tendril of frustration, but what's done was done. "At least that means we're both working toward the same goal. Sometimes I think if not for this team, I would never see Ava."

It was a depressing thought, but one she knew was true. If not for the way they had stumbled into coaching together, Grace doubted she would be spending as much time with Ava as she had been. It was the worst type of heaven and best type of hell to be so close to what she wanted and yet still so far.

Janae hummed, drawing Grace's attention. She had a sly look on her face as she observed Grace.

"What?"

"Nothing. You just talk about her a lot."

Busted. "Do I? I don't think I do." She tried to play it off but clearly didn't do very well based on Janae's smile. "What? I don't trust that smile."

"And you shouldn't," Janae confirmed. "I'm just wondering if there is something more there. Maybe a little hanky panky on the lanes."

Grace sputtered out a laugh but shook her head. "There is a distinct lack of hanky panky." At Janae's look, she quickly added, "not that I want there to be any hanky-panky to begin with. We're just colleagues."

"Right."

Grace chewed furiously. Clearly, she wasn't fooling anybody. Now, the only question that remained was just how many others could read the foolish emotions on her face. Maybe that was why Ava was so guarded around her. With a groan, Grace put her sandwich on the desk and dropped her face into her hands.

"Is it that obvious?"

"What? That you want to bone Ava?"

She peeked at Janae from between her fingers. "Who even says bone anymore?"

"Very obvious."

Grace's next groan was louder as she thought back to their team members and their insistence that Grace and Ava had something going on. Of course, it was probably her fault. Her emotions could likely be seen from space.

"Good thing she likes you too." Grace jerked her head up. Janae was still calmly eating her lunch, looking unconcerned with the direction the conversation was going. *It must be nice to be so unbothered*, Grace thought to herself. She felt like her existence had been nothing but a big ball of anxiety and confusion since moving back.

"What makes you say that?" She nearly winced at the hope in her voice. Grace clung to any small hope that her relationship with Ava wasn't totally in the gutter. "Has she said something?"

Janae shrugged. "If she has, it wouldn't be to me. The few times I've seen the two of you interacting, there was something there. Call it a hunch if you will."

Grace wasn't sure she could stack her hope on a hunch from someone who wasn't around Ava on the regular no matter how much she wanted to. If Brad had said something similar, she would have jumped at the idea completely.

"You should go for it and see what happens. You never know."

The thought made Grace swallow hard, but if things were difficult before, they were damn near impossible now. Now they were coworkers, which would make things even worse if they fell out any further. She didn't reply, instead focusing on her sandwich and the what-ifs that cycled through her mind.

"Before I forget, I'm having a paint-and-sip get together at my place this Friday night. You're more than welcome to join."

That sounded just like something that would help take Grace's mind off her current obsession. Jessica kept telling her she needed to get out, and this was the perfect occasion.

"Count me in. That sounds great."

The rest of the week had been rough, but now it was the weekend, and for the first time in a long time, she had plans.

"Good game, girls," Ava said, drawing Grace's attention. She was throwing reassuring smiles, though only a couple of the girls smiled back. It had been a hard blow to lose the game after the high of last week and getting their new equipment. When Ava looked at her, nodding toward their team members, Grace jumped in with her own reassurances.

"We're super proud of you all."

"But we lost," one of the girls said before sitting back in the chair. She crossed her arms and looked over toward the lane they had been on mere moments before. It had been a tough game, and the oil patterns seemed to be more of a hindrance than a help to many of them. It was all part of learning the game, but Grace knew firsthand that sometimes that first loss was the hardest one to swallow.

Grace nodded and patted her shoulder. "Doesn't change the fact that I am proud." She looked at the other girls. "You all did amazing, especially with using your personal equipment for the first time. Consistency will come with practice, and you should be proud that you're doing so well."

"Exactly," Ava agreed. "Plus, this is just the preseason. We have all next week to practice and get the feel for our games."

"Keep your heads high, and we'll see you at practice on Monday."

As the team members filed out, Ava came to stand closer to Grace. Silently, they watched the team leave, exchanging byes with them until they were the only two left. Beside her, Ava sighed heavily.

"That first loss is always a doozy." She shook her head and looked up at Grace with a small smile. "At least they got it out of the way."

"True. I don't think we were any better about our first defeat." Grace sent her a sly look. "I seem to remember someone being in tears."

Ava snorted before pushing Grace with her shoulder. "Like you were any better."

It was true. Grace had similarly had to hold back tears when they had their first loss. It had been a hard blow, but one they bounced back from, and so she knew the girls would too. "Touché."

For a moment, they stood there, nearly shoulder to shoulder as they stared at one another. It was the closest they had been to one another since waking up in bed together, and it was a closeness Grace was beginning to crave with each interaction. She could feel her body wanting to bend into Ava's orbit like an asteroid crashing to Earth after being locked in its pull. This close, she could see the darker flecks of brown in Ava's gaze, and it made her want to look harder and probe deeper until she came to the very essence of who Ava was. If not for the beep of her phone, she might have fallen in completely with no way of getting out again.

"I should get the scores from the desk."

Ava nodded slowly before blinking quickly. She glanced around. "We should probably sit and talk about them and see if we want to change the lineup."

"That sounds great," Grace began before she quickly back-tracked. "Oh, wait. I can't tonight."

Ava's smile dimmed. "Why not?"

"I'm supposed to be going to Janae's for a get together to-night. I already told her I would go."

"Ah."

Ah. On the surface, the response sounded so normal, but there was some undercurrent there that had Grace perking up and taking note. "But we could meet tomorrow?"

"I have to babysit Jordan tomorrow while Dani works an extra shift. He made me promise to take him to the aquarium."

Grace raised her eyebrows. "Like the Georgia Aquarium? All the way up in Atlanta?"

"The one and only." Ava ran a hand over her face, though her expression looked painfully fond as she continued. "Somehow, that kid manages to talk me into taking him places every time I'm in charge of him."

Grace chuckled. "Sounds like he's got Auntie wrapped around his little finger."

"True. We won't be back until late so we should probably just go over things on Monday during practice."

Grace had been about to suggest having dinner together on Sunday, but she pivoted and simply agreed to meeting back up on Monday. Grace's initial excitement at having plans that evening was dampened, and she tried not to think about it as a missed opportunity since she wanted to make friends and have her own social circle.

Not everything in her life needed to loop back around to Ava.

"Monday it is, then."

Ava nodded. "Monday."

Twenty

The weekend had been rough. Ava always enjoyed spending time with Jordan and, despite what she'd told Grace, she didn't mind taking him to places when Dani was working. It had become a ritual of theirs that when Dani had to be on call or cover a shift, either Grace or Vini would take Jordan up to Atlanta or down to Savannah for a day of fun. When she had relayed the information to Grace after the team had left, Ava had been tempted to invite her along. It was a ridiculous thought and not one that had been born from clear and careful consideration. No. It had come from pure jealousy.

Ava hadn't spent much time around Janae. She obviously knew who she was and had even conversed with her a few times, but they never really ran across one another on the day-to-day. She had seen Janae a few times in their hallway but had stopped to think about it. Aggravatingly, the whole thing had been on her mind the entire weekend. She had taken Jordan on a surprise trip to the zoo as well, but still, her mind was filled with Grace.

"Hey, Coach Ava."

Ava pushed away her thoughts and forced a smile to her lips. It wouldn't do to seem down during practice. The team was probably still reeling from last week's loss, so she wanted to be as upbeat as possible for them.

"Hey, Rory. Good to see that you remembered to bring your bag with you." Rory nodded with an excited smile as she pulled the rolling bag along behind her. Everything they needed was contained in those bags, and it made Ava proud to see Peach Blossom High printed on the outside. She had wanted this for so long, and she needed to get her head in the game to push through. The team wouldn't make it if she faltered. Thoughts of Grace and what she might have done over the weekend would do nothing to help with her productivity.

Ava called out greetings as the other girls filed in and got changed into their bowling shoes. It was almost like clockwork now. They would separate into two, enter their names into the kiosk, and get going. It brought an immense feeling of pride to Ava's chest to see them moving confidently.

"Ava. Hi."

Her heart thumped unnecessarily, but Ava schooled her expression into one of calm indifference before turning to face Grace. "Hey, Grace. Good to see you."

"You too."

Ava had told herself she was going to play it cool, but she couldn't help the way her eyes drifted over Grace's leggy frame, taking in jeans that had to be tailored the way they hugged her thighs and a loose T-shirt with a V-neck that was aggravatingly distracting. Her hair was loose this time, falling softly over her shoulders.

"How was your weekend?" It wasn't a question that Ava had planned to ask. In fact, she had told herself she didn't care what Grace had done over the weekend, and they didn't even have to speak of it. Clearly, her brain and her mouth needed to have another discussion about who was in charge.

"It was great," Grace replied as she stepped up and turned her attention to their team members. The girls were chatting softly, some of them practicing their stances as they waited their turn. Tabitha had turned and was looking at Grace and Ava with a small grin. "The paint-and-sip event was a lot of fun. I thought it might even be a fun team-building activity to do with the girls minus the wine."

Begrudgingly, Ava had to admit that it did sound like a good activity to do with the team. "That's a great idea. We'll have to look into it more and see about setting it up."

"I'll talk to Janae and see if she has some suggestions."

At Janae's name, Ava felt herself tensing. She let out a slow and steady breath before nodding sharply. "Wonderful." The thought was anything but. Unfortunately, she couldn't say that, so she opted to change the subject.

"Did you bring the scores from last week?"

Grace pulled them out of her bag before setting it down. She leaned closer to Ava and gestured to the writing in the margins. "I looked over them on Saturday and scribbled down some notes."

Ava narrowed her eyes as she reviewed them. She agreed with a lot of what Grace was saying until she got to one of her final notes. She looked over at her. "You want to switch Rory out?"

"Just for the first game of the season," Grace explained. "I think she has trouble setting up her initial throw and she's only closing frames about half the time."

"True, but she has one of the most consistent throws on the team," Ava pushed back. "When she's on, she's *on*."

Grace nodded, but she pulled several more score papers from her bag. "I don't disagree, but the problem is, if she isn't on, she flounders. I don't want to pull her for good, but I think maybe she needs more practice before starting."

Ava opened her mouth, ready to argue when another voice interrupted her.

"Spoken like a true coach."

Ava turned in time to see Grant walking over to them. She didn't attempt to keep her smile, instead letting it slip into a scowl as he bypassed her and leaned into Grace's space. She barely kept her eyes from narrowing as he and Grace hugged. When he pulled back, he barely acknowledged Ava.

"Grant, what are you doing here?"

"I was hoping to catch you again and see how you were doing," Grant replied, smiling in a way that reminded Ava of Robert. It was a condescending smile with way more teeth than necessary. She hadn't liked the man before, and she didn't like him any better now. "We still need to grab a bite and catch up."

If he had been Grace's coach before, that meant he was probably in his forties or fifties. The fact that he was so insistent on having dinner with Grace gave Ava the ick.

"Right, well I have a team to coach." He looked at Ava

and, for a moment, something shifted behind his smile. In that instant Ava knew without a single doubt that she hated him. "Excuse me."

Before either of them could say anything more, Ava stepped around them and moved closer to the students. She could hear the deep tones of Grant's voice and Grace's higher pitch, but thankfully the sounds of chattering and balls rolling down the lanes dulled her hearing so she couldn't make out any words. She kept her attention on the team, doling out advice here and there without another glance behind her. Even when he finally left, the vibe had been thrown off.

She and Grace chatted briefly, but never got back to their previous conversation. Ava knew it was only a matter of time. They needed to figure out their lineup before the first in-season match next Friday. That meant an argument or two. Ava wondered if they would be able to disagree without it turning into a major ordeal.

When practice was over, Ava got the scores this time and added them to the growing stack in her hand. The team members filed out quickly, and she turned to find Grace, but when she was nowhere to be found, Ava sighed and decided to just make her way home. She hadn't expected to step outside and see a frowning Grace muttering as she looked under the hood of her car. She paused for a moment, wondering if she should just let it go and keep moving. When Grace looked up, she knew she couldn't just leave.

"Is everything okay?"

Grace's smile was full of relief. She shook her head and then gestured to her car. "I don't know what's going on, but this piece of shit won't start."

Ava raised her eyebrows. It was the first time she could really remember hearing Grace curse, and for some reason she wanted to hear it again. But in a different context. She forced those thoughts away and focused on the problem at hand. "Well, I can probably help you out," Ava replied, looking at the vehicle. The car was new or at least newer than her Prius.

Grace looked surprised. "You know about cars?" she asked.

Ava laughed and shook her head. "I don't know shit about cars, but I am related to someone who does." She pulled out her phone and quickly dialed Vini's number. The phone rang twice before Vini answered.

"I'm working you know. I don't have time to be dealing with whatever your drama of the week is."

Ava rolled her eyes before turning and walking a slight distance away from Grace to give herself a bit of privacy. "It's not drama. I need your help."

"You need my help?" Vini asked. "Last time I tried to help you told me to fuck off."

"You tell me to fuck off all the time," Ava countered. "But I don't need your help with my life. I need your help with a car."

"I told you to trade in that piece of shit Prius for something else."

"Can you not right now? And anyway, it's not my car I need help with. It's Grace's car."

"What the hell did you do to her car?" Vini's voice went shrill, and Ava winced as she moved the phone away from her ear. "You know sometimes I think you're going a little too far with this rivalry between the two of you."

Frustration had her rubbing a hand over her face, but Ava willed herself to keep calm. It wouldn't do any good to get riled up. "We've already squashed that. Her car won't start. We're here at the bowling alley, and I'm just trying to see if you can come and help her."

That seemed to calm Vini down, and if not for needing her help, Ava would've called her on it. What was it with everyone immediately thinking when something went wrong, she was at fault? "Oh, okay. Well, sure, but it will be about an hour before I can get there."

Ava turned and called out to Grace over her shoulder. "Vini says she can get here but it'll take about an hour. Does that work for you?"

Grace shrugged. "There's really nothing else I can do but wait." She pulled out her own phone and started typing on it.

"She says that's fine. You should probably bring the tow truck just in case."

"Oh, so now you're telling me how to do my job?" Vini hung up the phone before Ava could reply, and she rubbed her forehead. She could feel pressure from an oncoming headache already and it was only Monday. Sometimes she wondered why she even bothered. *That's what I get for trying to be nice*, she thought before turning back around in time to see Grace smile down at her phone. The look made her pause, and she had another moment where she realized just how nice Grace's smile was.

Ava walked back over to Grace. "Maybe you should wait

in the bowling alley until then. It's hot as Satan's ass crack out here."

Grace looked up at her with a wide smile before slipping her phone back in her pocket. "You always did have a way with words. I suppose I should though. The humidity alone would probably be enough to suffocate me at this point." She turned to head back inside before pausing and giving Ava a thoughtful look. "You know, since I'm going to be waiting here, and if you don't have anywhere you need to be, maybe we could bowl a game or two. For old time's sake."

It was on the tip of Ava's tongue to say that she hadn't said anything about sticking around and waiting with Grace, but the truth was she wanted to. Bowling a game sounded like a perfect plan, and truthfully, she had nowhere else to be. Sending a prayer up to whoever was listening to give her the strength to not make a fool of herself, Ava shrugged and nodded.

"I mean, if you're ready to lose again absolutely."

Grace's smile turned sharp, and Ava's stomach clenched. This was what she missed, the feeling of competition. It was a feeling that only Grace seemed to conjure from her.

"Well, after you, then," Grace said, tipping her head and gesturing for Ava to precede her back into the building. Once they were again enveloped in the coolness of the alley, Ava waved at Terry to catch his attention.

"What are you guys doing back here?"

"Ava decided she wants to get a taste for losing again so we're back to bowl a game or two while we wait for Vini," Grace replied. "My car wouldn't start."

Ava rolled her eyes and looked at Terry. "Can you just get

us a couple pairs of shoes, Terry? Grace here needs a lesson in humility."

He laughed and shook his head but quickly got them two pairs of shoes and told them which lane to head toward. Ava's heart raced as she switched shoes. She glanced up at Grace from beneath her eyelashes as she tied her strings, noting that Grace seemed to be just as excited as her. She was unsure if the excitement was more about bowling itself or bowling with Ava. That was an important distinction.

As they entered their names in, it was almost like no time had passed. Ava mused on how similar and yet different this feeling was. Despite having been on the same team, Grace had always been her main competition, at least in Ava's mind. It had been all fun and games, until it wasn't. Even with how things ended, Ava had to admit that facing Grace on the lanes had been one of the only things to truly get her heart racing.

By the time she got back from choosing a ball to throw, Grace had rolled up her sleeves. She gifted Ava with a wide smile. "Age before beauty?"

Ava snorted. "Are you forgetting that you're older than I am?" She gave Grace a pointed look before lifting her ball and stepping forward. "But whatever, I'll go first this time." She ignored Grace's soft chuckle and stepped to the line.

It was like settling into a worn jacket, familiar and comforting all the same. Ava took a deep breath and lined up her gaze before starting her approach. The feel of the ball as she released it was like nothing else in life. She enjoyed bowling in the weekend league, but this strange mix of camaraderie and rivalry was something she only had with Grace. There had been a few people in the league that she enjoyed beating, mostly because they were assholes. But this was completely different. It was something she hadn't realized she missed.

When the pins crashed, falling all at once like she willed them, Ava turned back, eyeing Grace with a triumphant grin. "Looks like I'm starting off strong," she said with a snap of her fingers. Grace picked up her ball and walked past her.

"I guess we'll see how great your stamina is."

Those words could be used in so many ways and, despite herself, Ava couldn't help the frisson of arousal that slid down her spine. She watched enraptured as Grace took her start and slowly made her way to the line. Watching Grace bowl had always drawn her attention and now was no different. Long legs seem to drive her forward with a power that Ava never quite matched. Grace was like a force of nature. When she let go of the ball, it popped satisfyingly from her fingers, traveling a wide arc before hitting the pins right between the sweet spot, throwing them back with a crash. Grace turned and favored her with a grin and Ava knew then that this attraction wasn't something she could just ignore.

She had hoped, with the history between them, they could just move past the bullshit and settle into a civil working relationship. She was slowly realizing that while a friendly relationship wasn't a bad thing, she wanted more.

"It's your turn," Grace said, snapping her out of her reverie. Ava nodded, picking up her ball and pushing everything from her mind as she settled into her stance.

Time seemed to slowly trickle by with neither of them pulling too far ahead of the other. Even as teammates, they had always been evenly matched. By the time they got to the tenth frame it was always anyone's game, and this time was no different.

"Maybe we should do a little wager on this one." Grace crossed her arms as a sly smile slowly slid across her face. In the past, it wasn't uncommon for them to wager something for the eventual victor like a snack or a favor. But now Ava had an assortment of ideas in her mind that were definitely not family friendly.

"Like what?" Ava asked.

Grace paused for a moment, studying Ava's face before she shrugged. Her expression didn't change, but Ava could feel something in the air shift. "What about dinner this weekend?"

Shock jolted through her. If it were anyone else, Ava would think that they were flirting with her. But this was Grace. She decided to go with it instead of trying to decode what Grace might actually be saying. "You want to wager dinner?"

Grace nodded. "If I win, you buy me dinner this weekend wherever I want." Ava raised an eyebrow as she thought about it. Grace continued before she could respond. "And if you win, I'll buy you dinner this weekend wherever you want."

"Oh, so you've just decided we're getting dinner this weekend regardless?" Ava teased.

"Yep," Grace confirmed with a twinkle in her eyes. "I think it's high time we hang out together outside of a bunch of teenagers or Brad and Thomas."

Ava could've said something biting, but she cut the thoughts off before they could fully form. Things were going well, and she wasn't going to sabotage herself when she was getting what she wanted without having to ask.

"Alright, you're on."

Grace's smile set off butterflies fluttering furiously in Ava's chest. And the thrum of competition had her fingers wiggling in preparation for her next frame. She could almost see sparks as electric anticipation scorched the air. There were no heavy stakes here, and she could go all out without being accused of showing off or leaving anyone with hurt feelings. She knew Grace understood and would be going all out as well. It had her grinning like a loon as she set up her shot.

Time ticked by, each second loud even amongst the crashing of the pins, and Ava gave it everything. She racked up another strike before closing out her tenth frame with a solid spare. When she turned to Grace, admiration was clear in her gaze, and Ava couldn't help the way she stood a little taller. It was ridiculous, this desire to impress. She didn't normally give two shits what other people thought of her. But she did now. With Grace.

She always had.

"You did good, kid." Grace's teasing jab spurred Ava to shake off her thoughts and get her head back in the game. They had a wager going, one she was even more interested in seeing through now that she had come to her revelation. "Watch the master at work."

"Do you always refer to yourself in third person? It's a little concerning."

Grace waved her back as she walked up to the line. "No jeers from the peanut gallery."

Ava snorted softly but stood back and kept her eyes trained on Grace as she settled into her stance. Watching Grace bowl had always caught her eye and maybe if she had been more self-aware when they were younger, she would have understood why.

Grace was always elegant, especially now with her lithe build. But when she moved toward the line, she was all tightly coiled aggression and power. She seemed to move so suddenly, taking three long-limbed steps before the ball seemed to explode from her hand, barreling toward the pins as if gravity itself were propelling it forward. When it struck, settling into the sweet spot with laser-like accuracy, the sound was almost impossibly satisfying. Her pins went down in a blaze of glory as she turned and fixed Ava with a smug grin that did things to her. Tingly things that she refused to name.

"Oh, so you think you're tough shit now because you got one strike?" Ava called out, unable to stop herself from baiting Grace. It was like an urge she couldn't help but scratch at every opportunity. "Two more. Can your stamina hold out or do you need to take a quick break?"

Grace cocked her head to the side and gave Ava a look through narrowed eyes. "I'll show you how much stamina I have." The muttered promise made Ava shivery in all the best ways, but Grace turned before she could muster a reply.

The air seemed to shimmer with tension as Grace set up her next shot. Ava knew if she had been facing her, Grace's gaze would have been trained on the target arrows on the floor. Those dark brown eyes always seemed so intense when she was concentrating, and Ava knew that if they had been on her, she would have felt them like a physical touch. She wondered if the floor would feel different if she ran her fingertips over it. Surely, a gaze that heavy had to carry some weight. It was no doubt heavier than the weight of this change, the flirting banter that flowed back and forth between the two of them like soft waves lapping at the shore. Sure, they had teased one another when they were younger, but it never had the undercurrent of promise like it did now.

Ava's eyes locked onto Grace's form as she slowly approached the line and released. Once again, the ball took aim, but this time it seemed to hit a slick of oil, skidding farther than before and hitting the pins at an angle that left the front three remaining. Grace turned, giving a rueful smile.

"That was unexpected."

"Looks like you couldn't quite keep it up," Ava teased as she shrugged. "It happens to the best of us."

"You are so going to get it," Grace replied with narrowed eyes. She set up her final shot, slowly moving through her normal form before closing out the frame. Ava had expected no less. She had been excited at the prospect of having dinner with Grace regardless of the outcome, but she couldn't deny the fact that she wanted this win.

"I guess dinner is on you, then."

Grace didn't look the least bit upset as she stood in front of Ava with her legs slightly separated and her arms crossed. Ava swallowed hard and tried not to let her gaze linger. That was a posture that screamed sex. There was something about seeing a good-looking woman in such a powerful pose that got things going for her. It was right up there with seeing women in suits.

"I guess so," Grace finally replied. "Seems you do still have it."

Not one to miss an opportunity to boast, Ava cocked her hip out and gave Grace a look. "You mean you didn't realize it just by looking at me?"

Grace's eyebrows raised and her smile slowly morphed into a smirk. "I realized a lot of things when looking at you, but none of them had to do with bowling."

Pure unadulterated heat shot through Ava's frame with enough force that it almost knocked her off her feet. Normally, when someone flirted with her, she didn't realize it until days later when the interaction was over, and the other person was long gone.

This was blatant.

Or…she thought it was. There was still some lingering doubt along with a healthy dose of wariness about playing with fire. So many things could go sideways if she were wrong. Even more could go wrong if she were right. What was Grace playing at here, and why was Ava so gung ho about playing along?

"Oh?" Ava asked, pretending like she wasn't interested in the response. She tilted her head down and ran her finger over her ball. "And what are some of the things that you figured out when you looked at me?"

Grace's hands dropped down to her sides, and her smirk slowly changed into something less sharp, something fonder than it had any reason to be. "Are you sure you're really ready for that conversation?"

Now Ava couldn't possibly pretend that she wasn't intrigued. "I mean unless you're going to tell me that you figured out where you wanted to hide my body, I think I'm ready for it," she replied. "I'm a big girl now. I can handle it."

Grace laughed, throwing her head back and giving Ava the perfect view of her long, slender neck. Ava itched with the darkest desire to get her mouth all over that bit of skin and feel just how soft it was. Heaven help her, but the attraction was impossible to ignore. She was almost ready to say to hell with the consequences. In truth, this reunion had been a long time coming, and if this was going to blow up in her face, she was at least ready to enjoy the ride down to hell.

"Sometimes I wonder where you come up with these things," Grace said, shaking her head. She gestured back to the lane. "You looked good out there. Comfortable."

"You do remember I bowl on the weekends, don't you?"

"Can you just let me compliment you?"

Ava hummed but gestured for Grace to continue. It seemed like a backhanded compliment, but if she was being sincere, Ava would let her attempts go without commentary. Grace chuckled again and shook her head. "You are something else." She licked her lips, drawing Ava's gaze. "So, dinner on Saturday. You have some place in mind?"

She could have made it easy on Grace and just blurted out the places she liked, but something in her wanted to make her work for it. It wouldn't be any fun if she just gave in completely. That wasn't Ava's style.

"Maybe," she conceded before throwing a curveball. "Maybe I want to see what you think my win is worth. I could pick the most expensive place so I could be wined and dined, but I'm leaving the choice up to you."

Grace stepped forward, and Ava felt the air between them shift. This wasn't the thrill of competition she was feeling. That had been long replaced with something new. Something heady and waiting to be acknowledged. She took in a deep breath to calm the frantic thrum of her heart and gazed unblinkingly at Grace.

"If you wanted to be wined and dined, all you had to do was ask."

The conversation was moving into dangerous territory. No, it had moved well beyond that. It was moving into the type of territory that Ava only thought about when she knew she was alone with plenty of batteries. It was not something she should be engaging when she was in a semi-crowded public location where anyone who happened to focus on them would get unfettered access to her losing what little was left of her chill. She needed to rein in her wayward mouth before it started promising things it had no business throwing out there, like her hand in marriage. But it was so damn difficult to recall why she should be on her guard when Grace leaned closer to her and stared at her like she was ready to risk things she had no business risking.

"Ava, I think we should—"

"Here you guys are. I was outside looking for y'all."

Disappointment and gratefulness dueled as Ava shifted her attention to where Vini was rushing over to them, her hands on her hips and an annoyed frown on her face. She was the best and worst distraction from a moment that Ava would no doubt replay in her mind. Never had a week seemed so long before. How she would get through the next practice and game, Ava wasn't sure. She was barely keeping her cool before, if she were being honest with herself.

"It was hot out there, so we decided to come in and bowl a game or two until you got here." Vini tilted her head before giving Ava a once-over. "Grace wanted to relive how it felt to lose to me."

Grace's laugh broke some of the tension, and when Vini turned to her, Ava let out a breath.

"Well, I'm here now, so you ready for me to check out your car?"

Grace nodded before switching back into her regular shoes. She glanced over at Ava and gestured to the door. "You coming with us, or do you need to head out?"

Ava shook her head. "I have some grading I need to do, so I'll probably just head home." She sat down on one of the empty seats and leaned over to untie her bowling shoes. She paused and looked up at Grace. "I'll see you tomorrow?"

The smile that answered her damn near took her breath away and left Ava following Grace with her eyes as she and Vini exited the bowling alley. She didn't doubt that Vini would have some words for her when she got home, but Ava didn't care. She needed some time and space to think about the fact that in a few days she was going on what was effectively a date with Grace.

Twenty-One

"You have some explaining to do."

Ava refused to look up from her grading. She had only just been able to concentrate on it after spending an entire night and most of the current day analyzing every interaction she'd had with Grace yesterday. When Vini had gotten home, she had favored Ava with a knowing look but blessedly kept quiet, leaving Ava wondering what she and Grace might have talked about. She knew asking Vini was out of the question. That would have been admitting that she was curious.

Her thoughts had been plagued with nothing but Grace even during class. The few times Ava had spotted her through the doorway, she hadn't known how to act. Grace hadn't noticed her the first time, but the second time, they were both at their respective boards, and when their gazes met, Ava felt the moment go through her like a shock. She had frozen in place for a moment in the middle of whatever she had been writing out. If not for one of the students calling for help, she didn't know how long she would have been standing there looking like a deer caught in headlights. When she blinked, breaking the spell that had fallen over them, Grace had gifted her with a smile that damn near knocked the breath from her.

"Explaining about what?" Ava said finally, still not lifting her head. She hadn't gotten anything done during her actual grading period and now she was stuck grading papers when she had planned to have them done before she got home.

"Grace."

The scritch of her pen faltered slightly, but she recovered quickly, marking a check on an answer she hoped was actually correct. She wanted to do anything but talk to Dani about Grace, but she was worse than Vini when she got it into her head that she needed to discuss something. Relentless. Bullheaded. That fit Dani to a T. When a shadow fell over her, Ava sighed and finally looked up, annoyance clear on her face.

"Seriously? I have work to do."

Dani pursed her lips. "And?"

"And you're keeping me from doing that." Ava waved her hand at the stack of ungraded papers beside her. "I need to get these done so I can enter them in and hand them back tomorrow."

"So, you're trying to avoid the subject, then?"

For fuck's sake, she thought to herself. There clearly was nothing she could say that would knock Dani from this path she was on. "I'm not avoiding anything. What about Grace?"

"Vini tells me she found you two looking very cozy yesterday when she came to help you out." Dani leaned against the table and crossed her arms like she was some detective chasing a new lead instead of an annoying older sister gossiping for no reason. "She also mentioned something about a dinner?"

So much for keeping her business to herself. "We had a little wager when we were bowling. Loser buys dinner Saturday. It's no big deal."

"I know you don't expect me to believe that? Not after the fact that you named her public enemy number one for how many years? No, this is big. I can smell it."

Ava wrinkled her nose up before gathering her papers and preparing to move to her room to actually get work done. "You're smelling your upper lip because there is nothing going on. Lesbians can hang out as friends you know."

"Don't give me that shit. Lesbians can. You and Grace though are on a whole different level, and you know it. Where are you going?"

Ava tucked her papers close to her chest as she stood up. She pasted an affronted scowl on her face and tried not to look like a cornered animal trying to escape. "I'm going to my room to try to finish grading these papers so I can go to sleep before midnight. I don't have time for you and your weird attempt at whatever this was."

She could feel Dani's gaze follow her as she pushed away from the dining table and headed for the doorway. She walked slowly and steadily so she didn't look like she was fleeing the scene. She thought she was home free when Dani called out one last parting shot.

"Make sure you wear matching underwear."

"What the fu—"

"And switch out the snacks in your backpack. They're probably stale at this point."

Ava stumbled before glaring over her shoulder. "I hate you so much sometimes." When Dani smiled back sharply, she beat a hasty retreat, not caring how she looked this time. She had zero desire to discuss anything else with Dani. Her already battered pride would never survive.

Ava managed to finish her grading behind the safety of her locked bedroom door, but she was still left contemplating their upcoming dinner not-quite date when Wednesday's bowling practice rolled around. Ava had only just walked through the doors of the bowling alley when two of her team members, including Tabitha, bounced up beside her. They wore identical smiles and Ava grinned, thinking they were excited for practice.

"Hi, Coach Ava. Look, we brought our ball bags."

"Good job. Make sure you clean the balls before you put them away each time." She gestured for them to head to the lanes, but instead they walked to the counter with her. She was surprised but kept up pleasant conversation. She was a coach now, so she supposed talking with them and bonding was par for the course.

"Did you see Coach Grace today? I think she did something new with her hair," Tabitha said randomly. The other girl agreed before Ava could say anything in response.

Ava frowned slightly as she thought back to the school day. She hadn't noticed anything different about Grace. She looked as good as always of course, but Ava wasn't always the most observant, so she pledged to pay closer attention during practice.

Tabitha gestured to Ava to lean in closer, and she did, wondering what Tabitha was going to say next. "Do you think Coach Grace is pretty?"

That was not a question she was expecting, and Ava had to work hard to keep her expression neutral. It wasn't something she was prepared to answer in front of students or anyone for that matter. She was still working through things herself without any outside interference.

"I don't think that has anything to do with our upcoming practice," she replied finally, keeping her voice even so they wouldn't assume she was chastising them. Teenagers were often so temperamental that the most innocuous of responses could set them off and leave them spiraling for hours.

When Tabitha continued, Ava started to wonder if she were being punked. Did Dani or Vini put this kid up to this? Were they trying to get a rise out of her? It wouldn't be the first time they had included some of her students in pranking her, but the pranks had never been like this before. They were usually mild and consisted of putting sticky notes on her desk or other vaguely annoying but overall harmless situations. This was something else.

Harmless was not having her surreptitiously second-guessing her actions as she tried not to get caught glancing over at Grace multiple times during their practice. She saw Tabitha and Rory giggling as they looked back and forth between her and Grace. It left Ava feeling self-conscious in a way she hadn't in years. She thought she had moved past the nerves of talking to other women. Then again, other women weren't Grace.

"Ava?"

"Yeah?" She blinked quickly, realizing she had missed something that Grace said when she found the other woman looking at her with concern. "Sorry. Did you say something?"

Grace glanced at the team before walking over to Ava and shielding Ava with her taller frame. "Is everything alright? You seem distracted."

The softness of Grace's voice was simply unfair. Ava didn't know what she was supposed to do with that other than melt into it like the most comforting blanket. Soft giggles reached her ears, and she realized that they were probably being observed by very impressionable eyes. She pushed her lips up into what she hoped was a reassuring smile and nodded.

"Totally." When Grace didn't budge, she tried again. "I'm great. Didn't get as much sleep last night thanks to Dani and Vini's bickering again, but it's fine."

Grace stared for a moment longer before relaxing slightly. "Those two never seem to quit."

Ava huffed out a laugh. "You have no idea. But continue. I'm good."

Grace nodded before turning back to the team. Ava redoubled her efforts to pay attention and ignore the team's looks. Whether they had meant to or not, the team's reaction left her feeling off-balance for the rest of practice and she wasn't sure how to regain her equilibrium. She forced her thoughts to calm and pasted a smile on her face as she stepped up to Grace's side. They needed to present a united front no matter what. She didn't want even an inkling of discord to get back to Robert to give him any ammunition to call the team into question.

The rest of practice was uneventful, and Ava was able to get in the swing of it. It was amazing to see the girls transforming right before her eyes, and Ava couldn't help but be excited. Her hopes were finally coming to fruition.

"Okay, team. Remember to rest up and eat well on Friday. We are up against St. Mary's, and they will not be giving up pins. Consistency is just as much if not more important than power."

"Coach Ava is right," Grace chimed in, backing her up. "You all are doing amazing."

The girls cheered before slowly gathering their things. Their happy chattering was music to Ava's ears, and she couldn't help but smile.

"Seems like you're feeling better."

"I was feeling fine before," Ava replied, looking up at Grace. They were close; closer than maybe was necessary, but Ava didn't step away. Having Grace in her space now felt less like a hostile takeover and more like inviting in a close friend. It was strange how things had changed since Grace had first come to town.

"Your hair looks nice." Ava was 90 percent sure that wasn't what she had planned to say, but when Grace reached up to tuck a bit of hair behind her ear before her lips parted in a shy little smile, Ava couldn't regret the lapse of mouth control. Not when it let her hear a soft thanks uttered in that pitch-perfect voice.

"I was kind of thinking about ditching the perms and growing my hair out naturally like yours," Grace said as her gaze traveled up to Ava's hair. She had taken more time to style it this morning. Her curls had been springy and mois-turized when she checked in her car's rearview mirror. If she was putting a little more effort into her appearance lately, that was nobody's business but her own. "Your hair is beautiful."

Words couldn't describe the onslaught of pleasure that filled Ava at hearing those words. It wasn't the first time someone had admired the care she took with her hair, but it was the first time a compliment about it had hit so strongly.

"You too." *Oh, shit.* "I mean, yours too. I like your hair as well. It's very…healthy." Ava internally screamed at her mouth to stop moving before she made an even bigger fool of herself.

Surprisingly, Grace didn't laugh. Her gaze slowly slid over Ava's face and stopped somewhere near her chin. Ava couldn't be sure, but it seemed like Grace was staring at her mouth. The thought had her licking her lips, and her eyes widened when Grace's gaze followed the motion.

"Bye, Coach Grace. Bye, Coach Ava."

Ava jerked back, feeling like she had been caught doing something she wasn't supposed to, and Grace looked just as guilty. They both separated, and Ava looked at the students instead as she willed the heat in her cheeks to abate as she said her goodbyes. She made sure not to look at Grace again until they were alone without prying eyes. When she finally turned her gaze back to Grace, she was still looking away, and Ava let her eyes drink their fill.

"So, have you decided where we're going on Saturday?"

Grace shook her head. "Not yet, but even when I do, I'm not going to tell you."

"Then how will I know what to wear?" Ava tried to ignore just how much it sounded like she was seeing this as a date. If Grace interpreted it that way and balked, then she would have the answer to a question she hadn't yet asked but was dying to know.

"You always look good no matter what you wear," she replied, but gave in a little to Ava's prodding. "It'll be somewhere nice. You won't need a ball gown...yet."

Ava snorted. "Funny." She couldn't help but smile at the sound of Grace's laughter yet she crossed her arms and pretended that the twinkle of it didn't make her feel lighter than air. Saturday couldn't come fast enough.

Twenty-Two

Grace was a fool. Happy, but a fool. She hadn't stopped to think about how it would look at Wednesday's practice when she spoke to Ava out of concern. She had seemed off, and it worried Grace. Ava was normally unflappable as a boulder in a hurricane. To see her not quite on her game had been concerning. But given the way some of the team had responded with giggles and hushed whispers, Grace was left wondering if she had given away more of her feelings than she'd planned.

"So, a little birdie tells me you and Ava are getting along."

Grace groaned as Mrs. Patrick's words reached her. She turned away from the head of lettuce she had been staring at. She was surprised to see it hadn't wilted with how long she had been standing there.

"What have you heard?" There was no point in beating around the bush. If Mrs. P was bringing it up, that meant something about Ava and her had been making the rounds. Grace didn't have time to be playing twenty questions. She still needed to figure out what restaurant she was going to take Ava to in a couple days. She also doubted she was going to get more than one shot at this, and she wanted to make sure that it was the best shot possible.

Mrs. Patrick's smile was too wide to be trusted. She walked over to Grace and patted her arm in a way that made Grace feel like a kid. Tendrils of annoyance wound around her thoughts the longer Mrs. Patrick was silent. She didn't like being gossiped about, and while she knew she couldn't control other people, it still made her feel like a specimen under a microscope.

"Mrs. P," she urged. She wanted Mrs. Patrick to give it to her straight, but Grace knew she would clam up the moment she thought Grace was catching an attitude. "Please. What are people saying?"

"I don't know what you think I might have heard, but I assure you only good things."

Grace narrowed her eyes as she considered her. It was true that Mrs. Patrick wasn't known for spreading gossip that could be seen as malicious. Still, with how fragile the peace felt between her and Ava, Grace didn't want to take any chances that something might cause that glass bridge to come crashing down beyond repair.

"Yeah, I don't trust it." She set her basket on the ground before crossing her arms. "Spill it. What are people saying about me and Ava?"

Mrs. Patrick shook her head, but her smile never waned. "Just that the two of you were getting along and how happy the girls are on the team. You know Tabitha was so sullen before. So quiet and kept to herself. But now, I see her little friends come by the store all the time just to chat with her. The team really has made a world of difference for her."

Grace was happy to hear that. Tabitha was a great kid and had been excelling so far in chemistry, as well as being one of the best on the team. "Oh, well that is very good to hear."

"She and her little friends might also have been chatting about how cute their coaches looked together," Mrs. Patrick continued as her expression turned sly. "They might have even been musing on how they could get those same coaches to realize they liked each other."

Now that threw Grace for a loop. She had noticed some of the members on the team asking questions and making comments that were a little out of left field, but she had just chalked it up to youthful curiosity about the adults in their life. Never did she think that they had an agenda when it came to what they were asking. Some of the conversations were starting to make a lot more sense.

"And when she told me how well you and Ava seemed to work together, I knew that was the reason why."

Grace didn't completely understand how all that was related, but she figured having coaches that didn't hate each other could probably do wonders for a lot of teams. If that's all the gossip Mrs. Patrick had heard, then it wasn't so bad. Grace wanted people to see the bowling team as a good thing. Great even. She didn't doubt that Robert wanted nothing more than to see them fail, and she didn't want to give him the satisfaction. It was slightly sweet and a little creepy that their students were so invested in whether Ava and her were involved. She couldn't deny she was equally invested, but she needed the kids to stay in their own lane.

"And the way you practically light up when I say Ava's name is as dead a giveaway as any."

That had her thoughts screeching to a halt. "I don't know what you... My face looks exactly the same as it always does."

Now Mrs. Patrick did give her a look that Grace didn't appreciate in the slightest. Yes, she liked Ava. There was nothing wrong with that. But she didn't get all giddy like a kid having their first crush when someone mentioned Ava's name.

She barely reacted at all.

She was an adult.

"Oh, hi, Ava."

"What?" Grace came out of her thoughts and looked around quickly. When she didn't see any sign of Ava, she glared down at Mrs. Patrick who had a smug look on her face. "That wasn't very nice."

"Who said I was nice?" Mrs. Patrick asked before patting Grace again on the arm. "Kind, not nice. Different things entirely. Now, are you ready to make a move or are you going to twiddle your thumbs some more?"

Grace looked to the heavens as if they would give her some kind of guidance for how to handle this situation. She wasn't about to lie to Mrs. Patrick's face, but once she put these feelings out there, there was no taking them back. One thing she did need to do was nip the team's gossiping in the bud without being hypocritical or making them feel bad. She remembered being that age and speculating about which teachers might be together. None of them had ever tried to set their teachers up though. Clearly, this generation of students was on a completely different level. She could almost admire their tenacity if not for the fact that she was part of the plan unwillingly.

"Well thank you for letting me know, Mrs. Patrick. I probably need to have a conversation with the girls and let them know that meddling in grown folks' business is something they should not be doing."

Mrs. Patrick's smile turned wistful as she gazed up at Grace. "It's so strange to hear you say that and realize now you are an adult. I remember you and Ava coming through with some gossip of your own. My how things have changed."

Grace had the good graces to be slightly chastised. Mrs. Patrick wasn't lying. She and Ava probably had run around mouthing off a little more than they should have. It was disconcerting to realize she was now in the position of having to put a stop to that bit of fun with her students now, but it needed to be done. Gossip had a way of snowballing, especially in a town this small. That was sometimes the only entertainment that some people got.

"You go on and finish your grocery shopping," Mrs. Patrick said, drawing Grace's attention back to the fact that she hadn't finished grabbing even half of the items she needed. "And try not to give Tabitha too much of a hard time. She's a good kid."

Grace agreed before picking up her basket. "I agree. Don't worry. I'll talk to everyone as a group, so I don't single anyone out."

Mrs. Patrick gave her a look so fond that it almost brought tears to Grace's eyes before heading back to the front of the store. Grace watched her go before turning her attention back to the produce in front of her. She tried to pick up her train of thought from before, but she was drawing a blank.

"I should have made a grocery list."

Grace meant to talk to Ava about what Mrs. Patrick had told her, but every time she picked up her phone or saw Ava from across the school hallway, she choked and ended up waving awkwardly before shuffling away. Her friends back in New York would hardly recognize her if they saw her now. She had always been the confident one even as much as she went with the flow. In hindsight, she didn't understand how she and Emily had lasted as long as they had with the lack of confrontation when things weren't quite working. She wouldn't be making the same mistakes again.

As soon as she talked to Ava.

"Great job, Tabitha!"

Grace shook herself out of her musings and focused back on the lanes. They only had a few frames left, and the pin totals were close. She could feel in her bones that this was going to be a repeat of history, and it filled her with a small bit of apprehension. Ava hadn't treated this game against St. Mary's any different than the other games against other teams in their region, but they also only had a little more than one month left of the regular season before district tournaments began in mid-October. That would kick everything into overdrive before they knew it. District tournaments were the lightning round with four straight days of games and then a week of rest before the state championship began. Somehow, time had gone by so quickly, plunging them into the beginnings of fall. True, the trees hadn't yet started their great color change and the sun was still at times unbearably hot, but Grace could feel autumn coming on the breezes that blew in cooler in the evenings.

A cheer from the other team heralded another strike for them, and Grace sighed softly as she calculated the changes. Ava glanced back at her and twisted her lips up with a shrug. They couldn't control what the other team did, but they could encourage their girls to give it their all, so that's what she did.

"Alright, Rory. You got this," Grace called out, giving the girl a thumbs-up. Rory nodded sharply, her expression focused as she picked up her ball and slowly walked to the line. Grace watched her closely, slowing her own breathing like she had taught Rory to do to center her thoughts. Rory's form was nearly flawless as she tiptoed to the line and bent at the hips. Her release arched wide before cutting over and hitting perfectly. The shout of excitement when all the pins fell in a blaze of sound had even Grace's pulse jumping.

High fives were given all around as their next teammate stood for her turn. It was exhilarating to think that she was here now, coaching her own team alongside the woman who had been right there on the lanes with her. If not for where they were, Grace would have thrown an arm around Ava's shoulders in delight.

"Grace? Grace Jones?"

Grace frowned and turned to look behind her. The woman who had called her name waved. She looked vaguely familiar with her dark brown hair and pale willowy figure. Grace glanced at her team before walking toward the woman.

"Can I help you? We're still finishing our last game."

The woman put her hand on her chest and frowned like she couldn't believe Grace didn't recognize her. "It's me. Matilda. From St. Mary's."

Grace widened her eyes as she realized why the woman was familiar. "Oh, wow, hey. I didn't recognize you at all. It's been so long." They hugged briefly before Grace gestured back to her team. "I have to finish coaching, but we usually stick around for a bit after."

"That's perfect," Matilda replied. She pointed, and Grace turned to look at another high school girl with similar dark brown hair and pale skin on the other team. When the girl noticed they were looking, she ducked her head and waved before looking away. "My little sister is playing and when I saw who her opponent was, I knew I had to come say hello."

"That's great. Nice to see the bowling genes ran in the family." Grace took a step back. "I'll come find you then after the match and we can catch up."

"Sounds good," Matilda agreed with a nod.

Grace smiled before walking back to her team. When she stepped up beside Ava, Ava leaned over to whisper, "Who is that?"

"Old friend from high school," Grace replied before nodding to the girl on the other team. "She came to see her sister play and recognized me I guess."

Ava's expression didn't change, but she hummed instead of giving a verbal response. They stood side by side for a moment longer before Ava moved to give one of their team members some advice. Grace stayed focused on the game, ignoring any other sounds that would take her attention from their girls.

They were getting down to the last few frames that would determine the outcome, and the anxiety was starting to set in. She and Ava had both been good about letting the team know they should be proud of every game they bowled, whether they won or not, but she knew what was riding on this.

The small crowd surrounding the lanes grew quiet as the last two bowlers started their tenth frame. Grace couldn't decide if she wanted to review the calculated scores again or watch the action. The air was thick with tension. Beside her, Ava whispered softly, though Grace couldn't make out what she was saying. The bowler on the other team approached her first throw, and Grace noted how familiar her style was. When she released, the ball barreled forward with enough raw power to have Grace's eyes widening.

The girl had an arm for sure, but what she had in power, she lacked in accuracy. Her ball hit a dry pocket and skittered off course, taking out four pins and leaving the rest virtually untouched. Grace could see the frustration on the girl's face, and it was a feeling she understood. She picked up the spare, but her confidence seemed shaken and her final roll was evidence of that when she failed to down all the pins then as well. Grace swallowed hard as Tabitha moved to take her final chance at closing out the game.

Biting down hard on the pen in her hand did little to alleviate her anxiety, but when Tabitha paused at the line and glanced back over her shoulder, Grace whipped the pen from her mouth and gave Tabitha a sure nod and thumbs-up.

"You got this. Take your time."

Silence reigned as she approached, her footwork immaculate and steady. Grace felt a hand grip her arm, and she looked down in surprise to see Ava's hand. Ava's gaze was pasted on Tabitha, but her body radiated tension. Before she could second-guess herself, Grace put a hand over Ava's and stared as Tabitha swung her arm and released.

Cheers broke out from their seats as the ball traveled true, felling all the pins in a decisive smash of sound. Tabitha turned around, her smile triumphant as she clapped once. Grace nodded sharply before quieting the other girls down. Tabitha took her second throw, confidence infused in her frame as she once again left the lane spotless. Grace let out a breath in relief. That was the game regardless of the final throw, but she felt nothing but pride when once again, Tabitha left no crumbs, closing out her tenth frame amidst an outpouring of gobbles from her teammates celebrating her third strike. Grace couldn't help but smile at the familiar cheer for a well-deserved turkey.

"She did it," Ava exclaimed, shaking Grace's arm. She turned and threw her arms around Grace's shoulders as she jumped up and down before she turned and high-fived the team. Grace was left stunned and ecstatic. This was far from the end of their season, but the girls had showed up and showed out. Grace's smile spread slowly until it hurt her cheeks with its width.

"Great game," the other coach said, holding out his hand. Grace dutifully shook it and said the same. The team followed her lead, exchanging pleasant "good games" with the other team members. The coach nodded to Grace. "Your girls are good, no doubt thanks to your excellent coaching."

Grace shook her head. "It's been a team effort, truly. Your

team is amazing as well. They played some great games and really gave us a run." She shook his hand again before they all began to disperse.

Ava was chatting with the team, so Grace decided to turn in their scores. She had only taken a few steps away when she was face-to-face with Matilda again. This time, she was scowling as she wrapped an arm around her sister. The conversation they were having didn't seem to be a happy one. Grace only caught the tail end of it as she approached.

"...if you're going to lose games like that, you might as well be on the public school team. That's not what Mom and Dad paid for." The younger girl had her head down, but she looked up from beneath her damp lashes as Grace stepped closer. Matilda sighed loudly, but she turned on a smile that was sickeningly sweet when she saw Grace.

"Oh, hey again. Don't mind her. We were just talking about how disappointing that ending was," Matilda explained as if Grace hadn't just overheard her not only berating her sister but also denigrating Grace's school. Instead of responding to her, Grace looked over at the younger girl who still had her head down. It was painful to see.

"You bowled an amazing game," Grace said, pitching her voice low. "Keep up your practicing and you will be a great bowler." At Matilda's scoff, Grace narrowed her eyes.

Matilda rolled her eyes. "You don't need to lie and coddle her like you do your students. She can handle being told the truth about her bad performance."

Anger coursed through her, but Grace tried hard to hang

on to her manners. "Her performance was fine. Everyone has off days."

"Maybe at the school you're at," she replied, curling her nose like she smelled something bad. The Matilda Grace had known before never said things like this. Had she? "But at St. Mary's, second is still last. You should know that."

"I know that I'm proud of all the girls who bowled tonight. They did their best, and that is the most important part." Grace held up the papers in her hand to cut Matilda off before she could say anything else. "I have scores to deliver and then a team to celebrate with. Seeing you was an experience. Good luck."

Not wanting to hear anything else, Grace sidestepped Matilda and made her way to the counter. She had a lot of things to think about thanks to this brush with the past.

Twenty-Three

Excitement and apprehension warred in Grace's mind as she dropped down onto her couch with a cup of coffee, her phone, and a good helping of anxiety. Friday night had been a bit of a wash after her run-in with Matilda. Grace had barely been able to focus on celebrating with her team with the conversation playing on a loop. She doubted Matilda was the only one with disparaging words about Peach Blossom High now that her eyes had been opened. It had made her think back to some of her experiences after she had switched to St. Mary's. So many comments that had seemed innocuous then had new meaning, and she didn't like it at all. Had she been blind this whole time?

She hadn't mentioned Matilda's jabs to Ava. She had been relaxed and practically giddy as the girls enjoyed pizzas and more cupcakes from Brad and Thomas. Grace hadn't had the heart to say anything that might change Ava's good mood. She especially didn't want to bring up anything stressful before their dinner. Snagging a not-quite date with Ava had happened so quickly she'd barely had time to process it. Now she was left floundering with no plan and the timer counting down to tonight when she was supposed to get Ava. She hadn't even told her what to wear.

"I so don't got this," Grace muttered before taking a careful sip of her drink. She let it slide over her tongue as she pondered her choices. She didn't have Dani's or Vini's numbers so she couldn't reach out to them. She was pretty sure, even if she did, asking them for help would be a bad move. The Williams sisters made teasing one another an art form, and she doubted adding fuel to that, even by accident, would endear her to Ava.

She didn't want to do something as simple as take Ava to Thomas's café. Selfishly, she wanted to make this dinner better than any of the other dates Ava might have gone on previously. Grace wasn't sure how much dating Ava had done, especially since moving back to town. It wasn't like there was a group of lesbians out there who magically appeared when one of their own were single. The place had changed quite a bit, but it still wasn't Atlanta.

Grace knew she needed help if she was going to get this right. She glanced down at her phone before dialing a number and waited while it rang.

"Well, this is a surprise," Brad said, his voice tinged with humor. "I gave you my number weeks ago, and this is the first time you've actually used it."

"I'm sorry," Grace said hesitantly. Brad laughed, and she could almost see him shaking his head, his curls moving back and forth as he gave her a good-natured grin.

"It's fine. I'm just fucking with you. What's going on?"

Grace bit the bullet. She needed to come clean if she was going to get the kind of advice she was hoping for. "So, I sort of promised Ava I would take her to dinner tonight."

Brad was silent, and Grace moved the phone away from her ear so she could look at the screen to make sure he was still there. "Are you there?"

"Oh, I'm here," Brad replied. "I'm just a bit in shock that you guys might've gotten your shit together."

"It's not like that," Grace insisted, though she wished it were exactly like that. "We were bowling and sort of had a little wager between the two of us."

"Go on. I want to hear all about these bowling wagers. Sounds kinky."

Grace had just been about to take a sip of her coffee when his words reached her. She jerked at the word *kinky* in reference to Ava. She looked down at the drops of coffee on her shirt and sighed. "I'm going to need you to not do that again before I burn myself."

Brad laughed, not sounding the least bit apologetic. "I mean, you did say you two were betting things. Was it clothes? Who took what off first?"

"It's not like that," Grace insisted. "Every now and then when we were younger, we would place bets on who would win and what the winner would get. It was totally innocent."

"Emphasis on the *was*. Let me guess," Brad replied. "You won the game this time?"

Now Grace knew she couldn't make it sound innocent. "Actually, I sort of…maybe, rigged the game," Grace admitted. She hadn't quite known what she was doing when she initially set the wager. It wasn't until Ava drew her attention to it that Grace realized she had created a situation where no matter who won or lost, they would still be spending time together.

Ava hadn't pushed back, leaving Grace to wonder if she was okay with it. Then again, Ava wasn't the type of person to let anyone bully her into anything that she didn't want to do. Grace was pretty sure if Ava hadn't wanted to have dinner with her, this would not be happening.

"Are you telling me that you rigged the game to guarantee you would win?"

She winced. When Brad said it like that, it seemed so sordid. "I mean, not rigged exactly—"

"Oh, no. This is great," he insisted. "I was worried you would be a total pushover, but you have some bite to you, Ms. All-American."

Grace wasn't sure what to make of that new title, so she decided to ignore it. "Right, so as I said, we're supposed to get dinner tonight, but there's a problem."

"Let me guess," he replied. "You want me to help you pick out the perfect location for this sexy dinner date."

She switched the phone to her other hand and leaned back against the couch cushions. "I don't know about it being sexy, but I'm afraid of getting this wrong."

"Well, I mean I don't think you could get it wrong," Brad said. "It's just dinner."

"Yeah, but you know how Ava is," Grace pressed. "If it's bad, I probably won't get another shot at this."

He made a considering noise before he conceded, "True.

There is one restaurant that Ava likes, and she only goes there for special occasions. It's a couple towns over though." Grace let out a sigh of relief. She knew Brad was the person to go to with this. "It's called Monell's. Really cute place. Very grown and sexy-date-night-approved. Thomas and I like to go whenever we want to spice things up."

Grace could feel her cheeks burn at the thought of spicing anything up with Ava. "I don't know about spicing things up. I'm just trying to get things on salt, pepper, and garlic level."

"Well not spicy per se," Brad insisted. "But after ten, if you're still there, they move the tables and turn the place into a jazz club with room for dancing. If you want this to be an actual date, which I'm pretty sure you do, given how much you're freaking out about it, it's the perfect place to take Ava."

It did sound wonderful. "You're sure?"

"Honey, picture this—good food, wine, and dancing close together under the soft dim light."

Grace's breath caught as she imagined the scene in her mind. It was almost like a dream; one that she had never imagined happening. "It does sound like a great place to go. If I take her there, do you think that she will wonder if I'm trying to get in her pants or something?"

"Aren't you?" Brad asked without pause. "I mean, unless I'm reading this wrong, which I know I'm not. Your anxiety reads more like first-date jitters and less friends going out for a night of dinner and girlish fun."

Denials sat ready on Grace's tongue, but she couldn't give them a voice. Brad clearly was hoping for something to happen between her and Ava, so why was she bothering to pretend?

"You're not reading it wrong," Grace admitted. "I do want it to be a date, but the way things have been between us has me a little worried."

"Listen, there's nothing you can do about the past except try to resolve it, get on the same page, and then move forward. As much as I love Ava's stubborn ass, if she continues to wallow on the things that happened between the two of you when you were literal children, then maybe it's time to let her go."

Grace knew he was right. She also knew she would regret not giving it a try. "Alright. So, Monell's, huh? That's the place to go?"

"Oh, yeah. You take Ava there, and she'll be putty in your hands."

Grace liked the sound of that. Having Ava in her hands in any way sounded perfect. "Alright. Thanks, Brad, and do me a favor. Don't tell Ava I gave you a call."

"It'll be our little secret," he promised. Grace hung up the phone and immediately got to work. She made a reservation and then sat back and tried not to let her hopes get her too high in the sky to where the possible fall might just kill her.

Grace pulled up to the Williams house and took a deep breath before getting out of the car and walking up the steps to the front door. She fixed her maroon blouse and wiped her sweaty palms against her dark wash jeans before pressing the doorbell.

Immediately, the door swung open, and she looked down into the face of the cutest kid she had seen in a long time. He looked up at her with big brown eyes before his lips twisted in a smirk. *Oh, yeah. This is definitely a Williams*, she thought to herself.

"Hi there. Is Ava here?"

"Who's at the door?" a deep voice called out from somewhere in the house.

"It's some lady," the boy called out before welcoming Grace inside.

"Are you sure you should be letting me in?" she asked with a smile to let him know she wasn't chastising him. "I am a stranger, after all."

"Jordan Williams. What did I say about opening the door without an adult present?" Dani Williams walked into the foyer and Grace looked up at her with a sheepish smile. "Well, I'll be damned. Wow, you grew up good, kid."

Grace choked out a laugh before letting herself be swept into a strong hug. Dani didn't look a day over thirty as she leaned back and gave Grace a wide grin. "Long time no see."

"Mama, who is this lady?" Jordan asked, looking back and forth between the two of them. Dani chuckled and gestured to Grace.

"This is Grace. She and your aunt Ava were best friends when they were kids." She looked back at Grace and gestured to Jordan. "This is my son, Jordan."

"Nice to meet you, Jordan," Grace said, nodding to him. "I've heard so much about you from your aunt Ava. She says you're incredibly smart."

"I am," he replied. Dani snorted before gesturing for Grace to follow her to the living room.

"Jordan, do you have any homework you need to finish?"

"No."

She gave him another look. "Are you sure about that? If I go look in your folder, is everything going to be done?"

"I'll be right back," Jordan replied before sliding out of the living room. Grace chuckled at his hasty departure and shook her head.

"I guess some things just never change."

"True. Though some things do," Dani replied. "Seriously, kid. You were always cute, but damn, girl."

Grace's cheeks heated. "Thank you," she replied, not knowing what else to say.

"Dani, I thought I heard the doorbell ring," Ava's voice called out. Grace turned just in time to see Ava walk into the living room, and she almost choked on her next breath.

Ava was always pretty, but outside of the classroom, Grace could really stop and stare. Ava had slicked her hair back and gelled down the baby hairs that framed her face perfectly. She had on makeup with gold eyeshadow drawing attention to eyes Grace would happily sink into, and a dark red lip that drew Grace's attention without trying. Ava's skin seemed to shimmer or maybe it was the gold strap top that made her skin look as if it were heated by an inner warmth. She had on similar dark wash jeans, though these looked painted on, showing off ample curves and leading down to her feet where gold strap heels completed the look. Grace had known she looked good when she left, but Ava was something else entirely. Golden goddess was the only thing that came to her mind.

"Wow," Grace said quietly before she could catch herself. She heard a snort from beside her, but her attention was completely focused on the vision standing in front of her. Ava's lips curled up in a satisfied smile.

"Are we going to go or are you going to stand there and stare at me the whole night?"

It took Grace a moment, but she recovered and gestured to the door, bowing slightly. "Let me not keep the princess waiting."

"I'll show you princess," Ava retorted. Grace saw Dani shake her head, but her smile looked pleased. Grace nodded to her before following Ava out the front door and down the porch steps.

Once they were safely in the car and on their way out of town, Grace realized she now had to come up with conversation. There was no one else to help be the buffer between her and Ava. It was time to see if they had something other than their past rivalry and hard feelings.

"So, how are you enjoying teaching so far?" Ava asked before Grace could come up with a question. "I heard from Alyssa that you and Janae have gotten pretty close."

"It's been going good," Grace replied, happy that the conversation was starting with some easy, leading questions. "Janae has been nice and helped show me the ropes. She seems cool."

"I suppose so," Ava replied. "I don't know her that well. Brad had mentioned he saw her in our hallway a few times this week."

Grace chuckled at the way Ava emphasized *our hallway*. "Are we possessive about hallways now?"

"Absolutely. Haven't you noticed how nice and quiet ours is? It's far enough from the main office that Robert doesn't come around too often. The farther I can be away from that man, the better."

Grace couldn't deny that. She had enjoyed not having him start wars on her behalf for the past couple weeks. His ultimatum still lingered over them, but without his presence to back it up, she had found it easier to ignore.

"Anyway, I was just curious."

"Just curious," Grace parroted, amused. She was sure there was a thread of jealousy in Ava's tone. If the same question had come from Emily, Grace would have been completely sure of that assumption. Ava always threw her off and left her guessing. But Grace had said she was going for it tonight. There was no time like the present to call Ava's bluff.

"She has been great with helping me out. Sometimes you need a helping hand until you get on your feet, you know?" Ava hummed noncommittally, though Grace could see her mouth tighten. Not one to stop at the first hint that her hypothesis might be correct, she decided to test her theory a bit more. "She mentioned going to an outdoor movie next week. You should join us."

"It's rude inviting other people on your dates."

"Who said anything about it being a date?" Grace couldn't help but smile wide at Ava's tone. Ava's mouth clicked shut. When glanced over, she took one look at Grace's expression before rolling her eyes.

"You did that on purpose, didn't you?" Ava asked.

Grace shrugged but couldn't help but feel smug. "Maybe. Are you impressed?"

Ava gifted her a sharp smile. "A little, yeah."

The conversation drifted to other topics, mostly about the upcoming games and the team. Grace wanted nothing more than to delve into the heavier subjects, but conceded that doing that while they were both in the car in the middle of nowhere was probably not the best idea. If things went sideways, that would make for a very uncomfortable ride.

When Grace turned off the interstate, she sent a prayer up to whoever was listening that Brad's suggestion would ring true. She turned right and almost jerked the steering wheel when Ava gasped.

"What?" Grace was on alert as she looked around to see if there was something she missed. "What happened?"

"Are you taking me to Monell's?" Ava asked. Her voice had gone high with excitement, and Grace let out a silent sigh of relief. It looked like Brad hadn't been bullshitting.

"Are you impressed?" There was that question again. Grace couldn't help the needy desire for approval. She had a lot riding on this. Her anxiety melted away at Ava's clear excitement.

"How did you know I like Monell's?"

Grace shrugged. "Let's just say a little birdie told me."

"So, you asked Brad."

Grace didn't confirm nor deny it as she continued to the destination. They pulled into a nearly full parking lot and Grace was happy that she had called ahead and gotten a reservation. Clearly, this place was popular, and she was looking forward to it even more.

After opening the door for Ava, Grace took the chance to place a hand on her lower back. Ava's warmth was intoxicating. It made her want to lean in and feel that heat against her cheek. She kept her touch light as they made their way inside. Grace couldn't help but marvel at the decor. The outside hadn't looked all that impressive but inside was a different story. The lights were dim with the dining room being lit mostly by candlelight. It left a nice hazy glow. The servers were dressed smartly in all black and the tables were spaced apart enough for intimate conversations. It was exactly the type of place Grace had hoped for.

They were quickly shown to their table, placed their drink orders, and settled on an appetizer while they reviewed the rest of the menu. Grace decided to take advantage of having the few minutes to themselves to kick off the conversation.

"I just want to apologize again." Ava cocked her head and looked at her. "You know, for how things ended between us and how they started again."

Ava shook her head. "Robert was the instigator of this most recent mess. I know that now."

"Still," Grace insisted. "When I heard you had been trying to get the team started, I should have approached you before even going to him. That was on me."

"Well, I appreciate it. It all turned out good, at least."

Grace nodded. "It did. You know, I was excited to see that you were teaching here. Didn't think that I would be put right across the hall from you though."

Ava's snort brought a smile to Grace's face, and the conversation paused briefly as the waiter returned with their drinks. Grace had decided to forgo alcohol as the designated driver and sipped on her ginger ale while she thought about what else to say.

"I had wondered if you knew," Ava replied from behind her glass of wine, the deep red looking almost black in the dim candlelight.

"I expected we would run into one another sooner or later." Grace ducked her head and grinned sheepishly as she thought back to that reunion. "I just hadn't expected it to be that much sooner."

"I'm sure."

Deciding to be bold, Grace continued coming clean. "I'm not going to lie. I had always hoped that we would run into each other again and maybe find closure."

Ava tilted her head to the side and regarded Grace from across the table. Her dark eyes seemed to glow in the dim candlelight. It made it hard for Grace to concentrate on the next words as she admired Ava's beauty.

"So that's what tonight is all about, closure?"

"No." Closure had been something she was looking for in the beginning, but now Grace wouldn't be satisfied with just that. She didn't want them to move on as acquaintances who only spoke when absolutely necessary. She wanted a shot at a brand-new beginning. "I want a second chance."

"I don't know if we—"

"I lied when I said we should just forget about the kiss," Grace blurted out, interrupting her. Ava's eyes widened as she leaned back in her chair. Her lips parted, though no other words came out as she stared at Grace. "I think about both of them, all of them, every day."

This was it. Grace had put it out there. These feelings that had rumbled beneath the surface were now being brought to the light, and she was terrified. She was terrified about being shot down. Harshly. She was terrified of being shot down nicely and then having to see the pitying expression on Ava's face as they continued to meet. This was a whole new level of fear that had never been present in any of her other relationships.

Ava was still silent, but she had turned away, glancing around the restaurant as if looking for a sign to tell her what to say. Grace needed one too. She didn't know if she should wait until Ava had gathered her words or reel it all back in and stuff it down deeper this time. When Ava finally met her gaze again, there was something new shimmering within her eyes.

"This is a lot."

"I know," Grace agreed. "But, it's been ten years, and no one has ever made me feel like you do. I tried to ignore it, but I can't anymore. I have feelings for you, and I'm pretty sure you have feelings for me too."

The ball of feelings was released and rolling its way down the lane. All Grace could do was wait impatiently to see where it hit.

Twenty-Four

Saying yes to this date had been a terrible idea. A terribly, wonderful, frightening idea that left Ava, mouth open, with no words to say.

Grace sat across from her looking too damn good in the low light of the room. Her gaze hadn't left Ava even once after she dropped her bombshell. There was so much riding on her and Grace being able to lead a peaceful and civil coexistence and complicating that with romance seemed like a good way to set their worlds on fire.

But what a way to go.

That little voice inside of her that wanted to feel the burn inched her closer to giving in. She wanted to. She had been on cloud nine after winning their wager. So why was she holding back? With all the words she knew, why couldn't she find the ones to admit that her feelings were just as strong as Grace's? It wasn't until she looked up again that she found the resolve to come clean. Grace looked poised for a devastating blow. Ava couldn't lie to her.

"I have feelings for you too."

Grace's smile was like spring. Ava could almost feel its warmth, and not smiling back wasn't an option. She could feel her lips spread wide, and she chuckled at her own childish excitement.

"Don't give me that look. I still think this is a bad idea." She hated to put a damper on things, but it was better than starting out with a lie by omission. They had to get everything out there if they wanted this to work. "There's still the issue of teachers and coaches dating one another."

"Isn't Alyssa married to the librarian?"

"Yes, but they married before they started working together," Ava pointed out.

Grace shrugged, seeming very unconcerned. Ava wished she could feel the same way. "I don't see the issue as long as we aren't caught getting jiggy with it in a classroom."

Wine went down harshly as Ava fought against her need to swallow and laugh at the same time. She coughed as she came up for air and gave Grace a withering look. "Who the hell says *jiggy* anymore?"

Grace's smile was unrepentant as she turned to the waiter who had come back to take their order. Ava fought the urge to stick her tongue out because again, she was an adult. She couldn't deny that Grace had gotten what she clearly was going for. Ava was relaxed and quite entertained.

The conversation was steered away from illicit classroom affairs as they talked about some of the places their lives had taken them while they were separated. To Ava's shock and pleasure, she realized they had even more in common now. The small ember of attraction that seemed ever-present was now finding plenty of brush to set ablaze, and Ava couldn't take her eyes off Grace. If she had to come up with a word to describe her feelings, only one came to mind.

Smitten.

She was gone over Grace. How had she not realized her animosity hid these feelings of want? She'd always considered herself self-aware, but now she had questions.

"So, tell me," Ava started when their empty plates had been taken away. "Why did you decide to move back? It seems like you had a good thing going back in New York."

Grace took a sip of her drink before she leaned her elbows on the table. She played with the rim of her glass, finger tracing around its circle and nearly distracting Ava from her curiosity. "I did, but it never felt right. It always felt like someone else's life instead of mine."

Ava frowned. "What do you mean?"

Grace's finger paused before starting its tracing again. "I enjoyed academia and research, but there was always so much pressure about where I was going next. It was probably less from my colleagues and more from friends and family." Their gazes met and held. "Plus, my ex wanted to get married."

Ava had figured as much, given the bits and pieces she gleaned from social media, but hearing it was jarring all the same. Something inside her clenched at the thought of Grace marrying someone else. As selfish as the thought was, she was glad Grace was talking about her in the past tense.

"Do you not want to get married?"

"I do," Grace confirmed, gaze not wavering in the slightest. "But not to her."

Ava willed her heart to calm. Getting flustered at the thought of marriage was ridiculous. They had flirted and even locked lips, but that did not make a relationship. Ava was about to say as much, but their waiter returned to let them know the dancing would start soon.

"Do you want to head back?"

"And miss the dancing?" Ava asked, pretending to swoon with her hand over her chest. The laugh from Grace made it worth it. "I still remember how bad you were at dancing. Junior prom was hilarious watching you flail around."

Grace shook her head, stepping closer to Ava. The warmth of her hand once again found a place on Ava's back, and she had to stop herself from leaning into it. She didn't stop herself from imagining that touch running over other parts of her skin. The memory of being held in those arms still plagued her at night when she lay awake alone. That wiry strength was one she could happily get used to and she leaned into Grace's hold before the other woman could pull away. Their gazes met as music slowly filled the air. Soft murmurs of others finding dance partners reached Ava's ears, but her focus was solely on Grace. She lifted her arms and put them over Grace's shoulders.

Grace's hands rested on Ava's hips as they slowly started to sway. The lights seemed to grow dimmer and the room smokier as they shuffled from one foot to another in a dance they both seemed to know. Ava breathed deep, catching notes of Grace's scent, and she shifted her hands to cup them around the back of Grace's neck. Her knees felt weak, and she marveled at the fact that somehow she had found herself right back where she started.

"I never thought we would get here," Grace said softly, giving voice to Ava's own thoughts. It was almost eerie how they seemed to be on the same wavelength.

When their lips met, both paused as if waiting for the other to pull away and offer apologies or excuses for the light touch. For Ava, there were none. She wanted this, and she was so damn tired of fighting. It was clear that neither of them were going to be able to stay away from one another, so why not give in and see where things would lead?

One of them let out a soft groan and that seemed to spur things on. They shifted, lips slotting together more fully, and Ava couldn't stop the hitch in her breathing. It was pure heat. Grace's lips were soft yet her touch firm. Arms wrapped more firmly around her waist, and that same hand that branded her lower back now moved to tattoo its warmth between her shoulder blades. Ava had to lift onto her toes to press harder, wanting to imprint the taste of Grace onto her senses. When she parted her lips, Grace took that as the invitation it was, her tongue slipping between and brushing against the inside of Ava's top lip, sending shivers of sensation through her. Ava would have happily made the leap up and let Grace catch her if not for the soft cough that came from beside them.

When they parted, the same waiter from before was looking at them with a sheepish smile. "Sorry to interrupt, but this isn't the kind of show we provide."

Ava chuckled as she and Grace apologized. He shook off their apologies and invited them to continue dancing, but Ava

was primed up and more than ready to forgo the dancing for
a few private moves.

"Should we move things to a more private location?"

Grace's smile unfolded like petals of a flower and without
speaking, she reached for Ava's hand. As their fingers linked,
Ava waited to feel the anxiety that had plagued her for the
past few weeks, but all she could feel was a sense of hunger
that had nothing to do with dessert.

Grace's back hitting the door was jarring but not enough
to slow the biting kisses Ava was leaving down her neck. The
forty-five-minute drive back to Grace's house had been mad-
dening. Ava had worried that the fire they had stoked in the
restaurant would have cooled completely by the time they
pulled into Grace's driveway, but when she had cut the engine
and turned to look at Ava across the console, Ava felt a flare so
strong she nearly folded over. They had both scrambled from
the car, racing one another up the front steps until Grace had
gotten the door unlocked and Ava's patience had run its course.

"Jesus. I thought I was going to crash the car," Grace panted,
her hands gripping and releasing on random parts of Ava's body,
sending her nerves alight. She finally cupped Ava's cheeks and
tilted her face up to press another kiss against her lips. "I can't
believe we're finally here. You're finally in my arms."

Words weren't something Ava wanted to do right then.
Her skin tingled with arousal, and she could feel her body
clenching in all the right ways. If this was going to blow up
in their faces later, then she was going to get hers right the
fuck now. They had drawn this out long enough and she was

done worrying. Grace's tongue pressed against hers again, and she suckled softly, enjoying the resulting rumbling groan. She gripped Grace by the belt loops and pressed them tighter together until not even air could get between them. She wanted to climb inside and feel Grace breathe.

"Upstairs." Grace pushed Ava back slightly before grabbing her hand again and leading her up the stairs. Grace had taken the master bedroom now, and for some reason it made Ava giggle even as they walked over to the king-sized bed.

"Please tell me this is a new bed. I don't know if I can I have sex on your mom's old bed."

Grace snorted and rolled her eyes. "If you can think enough to worry about whose bed it is, I am clearly not doing my job." She pulled Ava to her before cupping Ava's face again. "But yes, it is a brand-new bed. Weirdo."

"Not a weirdo," Ava mumbled before her mouth was occupied again in a kiss so deep she felt it down to her toes. She pushed Grace away before she fell into her, completely enjoying the way she landed back against the bed. She set her knee on the mattress before moving to straddle Grace's hips. Hands came up to her waist before sliding under her shirt.

"Is this okay?"

Ava smirked before gripping the bottom of the fabric and pulling it over her head. She let it fall to the floor before leaning down to brush her lips over Grace's. "Does that answer your question?"

She brought her hands up, fingers quickly making work of the buttons on Grace's blouse before they both slid it off her. Ava enjoyed the dark black lace that cupped Grace's small breasts. She traced the pattern, smile widening when she felt fingers dig into her hips. They kissed again, teeth clacking as Ava fell forward. Soft huffs of laughter carried them through unzipping tight jeans until they both laid together, legs tangled and nothing between them but time.

Ava could feel the heat pouring off Grace's body, and she slid her thigh between to feel its source. Grace's soft groan was the sweetest song, and Ava echoed it when lips brushed a heated trail over her shoulder. Grace brought a hand up, nails softly skirting against her side until they brushed underneath her breasts.

"Alright?"

Ava nodded before biting her lip. Pleasure shot through her as a thumb pressed against her, skating over her nipple just like it had Grace's glass. Other fingers joined the fray, pinching lightly and making her sigh. Grace shifted then and when wet heat covered that same nipple, Ava let out a noise she hadn't heard from herself before.

"You taste so fucking sweet," Grace groaned, the vibrations of her words spreading over Ava's skin. "I've wanted you for so long." Breathing was hard as pulses of want lit Ava up from the inside. She pressed her thigh up, enjoying the wet slide of Grace's mound over her skin. Grace's hands shifted to gripping Ava's ass and pulling her closer as Grace slipped her own thigh forward. Puffs of breath left Ava almost unable to speak. She gripped the back of Grace's neck, nails digging in as she felt herself tumbling closer to release.

They moved together like waves lapping furiously against the shore. Soft grunts of pleasure and moans the only sounds as the night closed in and Ava let herself fall. She gripped Grace's hair and pulled her up to kiss soft cries into her mouth. Grace answered with a softly uttered obscenity of her own as her fingers spasmed before crushing Ava against her body. It was over faster than Ava had planned, but the ringing in her ears stayed even after her breathing had calmed.

"Jesus," Grace muttered. When Ava opened her eyes, she locked onto the wonderous look on Grace's face. Her lipstick was smudged, and her hair was lopsided thanks to Ava's tugging. Still, she was beautiful. When Grace licked her lips, Ava felt another flair of arousal course through her. She loosened her grip and slowly brought her fingers forward to brush across Grace's kiss bruised lips.

"If you think after how long it took us to get here that I'm a one-and-done kind of gal, you have another think coming."

Grace raised her eyebrows as a grin spread under Ava's fingers. She drew one into her mouth as her eyes darkened. When she released the digit to cool in the air of the room, Grace replied, "I sure as fuck hope so."

Twenty-Five

Light nearly blinded Grace when she opened her eyes. She yawned as feeling slowly drifted back into her limbs and nearly jumped out of her skin when she realized there was an arm thrown around her waist. It took a moment for her brain to reboot, but when it did, she was more than a little pleased to realize she hadn't woken up alone.

After finding out just how sweet Ava really was, she had found herself on her back barely managing to hold on with the sight of that familiar mane of curly hair dipping down between her thighs. Grace knew her hair had to be a mess. She hadn't wanted to leave the cocoon they had wrapped around one another. Falling asleep beside Ava was amazing, but waking up to see that same curly head of hair laid out on the pillow beside her was even better. Grace knew she probably looked foolish with her wide smile as she stared at Ava's face gone slack with sleep, but she would gladly accept that honor if she got to see this again.

Ava's nose crinkled before her eyes opened. Her dark gaze was unfocused for a moment before it locked onto Grace. Any anxiety about last night being a mistake melted away when Ava smiled.

"It's rude to stare." Her voice was rough as it washed over Grace. If not for being so tired, she would have rolled over and asked Ava for another go just to hear her name spoken in that sultry tone. Instead, Grace turned over and curled an arm around Ava's waist.

"Then stop being so beautiful." She loved Ava's laugh. It was like all the best things wrapped up in one sound. "I should probably brush the morning out of my mouth."

Ava's gaze dropped down to Grace's mouth before she looked up again. "I probably should too since—"

"Grace!"

The front door slamming was enough to have her shooting out of bed, but hearing her mother's voice nearly sent Grace into cardiac arrest. She quickly sat up and felt the bed dip when Ava did as well. The sheet slid off her body, baring Ava's still-naked body to Grace's gaze.

"Is that your mom?"

Grace nodded slowly, wondering if they were both hallu-cinating. Surely, she hadn't heard—

"Grace, honey. Are you home?"

"Fucking hell. It is my mom," Grace said. "I don't know what she's doing here."

Ava frowned before her eyes widened. "Oh, shit. The door."

In a flurry of movement, Grace jumped up and shot toward

the door, locking it just moments before she heard Millie's voice on the other side. "Yeah, Mom. I'm here."

"Well, come on down, then. Nolan and I brought breakfast."

Grace glanced back at Ava. "Yeah. Alright." When Ava gave her a look, Grace shrugged. There was nothing else she could do with them downstairs blocking the exits. No matter which door they tried to use, they would be seen.

"You okay with me coming down or should I just launch myself out of the window?"

"Maybe we both should," Grace muttered before she shook her head. "I'm not trying to hide this if you're not."

Ava snorted, but she slowly got out of bed and grabbed her clothes. "What the hell. Might as well give people something to talk about." She lifted her shirt from last night before glancing at Grace. "Do you mind if I borrow a shirt?"

Grace grabbed Ava a shirt and once they were dressed and looked somewhat presentable, they made their way downstairs and into the kitchen. Grace hadn't felt this nervous when she introduced Emily to Millie and Nolan years ago.

"Mom, you remember Ava. Ava, this is Nolan." Nolan smiled and shook Ava's hand while Millie stared. Her eyes went back and forth until she no doubt understood just why Ava was there so early in the morning. "What are you guys doing here so early? It's only nine."

Nolan put an arm around Millie's waist. "Your mother wanted to come check on you. Clearly, we should have called first." His grin looked knowing, and Grace had zero desire to deny it.

"I didn't know you were seeing someone," Millie interjected. Her smile might have fooled someone else, but Grace knew exactly what it meant. Millie was surprised and not in a good way. From the look on Ava's face, she had caught on to it too, leaving Grace to figure out a way to navigate out of the awkwardness that descended like a plague.

"Whatever you brought smells great," Grace said, desperate to move things along. She had been looking forward to convincing Ava to spend most of the day in bed with her, but as each minute ticked by, that plan slipped further away.

When they were sitting at the dining table, empty plates in front of them, Grace slowly relaxed, thinking the whole morning wasn't a total disaster. Obviously, that was when everything went to shit.

"So, Ava. I hear you are a teacher at the high school as well." Millie's voice was even as she looked at Ava over the rim of her coffee mug. "What is it you teach?"

"AP English." Grace had shifted until her thigh pressed against Ava's under the table. Neither of them had moved away while they ate, which had Grace smiling into her breakfast. Now she was hoping it would be enough to keep her from vibrating with nerves with each inquiry that fell from her mom's lips.

The questions themselves were deceptively curious. Grace knew her mom well and this was little more than an interrogation. She had done similar the first time Grace brought Emily to meet them, though Millie had warmed to her relatively quickly. Grace wasn't getting that same vibe now, and she didn't understand why.

"It's been great having Ava across the hall from me," Grace added. She caught Ava's eye, and they both smiled. "Distracting sometimes too."

Ava's smile fell at Millie's next words. "English teachers don't get paid much, do they?" Grace cut her eyes over to her mom in surprise. Why was she concerned with Ava's pay? The two of them were on the same scale. In fact, she and Grace might be making the same amount, given Grace's degree and Ava's years of experience.

"I make enough," Ava answered vaguely. "I teach because I love the students."

Millie chuckled, though there was a distinct lack of amusement in it. "Well, love doesn't pay the bills."

"No. Rich second husbands do."

Grace only had enough time to suck in a shocked breath before the room exploded with raised voices. She gripped Ava's arm as Nolan did the same with Millie. Ava's body trembled against her, but unlike the desire of last night, now there was only anger.

"Mom, what the hell?"

Millie pointed at Ava. "I know you are only here for the money. Don't lie." She fought against Nolan's hold but didn't get more than a couple steps forward. "I fought hard to get Grace away from this place, and I'll be damned if I see her get sucked back in again."

The words didn't make any sense. Grace was here of her own making. "Mom, what are you talking about? I came back for me. I love this place."

"This place," Millie spit out, face twisting in anger. "These people don't give a shit about you. They just care about themselves."

Ava surged forward and Grace had to scramble to retain her hold. "You are a stuck-up bitch and you always have been."

"Ava!" Grace was shocked. She had seen Ava angry, but not like this. When Ava turned to look at her, there was anger in her gaze but also pain.

"What? You know I'm right. Every time I would come over, your mom always had something slick to say about my parents or our friends." She looked back at Millie with narrowed eyes. "You moved her to that private school just to get her away from us. Why? Were we not good enough for you?"

"Of course, you weren't!"

Silence.

Grace could hear blood roaring in her ears as she stared in surprise at her mother. She had known Millie hated Peach Blossom, but she hadn't been aware she thought so little of it. "You and everyone else in this town can all go to hell."

Grace shook her head. "Mom, you don't mean that." When Millie didn't back down, she tried again. "There are good people here."

Millie's eyes seemed to flash at Grace's words. "Good people? Like the drunken asshole who killed your father or the rest of the town who patted him on the back and swept it under the rug? Which *good* people?" Those words seemed to sap all the fight from her, and she turned, falling into Nolan's arms.

Grace was left frozen. Her head buzzed with too many new details that she didn't even know how to make sense of. Was this why her mom hated coming back here? Was this why she had tried to sell the house and remove the last thing that tied Grace to this town and its residents? Grace's hold on Ava loosened but before she could make a move, Ava slipped from her grasp. Grace's fingers closed on air as Ava turned and left the dining room. Grace couldn't move, stuck in the frightening knowledge that something fundamental had just changed. When the front door slammed, she jerked forward, intending on following Ava and telling her not to go.

"Don't." Millie's voice was rough with emotion and her eyes rimmed red with tears. Grace wanted to comfort her like she had when she was a child and overheard her mother crying. This house had so many painful memories and yet Grace couldn't bring herself to stay away. "Let her go. There is nothing left for us here."

"Mom," Grace croaked. Her words were choked behind a sob that fought desperately to claw its way out. Swallowing it back took everything in her. If not for the muscle memory of having Ava in her arms that morning and the reminder of how content she had been in that moment, she would have stayed quiet. But she couldn't. Not anymore.

This move had been about more than just finding some downtime to figure out her life. She knew that now. All her life, she had been following what others wanted and expected. She had allowed herself to float along with the current, not stopping to think about what she truly wanted. If not for that little voice inside her that had cried out at the thought of continuing on in that vein, where would she have been right now? Engaged? Miserable? Coming back to Peach Blossom had been her choice.

She refused to regret it.

"I knew coming back here was a horrible idea," Millie said softly, drawing Grace's attention. Her eyes were still red, but her expression was determined. Grace knew her mom was no doubt gearing up for a last-ditch effort to convince Grace to leave. She didn't want to hear it.

"I need to talk to Ava. I need to apologize for what you said to her." Grace clenched her fists at her sides. "Why would you say that to her?"

Millie wiped the tears from her cheeks and Grace allowed her the moment to compose herself. Nolan was a silent figure behind her, and Grace was glad for his calming presence. It kept her from screaming in frustration.

"Because it's true, honey. You always had so much potential, and yet you spent so much time worrying about her. You would always talk about her, and I knew, if I let you, you would never leave this place. You would be stuck just like I almost was."

There was so much wrong there that Grace didn't know where to start. Would she have stayed? If they hadn't fallen apart right on the cusp of adulthood? She didn't know. But she ached for the lost opportunity to find out.

"I know dad's death hurt you," she started, carefully wading into a subject they had never truly talked about. "And I'm sure how some people acted made things worse, but Ava was a kid then, like me. She had nothing to do with it."

Millie shook her head, but Grace continued.

"I like her, Mom. I always have, and the fact that ten years have passed and I still feel this way makes me think I always will. You trying to get me to leave won't change that." Leaving was the last thing on Grace's mind. "You have to let it go."

Millie's rebuttals were swift, battering against Grace's will, and yet all she could think was how little it mattered. Her dad's death still affected her and knowing more details about it left a bad taste in her mouth for what her mom endured. Grace didn't begrudge her desire to leave. Her insistence at selling the house made sense as did her need to wipe everything from the past away.

Millie used Grace's lapse of attention to come around the table. She reached out, grasping at Grace's wrist. Her brown eyes, the same ones Grace saw in her own reflection every morning, stared up at her beseechingly. "There are so many places out there—"

"Stop," she replied, staunching the flow of her mom's words. Grace covered Millie's hand with one of her own and pulled it away. "Just stop."

She didn't know what else to say. She had so many questions about her dad and what had happened between his death and their moving away. She had always been afraid to upset her mother by bringing up details from the past, but clearly avoidance hadn't done them any good. Grace had thought there was only one past she needed to resolve. She had never been more wrong.

Finally, she looked at her mom and Nolan, resolve coursing through her veins at what needed to be done.

"Mom, we need to talk."

Twenty-Six

Anger and indignation burned brightly as Ava made her way into the house. The morning had started so promising after a night of revelations and pure pleasure. She had woken up on cloud nine until being so cruelly yanked back down to earth. She felt a sliver of guilt at having cursed at Grace's mom. It made her uncomfortable to know she had disrespected Grace's mom even while she wanted to go back and tell that lady she could go all the way to hell.

Even after showering and changing, Ava still found herself frustrated. She stared into her cup of coffee as she tried to think of what to do next.

"What are you doing up so early?"

"What do you mean early? It's past nine." Ava glanced up as Dani opened the refrigerator door. She pulled out some bacon strips and the carton of eggs before favoring Ava with a look.

"Right, but it's the weekend, so again I ask, why are you awake so early?"

Ava didn't care for the interrogation, but she could use a second opinion even if said opinion would come with a helping of assholery.

"Can I talk to you about something?"

"If it's about your date with Grace last night, then my opinion is yes. I think you should get all up on that and might I add, it's about damn time." She grabbed a pan, ignoring Ava's incredulous expression. "Also, use protection."

"What the hell, Dani."

She rolled her eyes at Ava's surprise. "I know you didn't think you were hiding your feelings about that woman. You've been sick over her since high school." She shook her head before popping the bacon into the microwave. "I know this family likes to live in its delusions at times but now you're taking it a bit far."

That was not what Ava was expecting. Sure, she probably spent more time than necessary talking about Grace over the years, but that didn't mean she was pining for her. Ava didn't pine.

"I'm just trying to understand why you thought I've been hung up on Grace for the past ten years. That doesn't even make any sense."

Last night and even this morning's madness had her rethinking everything. She had always thought herself fairly self-aware. How had she missed this? When Vini walked into the kitchen, Ava didn't have time to tell Dani to keep her mouth shut.

"What is Ava doing up so early?"

"Freaking out about her date with Grace last night," Dani replied, making Ava's mouth click shut. "I think they had sex."

Vini snorted and leaned back against the counter as she eyed the pan Dani was using. "On the first date? Ava, you hussy. What will the children think?"

"Fuck off," Ava shot back. She took a sip of her coffee, ignoring the laughter coming from the stove. Sometimes she wished she were an only child. "And anyway, I didn't say anything about sex."

Vini turned and pointed the spatula at her. "You didn't have to say anything about it. It's written all over your face. Though I had hoped you would be a little less grumpy after releasing a bit of tension. Was it not good?"

Ava's mouth was clearly not listening to her brain, because it rose to the bait, giving her away. "I can still be grumpy and have sex."

"That is not something a father wants to hear before eating."

Now Ava was embarrassed. Her face burned as she dropped it into her hands. Other than a disastrous birds-and-bees conversation with her dad at thirteen, sex was not a topic that regularly came up. She wasn't a prude, and neither was Daniel Williams. He had powered through the talk with the same dogged persistence that drove him to make the family's auto shop successful before passing it to Vini. Still, Ava had had enough awkwardness for one morning.

Vini seemed determined to keep the embarrassment coming as she turned around and gestured toward Ava. "She's being ridiculous about Grace again. We're only trying to get her to see reason."

"Ah." He sat down beside her before patting her hand. The gentle smile on his face was knowing.

"So, you all knew."

"'Fraid so, kiddo," Daniel replied with a soft squeeze. "If it makes you feel any better, I'm about seventy percent sure you get your obliviousness from me. It'll wear off eventually."

"Not likely!" Dani called out from across the kitchen, prompting Ava to tell her where to stick it. Daniel laughed and shook his head.

Ava sighed deeply. Regardless of last night, feelings didn't equal a successful relationship. She wanted a love like her parents where they seemed so perfectly matched watching them was almost like observing a dance. They had made it look so effortless, and while she knew that she didn't have a clue about the ins and outs of her parents' entire relationship, she knew they had loved one another until the end. Their vows had been fulfilled.

"You know, before Grace left, your mother and I wondered about the two of you." His admission was surprising, considering Ava hadn't expressed interest in anyone until college. "Don't look so shocked."

"You guys never said anything." She frowned. "Except when I complained about her."

"Which was a lot," Vini chimed in, laughing when Ava gave her the finger. "You did. *Grace got a higher score* this or *Grace thinks she's so smart* that. Mom used to joke that Grace's name was my first word because you talked about her so much."

Ava leaned her head back and stared up at the ceiling. "I guess I was the last to know."

"Your mom and I were the same way when we were kids. Battled for valedictorian for years, and I was convinced she cheated when she got it. Turns out she was just way smarter because she realized what our rivalry really was and called me out."

Ava lifted her head in surprise. "You never told us that."

His laughter was loud and bled away some of Ava's frustration. It had been a long time since he had sounded so joyous, and it was impossible to be upset in the face of it. She glanced over and saw Dani and Vini sharing small smiles of their own. It was the first time in a long time that talks of their mom brought happiness rather than pain to their dad's voice, and she was desperate to hang on to it even if it meant talking about her own feelings.

"I told your mom she was smarter than me all the time. She just waved it away," he replied, his thin lips twisting into a smile as his eyes gazed at something only he could see. "I thought for sure when I had to drop out of college to take over the shop that she would move on and marry an engineer or a doctor. I tried to break up with her, and you know what she told me?"

"What?" Ava leaned in, enraptured at hearing stories about a mother she missed with each breath she took.

"She told me, *Danny boy, I know you're delusional, but this is trophy-worthy.*" He shook his head. "Never questioned her choice in men again."

That sounded like her mom. It made Ava ache to know that she wouldn't be able to talk to her mom about her feelings for Grace, but she was happy to know that her mother had been aware. It kept something of her alive in a way that brought Ava comfort.

"So, you listen. Sometimes things don't turn out the way we want, but that doesn't mean it's a bad thing." He nodded before giving her hand a firm pat. "Sometimes they turn out even better. Like the breakfast I hope your sisters aren't burning."

Ava released a soft huff of laughter as she turned to watch Dani and Vini fight over the spatula. She had a lot to think about when it came to her feelings, but one thing was sure, she wasn't ready to throw in the towel. Not when she had just now realized what it could all mean.

Pep talk from her father aside, Ava had no idea how to handle bringing up the date or the morning after. She needed a game plan. But when she thought about Grace, all she could imagine was how good bliss looked on her face when she came. Ava had tossed and turned all night. She had awoken restless and horny, which did not bode well for her patience. To make matters worse, she had run into Robert in the hallway on the way to class and he had mentioned stopping by bowling practice that afternoon. She didn't want him anywhere near the team, but there wasn't much she could do. She knew she needed to let Grace know, but she had needed a moment to herself.

She regretted having her door closed for most of the day, but she was distracted enough as it was. The students deserved her utmost attention regardless of how she was feeling. Pushing through was a struggle, but when they seemed none the wiser to her mental state, she counted the school day as a win. That feeling lasted right up until she ran into Brad in the parking lot.

"You two did it, didn't you?"

She rolled her eyes but kept walking to her car. Unsurprisingly, he followed her. "You can say the word *sex*."

"And offend the sensibilities of some kid's pearl-clutching parents? Absolutely not," he replied. "Someone complained about me having pads and tampons in the gym bathrooms. Can you imagine if mister or missus *how dare you imply my child has bodily functions* heard me say the S word?"

Ava snorted, but she couldn't deny the truthfulness of his words. Most of the parents were relaxed and worked with the teachers rather than against them, but there were a few who seemed to enjoy trying to get people riled up.

"Fair enough. And yes, we did." Her admission seemed to give him new life. He gripped her arm, halting her movement.

"So, then why do you seem so down? Was it not good?"

Ava frowned. "Why is that always people's firs—" She cut herself off with a sigh. "It was fine."

"…fine."

"My legs shook."

He nodded. "Fair enough. Then why the glum look? It wasn't a one-and-done kind of thing, right? I don't see her as a player, but fuckboys come in all genders."

"Her mom showed up the next morning and basically called me a gold digger." Brad's eyes widened. "I ended up calling her a bitch and leaving. Left my gold top there too."

His grimace let her know exactly how in the shit she was. "Yeah, babe, that sounds like a lot for a first date."

Ava's shoulders slumped. "And the ridiculous part is that I still want to try with her. Any other person and I would have deleted them from existence as soon as their mom tried to open the door." When his grip loosened, she continued to her car, expecting him to follow. She wasn't wrong. When she reached her car and turned, he was there looking at her with more than a little concern.

"So, what do you plan on doing?"

"I'm going to apologize." Brad's shocked expression had her rolling her eyes. "Why are you so shocked? I do apologize sometimes. When I know I was wrong."

He held his hands up in surrender but gave her a look that screamed how little he agreed. She didn't feel like calling him on it. Saying she would apologize and then figuring out how to do so were two different things, and she was still clueless on how exactly to lead up to that or if Grace would even be open to it. So many unknowns left Ava wrong-footed as she approached the line that was the end of their past and the possible beginning of their future.

Twenty-Seven

Saying Grace was horrified didn't even begin to capture how she felt. While the resulting conversation with her mother was therapeutic in many ways, in other ways it left things so far up in the air she had to strain to reach. After her mother and Nolan had left, she sat at the table for who knows how long just thinking about everything that had happened. She felt for her mom, and she didn't begrudge her for never wanting to step foot back in Peach Blossom. Grace had lost her dad, but her mom had lost her husband.

When it came to the conversation about Ava though, she refused to give any grace. It seemed Millie had calmed after both Grace and Nolan had spoken, and while Grace knew her mom wasn't happy, she didn't say anything else insulting. Still, the whole episode had left Grace staring at her phone the entire night, wondering if she should give Ava a call. In the end, she did nothing.

She didn't know how to come back from this disastrous

event. The night had started out so promising, until it crashed and burned harder than the time she tried sleeping with a man. It left her on edge when she walked into work this morning. Her anxiety had been higher than the first day, and that was saying something. When Ava's closed door came into view, she had slowed to a stop in front of it. The meaning of it was clear. Ava didn't want to talk. Especially not to her.

Grace stood there for a moment, wondering if she should knock anyway and get the whole thing over with. She would apologize, and Ava would tell her sorry not sorry. They would go about the rest of the year as strangers, being civil when needed and not interacting more than that. The thought of it was painful, but really, what more could she expect? It had been one disaster after another since Grace stepped onto the scene. Even she was starting to wonder if this was the universe telling her to just leave things well enough alone. She needed some advice, but she had no one to go to.

She had taken a deep breath and made her way to her own classroom, instead of pushing things, and closed her door as well. Being alone with no one to oversee gave her time to breathe and think—two things she desperately needed. The day trickled by slowly. The students seemed to pick up on how low her emotions were. Normally, there was boisterous conversation that Grace would occasionally have to redirect to the task at hand. But today, the students seem to regulate themselves in a way that made her suspicious. She even caught Tabitha shooting her furtive looks and shushing some of her louder classmates.

On one hand, Grace appreciated her students understanding

she was human and had moments where she wasn't on it. On the other hand, it made her feel terrible that she wasn't controlling her own emotions enough to keep them from picking up on it. She prided herself on being able to get the job done no matter how she was feeling. Anxiety had always been a constant companion, and she had her own ways of regulating things. Now was unfortunately not one of those times though. Every sound grated on her nerves until she felt like she would vibrate out of her skin. She spent more time walking around the classroom just to get rid of some of that restlessness. The end of the school day couldn't come fast enough, although that left her with another problem to think about.

Bowling practice.

She made her way into the bowling alley with her head held high to cover up the fact that she felt low. Ava was already there, head bowed as she spoke softly with some of the students. When Grace walked up, they all turned and looked at her, making her steps falter. Is this what her samples had felt like as she studied them under a microscope? If not for her determination to seem unruffled, she would have turned and walked the other way.

Instead, she fixed a smile on her face and tried to pitch her voice as cheery and normal. "Hope you all had a great weekend and are ready for an amazing practice," she chirped, hoping her voice sounded steady enough to not give her false bravado away. Ava raised an eyebrow in response but didn't say anything, instead stepping back as the team prepared.

They had been doing this long enough that their practices were now like a well-choreographed dance. The girls knew exactly who was going to bowl in what lane and in what order. It meant that Ava and Grace just needed to observe unless they had something to specifically point out. Normally, they would speak with one another, discussing different strategies and preparing for the Friday meets. It was a far cry from how they were today—standing together and yet doing everything they could to make it seem like they weren't stealing glances at one another. It was uncomfortable in a way it hadn't been in months.

Just when Grace thought she couldn't stand the silence between them any longer, Tabitha walked over, her gaze going back and forth as if she could feel the tension.

"Is everything okay?"

Grace smiled, though it felt more like a grimace. This was not going well. She was surprised when Ava spoke up.

"Of course. Are you alright? Was there something you needed to talk to us about?"

Tabitha shook her head. "Just—" she paused, looking between them again "—normally you guys talk more."

Ava glanced over at Grace, her eyebrows doing a complicated dance Grace could only halfway follow. Before Grace could reassure her that they were fine, Rory joined the conversation, bouncing over in her normal exuberant way.

"Yeah. You guys are acting kind of sus." She gestured at Ava and Grace, looking like a bird about to take off into the sky. Whenever she spoke, she tended to use her entire body to do it. The only time she wasn't expending so much energy was when she was preparing to bowl. It was something that Grace always found amusing.

"Plus, normally you guys giggle like schoolgirls. Kind of like how my mom and aunt talk about people in the kitchen when they think we aren't listening."

That forced a bark of laughter from Grace, and Ava looked over her at her with a twist to her lips. "I think we're a little too old to be called schoolgirls," Ava replied. "And shouldn't you guys be practicing?"

"We will," Tabitha said. "We just want to make sure our two favorite coaches are okay."

"Aren't we your only coaches?" Grace chimed in, pointing out the obvious.

"Doesn't mean we can't still have favorites," Tabitha insisted. "Plus, it's like watching reality TV. You guys are totally our favorite source of entertainment."

Rory agreed before calling out to the rest of the team to weigh in. The more nods she saw, the more Grace was concerned that she was living her life in a fishbowl. She didn't understand what was going on. Teenagers confused her, even though she used to be one of them not too long ago. From the look on Ava's face, she was similarly in the dark.

"And you guys are really cute together."

"Alright. I think it's time you all got back to practice," Ava said, shaking her head. Grace noticed a small smile on her face and couldn't help the hope that bloomed in her chest. Maybe everything wasn't ruined.

"I agree. It seems like there is more chatting than practicing going on here."

The playful mood turned dark and uncomfortable with Robert's words. Grace wanted to ignore him, but she knew that would do nothing but invite more drama to her and the team. She braced herself and pasted another smile on her face.

"Robert, I didn't realize you would be coming today?"

He walked up, brown eyes assessing, and clearly whatever he saw wasn't to his liking. Tabitha and Rory slunk off back to the lanes, and she couldn't even blame them. She wished she could do the same rather than engage him in conversation.

"I informed Ms. Williams that I would be coming to observe today." He turned his fake-looking smile toward Ava. "I can't imagine why she didn't relay that message."

"It must have slipped my mind." Ava gave him a faux smile of her own, and Grace had to hide her snort behind a cough. The way Ava's lips twitched let her know she heard it loud and clear, and it was a small comfort.

His smile sharpened, showing far more teeth than necessary. "Well, I hope you don't forget about the deadline to make sure this venture of yours works." He looked over at the team, and Grace had the strangest urge to stand in front of him and hide them from his gaze. "Three months left, well, if you win regionals that is."

Ava's expression didn't change, but Grace saw her throat move as she no doubt swallowed down the words she wanted to say. Grace had a few choice words of her own, but she knew better than to set them free.

"It doesn't seem like they have garnered much school spirit." He glanced over at the girls again, and Grace crossed her arms, gripping each elbow to keep from dragging him away. "What a shame."

Ava and Grace both stayed quiet, not giving him the satisfaction of rising to his baiting comments. Grace wanted to, if only to correct him about his assumptions, but she knew it would do no good. Robert had made up his mind about them long ago.

"Three months," he said as a final parting shot before turning and leaving without bothering to say goodbye. Grace was happy enough he was leaving, but the playful mood was over. She hadn't gotten along with everyone at the university, but this was one of the first times she had disliked someone this much so quickly.

"I really hate him." Ava's voice was soft, so it didn't seem to carry to the team. "And what was that dig at school spirit? We draw an okay group to watch the girls bowl. Don't we?"

That did have Grace wincing. Most of the time, it was immediate family and friends who came for the Friday games. She could understand it. Not everyone found bowling exciting. Even some of her friends who were totally supportive found it difficult to stick around while she bowled an entire match. She didn't hold it against them, but now she needed to do something to change that. The girls deserved support.

An idea came to her. "The newsletter. I'll reach out to Janae and see if we can announce the upcoming matches there. Maybe even get something out to the city newspaper."

Ava slowly nodded. "Probably wouldn't hurt. I don't think we have any money left in the budget for that though."

Grace waved her concern away. "Don't worry about that. I got it." Ava looked like she wanted to argue, but maybe it was the threat of losing the team that made her agree. Either way, Grace was going to do what she could.

"I'll talk to Terry as well and see if we can have some sort of special here at the alley to entice people to stay and watch." Her gaze lowered. "People are pretty good at rallying even if it's not always for a good reason."

Grace breathed deep at the knowledge that Ava was subtly trying to bring up what happened over the weekend. It was vague enough that she could have let it slide, but Grace was done with taking a back seat with things. She moved to take the plunge when a shout from the girls startled them both. They turned in time to see Lauren, one of the sophomores, and Rory pushing each other. Without thinking, Grace hurried between the girls to separate them.

"What is going on?" Ava asked. She held her hands out, helping Grace keep the two girls separated before either of them decided to get another push in. The floors could be slick and even with the grip of their shoes, they didn't need anyone to accidentally trip and hurt themselves.

"Ask her!" Rory exclaimed, pointing at Lauren. "She's the one who started it."

Lauren strained against her other teammates' hold. "I'm not the one acting like a self-important bitch all the time."

"Lauren!" Grace didn't know Lauren that well outside of the team, but she had never heard the girl curse like that. "Okay, Rory, you and I need to talk. Lauren, go with Coach Ava. Everyone else, keep practicing."

It didn't take much prodding to get Rory to come with her, but she kept shooting Lauren angry looks when she thought Grace wasn't watching. When they moved far enough away that Grace was sure the other girls wouldn't overhear, she sat Rory down and asked what was going on.

"I don't know," Rory insisted. She sounded sincere enough that Grace believed her, but she knew there had to be a reason for the blowup. "We were good friends but lately she's been acting freaking weird."

Grace nodded. "Weird how?"

Rory shrugged and looked away. "Like she hates me for some reason. I tried to get her to talk to me, but she wouldn't so I just gave up. Ever since she got her new friends, she's been an absolute—"

"Rory," Grace said, interrupting her words. Rory gave her a sheepish smile. Grace recognized the confusion in her gaze. It was similar to the confusion that had been reflected in her own so many years ago when she and Ava had their own falling out. It was weird how the past and present mirrored one another, but in this case, Grace could see what was happening and maybe help stop it from getting to the point of a decade-long separation.

"Listen, sometimes friends have moments where they're not on the same page. It doesn't mean you stop being friends."

Hope surged in Rory's expression, and her gaze moved past Grace toward where Ava and Lauren were no doubt having a similar conversation. "What if she doesn't want to be my friend anymore?"

That was a tough question. Grace didn't want to give her false hope or dampen her spirits. She walked a fine line here. "Wouldn't it hurt more if you never tried?"

Rory seemed to marinate on her words before she finally

nodded. Grace was happy enough to count that as a win. When Rory stood and said she was ready to go back, Grace walked her over to the team. Ava and Lauren finished their conversation not too long after and when Lauren rejoined the group, things were tense for a moment before both she and Rory seemed to agree to let things be. Grace monitored things for a moment before she felt comfortable enough to take a step back to where Ava was observing.

"So, that was interesting."

Ava snorted. "Interesting wasn't the word I was thinking of." She glanced up at Grace with a twist of her lips. "Did you get anything out of Rory?"

Grace shrugged. "Sort of? You?"

"Lauren was apparently upset at how close Rory and Tabitha had gotten. Seems like a mild case of jealousy."

"Ah," Grace breathed out in understanding. "Rory said something similar but about the new friends Lauren has been hanging out with. Teenagers. So many emotions."

Ava's chuckle was soft as she turned her attention back to where the girls continued bowling. Occasionally, Rory and Lauren would look at one another, and Grace wondered if they would be okay. She hoped so. High school was difficult enough without having to think about what would happen after. Friendships were essential and Grace knew how much she had hated when hers and Ava's ended. It made her even more determined to work through yesterday's fiasco.

"We should talk." It was blunt, but there was no point in dancing around it. "After practice."

Their gazes locked, and Grace wondered if Ava would push

back. If Ava really didn't want to talk about it, they wouldn't. Grace would count it as a strike against the direction they were headed into before, but there was only so much she could do on her own. This was going to take both of them making an effort.

When Ava agreed, Grace's shoulders sagged with relief. She had forgotten what chance they were on this time, but she hoped to God it would stick.

Twenty-Eight

"Are you hungry?"

Ava nodded. "I could eat." They were standing closer than normal. It was as if Ava couldn't help the way she gravitated toward Grace. How she never noticed before was anyone's guess. They shifted inexplicably closer until the back of Grace's hand brushed against Ava's. The electricity from before was still there, dormant and waiting to be ignited.

"Bye, Coach!"

The shout had them pulling apart, Ava with a guilty smile as she waved at Rory. When the girl drove off, Ava came to her senses and realized they were just standing in the middle of the parking lot like a couple of fools.

"We should go."

Grace nodded, but instead of moving away, she was drawing closer. Ava couldn't turn away from those dark eyes that seemed to coax fire from her own and before she could stop herself, they were kissing.

This wasn't what she meant to do and yet all she could do was groan as a tongue brushed her bottom lip, begging for entry. She granted it, reaching out to grip Grace's shoulders as she pressed further into the kiss. Each brush of their lips had her trembling as warmth grew in her chest.

"We should stop."

Grace's eyes were half-lidded as she stared at Ava's mouth. "We should." She didn't sound like she believed it, and Ava was fully prepared to lose herself again in the unique taste that was Grace. "Or, we could take this to my place. Maybe have a second date."

Ava swallowed hard, not loosening her hold. "Our first one didn't end so well."

"I guarantee this one will be completely different." Grace leaned forward, and Ava's eyes fluttered closed. She had expected a kiss but when lush lips brushed the shell of her ear, she gasped. That was a weak spot for her, and she could feel her body giving in, eager to get more of what Grace was offering. A car honking brought her back to the fact that they needed to be somewhere more private.

Ava pressed a kiss to Grace's cheek before pulling her to the car. "Come on. I'm driving." Grace didn't fight her hold, instead crowding her back toward Ava's Prius. She pressed Ava against the warm metal before cupping her cheek.

"I need to drive my car home, but you know how to get there." Her voice was soft and decadently rich. It slid over Ava's skin like warm chocolate, making her pliable. She barely remembered getting in her car or driving toward Grace's place.

It wasn't until they were in Grace's bed pressed together from shoulder to hip that her brain seemed to come back online.

"How are you real?" Ava whispered, her fingers brushing over the elegant arch of Grace's eyebrow before following the path her eyes took. Fingers gripped her back, but all Ava could feel was the smooth heat of Grace's cheek and the thrumming pulse under the skin of her neck. She followed the path, pushing down the strap of Grace's bra so she could dip forward and press her tongue against her shoulder.

"I should be asking you the same thing," Grace murmured as her thumb caressed Ava's bottom lip. Ava leaned forward to suck it into her mouth. She enjoyed the gasp Grace let out. She gladly drank up every pleasurable noise as she removed the bra and panties that hid Grace from her.

Dark nipples called to her, and Ava was helpless to do anything but answer. She circled her tongue around, loving the hitching breaths above her. Her other hand reached out to gently twist the twin between her fingers. Their skin was growing damp with sweat. The rising heat between them and another scent, subtle but rich, called to her.

Ava lifted away before scooting back between Grace's legs. She pulled those long limbs over her shoulders taking care to press biting kisses against the sensitive inner skin. A hand cupped the back of her neck, gently coaxing her forward.

"What do you want?" Grace looked down at her with an incredulous look. It made Ava smirk. "Come on. You can tell me."

"You know exactly what I want," Grace panted, nails digging gently into the back of Ava's neck. She had to close her eyes against the shiver they caused, but when she opened her eyes, she didn't give in. She wanted to hear Grace say it.

"Then tell me."

Eyes narrowed but in the end, she got what she wanted. That sinful voice calling out her name.

"Ava, please. I want you to lick me." She groaned at Grace's words before lapping up the sweetness that she had never stopped catching hints of no matter how many times she tried. Grace was hot and, oh, so wet, slicking Ava's chin. She pressed in as far as she could, wanting to get to the core of who Grace was before drawing back and adding a finger. When Grace's hips lifted, chasing that pleasure, she added another, spreading them slightly so she could thrust her tongue back in and gorge herself on that taste.

When Grace's voice broke, cutting Ava's name in half, it took all of Ava's strength not to follow. She caressed those trembling walls and let herself be lulled by the soft pants of breath as Grace rode out her release.

If Ava had known that she could have this, she would have given in to temptation sooner. She had spent every night for the past two weeks at Grace's though they had spent more time beneath the sheets than talking. Ava knew there were things left unsaid that needed to be aired out, but she couldn't stop herself from falling under the spell of Grace's touch each time. They were careful to not be seen coming or going together as they were still unsure of how to breach the subject of them being coworkers, but so far Ava was content to continue as they were. Her sisters knew where she was and surprisingly, they didn't give her any shit about it. Her dad's satisfied smile whenever she came by to grab a change of clothes was enough to let her know just how okay they were with things.

No one else on the team had mentioned anything to her about she and Grace dating, but she did occasionally catch Tabitha and Rory smiling over at them. It was a little strange to think that her students were rooting for their coaches to date, but since they never said anything, she let it go. If she had been any less content, she might have realized that perhaps things were going too perfectly. There was still the specter of Millie's revelation to deal with, but Ava wasn't sure how to bring that one up, so she focused her attention elsewhere. The team had won their last two matches, and the turnout to watch had tripled. She knew some of the adults probably came for the drink specials Terry instituted on game days, but Ava was just happy that the team was getting support. Robert hadn't shown up again, but that was fine with her. The less she saw of him, the better.

As if her thoughts had summoned him, an email from Robert pinged Ava's inbox. She glanced at the clock. It was technically still working hours, though she could conceivably pretend she never saw the message. But she was having a double date with Brad and Thomas tonight. She didn't want the question of Robert's message hanging over her head. With a sigh, Ava clicked on it, surprised when all it said was to come to his office.

"You wanted to see me?" she asked when she walked through his doorway a few minutes later. He looked up from the stack of papers on his desk and waved her in. He was without smiles today, and as much as she hated it, Ava grew concerned.

"Yes." He stood up and closed the door. Ava stayed quiet, running through all the possible reasons he could have called her into his office. When he sat down, he paused before clasping his hands. "It has come to our attention that you might be engaging in activities that don't conform to school rules and procedures."

She frowned. "I'm not sure what you're talking about."

"A concerned community member let us know he saw you and Ms. Jones engaging in adult activities in a location frequented by students."

Shock didn't begin to cover how she felt. Sure, she and Grace weren't going above and beyond to hide their relationship, but they did their best to make sure no students were around when they were together in public, and they had never done more than chat at school.

"Given the complaints, I think it's best if you cease coaching activities and focus on your students' academics."

Ava couldn't believe what she was hearing. She stared at Robert, trying to make sense of his words. "Are you serious right now?"

He folded his arms and sat back in his chair. His unrepentant smugness had Ava contemplating homicide. "You've displayed a stark lack of decorum, which reflects poorly on our high school. While we appreciate your services as a teacher, your services as a coach are no longer required."

Ava was livid. "What is your problem with me?"

"I don't have a problem with you. I have a problem with your attitude and how you think the rules don't apply to you."

Now she knew he was full of shit. She had never been so much as reprimanded in all the years she had spent at this school. Whatever rules he was talking about, they were new to her.

"As it is, I think Ms. Jones is more than capable of leading the team solo."

"If Ava goes, so do I."

Ava whirled around, shocked to see Grace in the doorway. She hadn't even heard the door open. Then again, she had been focused on not losing her shit and giving Robert even more ammo to use against her. Ava's eyes locked onto Grace as she strode into the room, looking like a woman on a mission. Relief washed through Ava as Grace stopped to stand beside her. She glanced down at her and Ava instantly felt secure in the knowledge that Grace had her back. They were in this together.

"If you are trying to get rid of Ava as the coach because you think she's done something inappropriate and it involves me, it only makes sense for you to get rid of me too. Correct?"

Robert dropped his arms. "I don't think we need to go that far," he backtracked. Ava felt a sick little thrill at how panicked he looked.

"Why not?" Grace insisted. "In fact. You should probably just get rid of me since I was the one who kissed Ava first. If anything, it's my fault."

Ava wasn't normally one to let someone fight her battles, but it felt good to have someone else speak up on her behalf. As

Grace continued to build her case, all Ava could focus on was the fact that Robert had pretty much confirmed her suspicions. For whatever reason, he didn't like her. It wasn't the first time she had been disliked. Hell, Millie had all but confirmed it during the disastrous morning after Ava and Grace's first date. She knew she was a lot for some people, but it further cemented in her mind the thoughts that had been circling as of late.

She was done.

"I quit."

Her voice was calm and steady, a counterpoint to how she felt inside. She didn't raise her voice or attempt to talk over Grace or Robert, but they both quieted all the same.

"Ava," Grace began. Her mouth opened and closed on nothing, and Ava almost smiled at how funny she looked. She knew it was probably adrenaline that made the whole situation amusing to her, but it was better than breaking down in tears. She wouldn't give Robert the satisfaction.

"I've been thinking about quitting for a while, and this just confirms that it's the best route for me. As of next year, I will no longer be at Peach Blossom." She didn't feel any other words were needed. She had made up her mind and that was that. Before Robert or Grace could say anything else, Ava stood, nodded once, and walked out of the office.

She made her way back to her room, happy that she didn't run in to anyone. She gathered her things and made her way to the parking lot. When she got to her car, she paused, hand on the door, as she thought about everything that had just happened.

Ava wasn't surprised when Grace called out her name.

Maybe she had even been waiting for her. She unlocked her car door and opened it, but let Grace catch up and stop her from getting in the car and driving off. They were supposed to be meeting Brad and Thomas at Monell's for dinner, but she couldn't bring herself to get dolled up and be out and about.

"Can we move the dinner to your place?" Ava immediately asked her. Grace frowned. "I don't really feel like going out tonight." *But I don't want to be alone either.* She didn't say that, but she felt it with a strength that surprised her. Being alone had never bothered her before, but now it was the last thing she wanted.

Grace said nothing as she coaxed Ava into the driver's seat of her Prius. She placed a soft kiss on Ava's forehead and at that moment—when soft lips brushed a comforting heat across her skin—Ava broke. She let out a deep breath, expelling all the frustration she had felt for the past four years. There were no tears, though her eyes did burn.

"Of course. I'll let them know."

Her words choked up somewhere deep inside as she nodded. Grace closed her door softly before turning and heading to her car. She watched, still in awe at how things had changed in only a few short months. She was on the precipice of something big with one foot dangling in the air. She could almost taste the possibilities as well as her fear of what it all could mean.

The drive to Grace's house was quick and Ava hardly remembered any of it. She was moving by instinct as she pulled into Grace's driveway with Grace not far behind. They made their way into the house and before Grace could say anything,

Ava fell onto the couch. She leaned her head back against the cushions and closed her eyes on a sigh.

"Do you want something to drink?" Grace asked quietly. Ava shook her head, but before Grace could walk away, she reached out her hand, beckoning her closer. When Grace got close enough, Ava reached up and clutched at her hand before pulling her down to the couch. Grace landed beside her with a grunt and looked over, questions clear in her gaze. Ava didn't have any answers right now. All she had was the deep need for comfort and someone to tell her everything would be alright.

Arms wrapped around her waist, pulling her into a body she now knew almost as well as her own. Ava tucked her head under Grace's chin, letting her familiar scent wrap her in a cocoon of safety as she breathed deep.

"I got you."

It was those three words that Ava needed to hear as she finally let her tears fall.

Twenty-Nine

Shocked didn't even begin to cover how Grace felt about the events of the past few hours. When Janae had come skidding into her classroom to let her know what Robert was up to, she had booked it to the office in time to hear the slight tremble in Ava's voice that gave away just how affected she was by Robert's words. None of it made sense, a fact that Grace brought up in defense of Ava's character. It was the look of gratefulness on Ava's face that propelled her forward. After Ava had left, Robert backtracked quickly, leaving Grace to issue her own ultimatum before she left in search of Ava. Seeing her so emotionless reminded Grace of how she had looked when she caught sight of her at Mrs. William's funeral.

Strong. Almost unapproachable as she became the strength her family needed. But there had been cracks then as there were now that showed someone screaming out to be held. Grace wanted to be that strength. She wanted to be a lot of things.

"I still can't believe that bastard tried to remove you from the team." Brad shook his head as he plunked down his glass. His anger was bright and energizing. Beside him, Thomas was quieter but even his expression was hard.

Ava snorted, though the sound held no humor. "Not tried, did."

"No," Grace stepped in. She squeezed Ava's shoulder. "He backtracked when I said I would quit then. With the team gaining more traction and crowds, he wouldn't risk it coming out that his two coaches both quit thanks to him."

Brad made a rude gesture that had Grace smiling behind her drink. "That asshole is all about appearances and no substance. It would serve him right if the community ganged up on him."

"Are you really planning to leave?"

Thomas's question doused some of the anger of the evening. Ava had only mentioned that briefly at the beginning, but now it was the focus of the hour.

"Yes." Ava's voice held no inflection, and that's when Grace knew the decision had been made. There was no anger in that answer. Just calm acceptance. "This will be my last year."

Grace wanted to beg Ava to change her mind. She couldn't imagine being here if Ava was not, but that was selfish of her. She knew that.

"Dad is doing okay now, and Vini has the shop handled. It's time for me to figure out what I want." She glanced at Grace, and it was then that there was a flicker of emotion she didn't hide. Grace gave her a reassuring smile before brushing a kiss to her temple. A separation was the last thing she wanted before they had even put a word to what this thing between them was, but she would do what was needed to make it work.

A part of her wanted to bring up the team and how much they needed Ava, but she pushed that voice down deep and locked it away. "You have to do what's best for you now. No regrets."

Her worries about the progress they had made in their relationship being derailed by the space between them melted away as Ava leaned into her. They weren't kids anymore like last time. They were adults and if they wanted this to work, it would. Ava gazed up at her and Grace looked back, letting her see just how firm and secure she was in the knowledge that this would work.

"So, are you two ready to admit that you're dating?" Brad's voice broke their silence, and his smile was wide enough to force a laugh from Grace. Thomas was quiet beside him, but his smile was just as wide. Ava's shoulders shook as she chuckled.

"I suppose I didn't stand a chance," she replied. She leaned forward and picked up her glass before gesturing toward Grace. "You win."

Grace shook her head but clinked her glass with Ava's. "No, we win." She leaned forward, happy when Ava's lips met hers in a soft kiss.

"Final game of the season." Grace's heart was beating double time as she looked at the crowd. Putting out that ad in the school newsletter had done wonders at attracting more students as had the announcement in the town newspaper.

"Yup."

"This is a big one."

"That's what she said." Ava's joke had her holding back laughter, which seemed to be what she was going for if her smirk was any indication. They both looked around, waving at a few of the teachers who had come, including Janae. Grace had been surprised to see her mom in the crowd. Nolan had texted her that they were coming, but she hadn't believed it until she saw them seated. There was a tense moment when Millie's and Ava's eyes met, and Grace feared she might have to step between them.

Grace and Ava had talked about Millie's revelation and while she didn't think her mom would ever be Ava's favorite person, their discussion had seemed to smooth things out. Grief was something they all were well-versed in. Losing someone you loved sometimes brought out the worst in people, but it could also bring healing.

When Ava and Mille exchanged stiff nods, something in Grace's chest loosened. She knew there was still bad blood there, and she wasn't sure if her mom would ever see Peach Blossom as more than a cage, but it was a first step.

Even Jessica had come to see the team's final regular season match. This would determine whether they would move on to regionals. It was a big deal that they had gotten this far. Grace was proud of the girls for their hard work, and she was happy that she could make Robert choke on the fact that they called his bluff. They had won more than enough games to prove the team was outstanding, and there had even been talk around town about some of the students and parents wanting a boys' team next season. Grace would pay big money to see Robert's face when he got that suggestion.

"I'm so nervous," Rory said as she walked up to Grace and Ava. Her smile was small as she looked around the crowd. "There are a lot of people here."

"That's because they came to see us crush the competition." Lauren wrapped an arm around her shoulders. "We got this. Just imagine the pins are your ex-boyfriend."

Grace hid her laughter behind her hand, but she knew they heard it by how wide their smiles were. She was just happy that whatever had been going on between the two of them seemed to have resolved itself. The girls walked over to their teammates and Grace grinned when she saw Lauren's other arm fall across Tabitha's shoulders.

"Looks like they're good," Ava said, her gaze on the girls as well. "Your old friend is over there."

Grace turned to look where Ava was gesturing, and she saw Matilda standing with the St. Mary's crowd. When she saw Grace looking at her, she turned away completely. Grace snorted before turning back to Ava.

"Friend is a bit of an overstatement."

Ava looked at her for a moment before her lips twisted in a small smirk. "She finally showed you how much of a jerk she was, huh?"

"You could say that," Grace conceded. She knocked her shoulder against Ava's. "You could've told me, you know. The comments she and everyone else were making. I would've believed you."

Ava shrugged before glancing at her. "I wasn't sure you

would have. Your mom always talked about how well you were doing and how happy you were there, so I thought..." She trailed off. The uncertainty in her voice had Grace wishing she could go back in time. "We were already moving apart, so I thought ignoring it was the best for everyone."

Grace shook her head. "No matter what, you were still my best friend, Ava. I would have said something to them at the very least."

"Your mom would have had a fit."

"She would have had to deal with it," Grace insisted.

Ava's smile softened before she turned back to the team. "Maybe. Can't change the past. Might as well move forward." The back of her hand brushed against Grace's as she moved away. It left Grace feeling lighter and she held on to that feeling.

With a clap of her hands, Grace got her head in the game, letting her awareness of Ava settle into the back of her mind like it always did. They worked together, calling out encouragement and offering advice to the team as the first game went by and then the second. The crowd slowly grew more and more attentive as each pin fell. There were gasps of surprise when a spare was missed and loud cheers when two strikes were gotten back-to-back. The excitement was contagious and as Grace continued tallying scores, she felt the rush of it infusing her frame. She had thought she would never feel this way again outside of her own competitions, and yet there it was, lighting up her nerves and pushing her forward.

"You got this, Tabitha," Lauren called out as they headed into the final game. It was going to be close. St. Mary's was good and with Grant once again taking over coaching, Grace didn't doubt they had been drilled over and over about consistency. Seeing him once again heading the team had been a shock as had finding out he was the one who had snitched about Grace and Ava's relationship. Grace had had to rethink a lot of her previous friendships. Surprisingly, it had been Thomas who related the most, giving her a sounding board for figuring things out. Another brush against the back of her hand got her head back in the game and she sent Ava a grateful smile as she refocused.

The closer they got to the final frame of competition, the quieter the crowd grew. It was tense and the air snapped with nerves from players and spectators alike. Grace bit down on the cap of her pen as she watched the last two bowlers approach. Rory's gaze was focused as she slowly approached the line, and you could almost hear her footsteps.

"Focus. You got this," Grace whispered. When she released the ball, it was like the crowd was released with it. The crash of pins set off a loud cheer as they all fell.

Beside her, Ava let out a soft "yes," the sound quiet but full of pride. Regardless of what happened next, this was their team. Grace knew things would be different next year with Ava gone, but right now, she was going to soak it all in.

Rory approached the line again. With her breath held, Grace watched as the ball hit slightly off.

"Oh, hell," she said softly as the mass of pins finished collapsing leaving only two.

"Jesus." She and Ava looked at one another with incredulous expressions. This was every bowler's worst nightmare.

Seven and ten. Those two pins stood staring back at the crowd like defiant warriors in battle. Grace felt laughter bubble in her chest at the appearance of those two pins now. What were the odds?

Rory looked back at them in a panic. Grace understood why. Most people never closed out with these two, and Grace was no exception. From the corner of her eye, she saw Ava take a step forward, the smile on her face nothing but reassuring.

"It's okay," she uttered, tone calm and firm. "Just choose one."

When Rory's eyes flickered to her, Grace mirrored Ava, reassuring her that it was fine. Rory's eyes were wet and her smile watery, but she turned and again took aim, knocking down the ten pin with ease.

Grace knew from the scores that it wouldn't be enough, and St. Mary's side erupted in loud cheers when their final bowler closed out her tenth frame. Grace fixed a smile on her face that was surprisingly genuine. She felt nothing but pride in their team, and she pulled the girls into a huddle to say as much.

"But, we lost," Tabitha said after Grace's praise.

"Did you?" The girls looked at her in confusion, but Grace didn't waver. "St. Mary's has been bowling for years. This was our first and yet we gave them a run. It was so close that I have no doubt next year you will win."

Slowly, smiles replaced frowns as her words sank in. Ava encouraged the girls to go congratulate the other team. Handshakes and high fives were doled out, warming Grace with the knowledge that they did what they had to do and did it well.

"So, second place," Ava said, drawing her attention. Her eyes were bright as she looked up at Grace. Their hands brushed again as all around them congratulations were given. "How does it feel?"

The question was a fair one, and Grace didn't have to think long about her answer. "Feels a lot like first."

Ava's smile was radiant before her eyebrow raised. "We should probably celebrate."

"Probably."

Anticipation slowly built and Grace could feel herself leaning into Ava with each second that ticked by. All around them, the sounds of the crowd slowly bled away until all Grace could see was Ava.

"Cupcakes!"

Brad's voice was almost in her ear, and she and Ava blinked as a box was thrust between them. Brad's smiling face and the scent of baked sweetness was the only thing keeping Grace from jerking away. His expression was knowing as he looked between the two of them.

"No matter what, you guys are winners to us."

Ava rolled her eyes, but she stepped back as the team huddled around, hands reaching for their own piece of happiness. Grace couldn't feel disappointed when surrounded by the team she helped build or the new life she had created.

She held the box up, laughing as it was batted around by eager hands reaching in. When another hand cupped hers, adding stability, she warmed and looked across to see Ava's gaze on her. Tomorrow they would talk about the future, and when Ava's acceptance letter for her PhD program came, they would talk more. Things would change as they often did, but one thing wouldn't.

"We did it, Coach Grace."

Her gaze didn't leave Ava's as she smiled. "Yes, we did."

★ ★ ★ ★ ★

Don't miss Vini's story
coming in Winter 2025!

Acknowledgments

I never imagined I would write a bowling romance.

I also never imagined I would do a pitch event on social media.

If not for the amazing writers in Wordmakers, I might not have done either. If not for them, especially the awesome night owls who cheered me on even as the clock moved ever closer to midnight, Ava and Grace may have remained vaguely in my mind but never on the page or in your hands.

To the Write Owls, I am forever grateful to have met you. D. Ann Williams, Rae Shawn, and Meka James, thank you for not letting me second-guess myself into never getting started. You all help keep me grounded. To Mia Heintzelman, Sri Savita, Renée Dahlia, Ali Williams, and Lisa Kessler, thank you for cheering me on with each word I put on the page.

To all the Wordmakers, thank you for the chance to write with you and share each milestone. And Tasha L. Harrison, thank you for creating the space for us to all find one another.

Without Wordmakers, I don't think I would have gotten my second wind and the push to keep writing.

To my amazing agent, Taj McCoy: thank you for being a constant cheerleader for *The 7-10 Split* and beyond. To my awesome editor, Errin Toma, and the entire Afterglow Books team, working with you all has been a dream.

To think, this all started thanks to a conversation and a few (nerve-racking) tweets.

And last but certainly not least, thank you, readers, for making my greatest wish possible.

Karmen <3